BOYFRIEND MATERIAL

HAWTHORNE UNIVERSITY
BOOK 2

ILSA MADDEN-MILLS

Boyfriend Material
Copyright © 2022 by Ilsa Madden-Mills
Illustrated Cover Designer: Elle Maxwell

IMM Publishing
Paperback ISBN: 978-1-960512-02-4

Copyright Law:

If you are reading this book and did not purchase it, this book has been pirated and you are stealing. Please delete it from your device and support the author by purchasing a legal copy. All rights reserved. Without limiting the rights under copyright reserved above, no part of this publication may be reproduced, stored in or introduced into a retrieval system, or transmitted in any form, or by any means (electronic, mechanical, photocopying, recording, or otherwise) without the prior written permission of the above copyright owner of this book or publisher.

This is a work of fiction. Names, characters, places, brands, media, and incidents are either the product of the author's imagination or are used fictitiously. The author acknowledges the trademarked statue and trademark owners of various products referenced in this work of fiction, which have been used without permission. The publication/use of these trademarks is not authorized, associated with, or sponsored by the trademark owners.

Second Edition June 2023

88bee1be0e7f59b91ccff48a3d3d88625d7a351b57c28eaae8c124871b947dea

TRIGGER WARNING

This book contains scenes of sexual assault.

PROLOGUE

Before

Julia

Meet me at my locker. Can't wait to c u.

OK, I reply back to the text with a grin.

Five minutes later the bell rings, and I hand in my essay and dash out of class. A sea of maroon and green uniforms greet me in the hallway, girls in crisp pleated skirts and knee socks, guys in khakis and blazers. Welcome to Bellemeade Prep, a private school for the rich.

I avoid a cluster of students, stumbling and nearly losing my backpack as I hurry. Giddiness races over me, and for a second, I feel goofy for the excitement, then shove it away.

He's a piece of nirvana in a world I don't belong in.

It's okay to feel as if I'm floating.

I'm in love with him.

And today is the day.

We're going to do *it*.

It's been weeks of hot glances, erotic kisses, and his fingers in my panties in every private place we could find. The gym. The drama room. The yearbook room. Once in the cafeteria while I sat in his lap with a coat over my skirt.

The crowd parts and I see him leaning against his locker.

My breath catches.

Dark red hair frames a face that angels carved. Angular jawline, lush lips, piercing topaz eyes.

His lashes are long and dark and dramatically thick.

He's not a pale redhead. His skin is golden. Like a lion.

He could have any girl here.

I'm not the pretty cheerleader.

Or the social butterfly.

Or rich.

"Hey, gorgeous. Finally." He smiles as he curls his arms around my waist and gazes soulfully into my eyes.

"Hey," I breathe.

"School's over. Wanna go take a ride in the Aston Martin? We can put the top down and go wherever you want." His eyes lower. "*Do* anything you want."

I don't even have to think about it. "Okay."

His fingers playfully untie the black ribbon around the neck of my shirt. He tugs it off, then unbuttons the top two buttons. His hand snakes in and presses against my sternum as we move closer and breathe each other in. We need to touch each other. It's been this way since he sat next to me in poetry class after Christmas.

He dips his head to my neck, then bites my ear. "I want to fuck you in that car."

I gasp as tingles erupt over my skin.

I'm new to this school, but I've heard the rumors about him. That he's the king of breakups. That he has sex with girls, then moves on.

But they don't know him like I do.

He's perfect boyfriend material...

1

Present Day

Julia

You know you've hit rock-bottom when you're allowing yourself to be groped in an alley by a guy in a vomit-covered shirt.

Even worse, a *Kappa* shirt.

I play nice. Vomit boy has been my best customer of the night, laying an endless supply of dollars at my feet.

It's not enough. Not nearly enough. But it will be.

If it isn't, I might be dead by sunrise.

More likely hurt or disfigured, but none of those options are on my to-do list.

I need more money tonight . . . or this morning . . . or whatever is chronologically correct.

Sweat dots my face. It's the end of August in Sparrow Lake, Minnesota, so the temperature is dropping, but humidity lingers. Kappa-guy swims in sweat.

He pulls me to him and runs his tongue down my neck. It leaves a wet trail on my throat like a wriggling worm.

Shuddering in revulsion, I push him away. "Private dance only, remember? Nothing below the belt and no kissing—or licking."

Inside the club all they can do is look. Even during the lap dances in the VIP room they have to keep their hands on the couch. Those rules are told to them by a huge-ass bouncer and written in neon letters on a sign in the room. Not that I get many requests for private dances—until tonight.

Only it wasn't for a dance inside the VIP room. He wanted me to meet him in the alley.

When I started working at Platinum Nights, I drew a line in the sand. Some of the girls bring the guys out to the alley for "more" while the manager looks the other way.

I swore I'd never do it.

Guys like this, if you give them an inch, they take a mile. Every one of them thinks the world should bow before them.

They can be dangerous.

Especially when they're drunk.

I swallow down my disgust.

And morals.

Don't think about it, I tell myself.

Think about butterflies. The smell of daffodils. A sunrise over the lake.

When that doesn't work, I close my eyes and concentrate on the several hundred-dollar-bills he flashed at me as my shift was ending. Sure, I recognized him. We had a sociology class together this summer and he seemed manageable, even nice. He flirted with me but never took it too far—for good reason. Last semester I dated Parker Cavendish, the current Kappa president. You can guess what happened next. The frat black-balled me after we broke up.

Not that I care. Those parties aren't my scene anymore.

I thought doing a dance for him out here would be easy, but that's desperation talking. It's been a slow month as students migrate back to school, and I've run out of time.

"Lean back," I coo, nudging him back against the wall. *Get as far away from me as possible.*

"What if I don't want to?" He slurs as his gaze roams my body.

"Those are the rules."

"Show me your tits then," he demands.

Fine. I abandon all seductive de-clothing and pull off my shirt and bikini bra. In the club I wear pasties over my nipples, but those are in the trash already. He's getting his money's worth. A guy hasn't seen all of my boobs since, well, Parker.

I look around the alley. We're alone. Good. I think.

He licks his lips. "Yeah, baby, nice. Now get those shorts off."

Anxiety spikes higher as blood rushes through my veins. "I said topless only."

"For three hundred? And I can't kiss you? I might as well watch porn." He reaches for me again, and I rear back, laughing nervously.

"But a porn video can't say your name. Do you want this or not . . . Scott?" I bat my eyelashes as I make my voice sound breathless.

His eyes narrow. "All right. Get on with it."

My jaw clenches. He's rude and disrespectful. He makes my skin crawl.

"Let me dance. I promise, you'll be happy." I do a twirl and run my hands through my long brown hair as I shimmy my hips, doing a routine from Madonna's "Like a Virgin".

She croons about being touched for the very first time while I'm just praying Vomit Boy keeps his hands to himself. Singing the song in my head, I stare at a point over his shoulder and move my body from muscle memory. I end with a big, fake smile.

He jumps at me. His hands wrap around my waist as he whips me around so that I'm the one up against the wall.

"Your dance sucked, babe. You lacked enthusiasm." His hands move to my throat. "I expected more."

Fear slams into my skull. My heart beats like a snare drum. "Easy now. Play nice." I tug at his fingers and they loosen. A little.

"Suck my cock and I will."

"Not happening." I place my hands on his chest and push, but the guy's built like a linebacker, thick but compact. I may as well be shoving a tractor.

He leans in to nuzzle at my hair, pressing closer. His hand gropes my body, and I flinch. My gaze darts down the alleyway to the street as college girls hurry by and frat-hop without a care in the world.

I wish I could be one of them.

I was one of them.

I try to jerk away as he puts pressure on my shoulders, nudging me down. The brick of the wall scratches my back as his fingers dig into my skin.

"No . . ." I protest, but he cuts me off.

"Yeah, baby . . ." His hand moves between us as he pulls down his zipper. I fight the rising bile in my throat and beat at him.

I never should have agreed to this.

Even if I am at the end of my rope.

Disappointment in myself, mixed with anger for him, bubbles up inside me like lava.

I angle my head up and hold his bleary eyes as I grit my words out. "You asshole! I don't have sex with clients."

He reaches into the confines of his pants. I smell his rankness, loosely veiled by too much body spray.

I try to jab him in the nuts, when . . .

"That you, Scott?" a male voice calls from the street.

He lets go so fast that I fall to the side and land on the asphalt.

He's spared the pain in his crotch, but I get it screaming up both of my elbows. My backside is covered with bits of crumbled concrete. Blood blooms on my knees.

These damn shoes. With hands that tremble, I undo the gold stilettos from my feet. Scratches line the shiny plastic coating and one of the heels has broken off.

Cheap. Useless. A metaphor for my life.

I toss them in front of me as I crawl towards a dumpster.

"Yeah, it's me. Hold the fuck on. Be there in a minute," Scott mumbles to his friend, then looks back at me. "Hey! Where are you going? We're having fun, baby."

I stare at him. At his flushed face and vomit-covered shirt.

How did I get *here*?

When I was a kid, I dreamed of college. Of being my own person.

But this? This is a joke.

Taylor's voice sounds in my head: *You are your own universe, Julia. You're made up of black holes and glittering galaxies. You are beautiful. Vast. Limitless.*

He tells me this when I get low. I'm pretty low now.

Clenching my hands, I rise up.

"Give me my money," I say as I snatch my bra and strap it on.

"What? Come on. Let's try this again, yeah?" He puts on his friendly face, and I start at the way he switches from jerk to nice guy.

"No," I mutter.

The voice comes again. "Scott! Get your ass out of the alley. Your girlfriend just showed at the frat house."

He blinks hard. "Fuck." He tucks his dick in his pants and zips, then gives me a smirk. "Catch you later, baby."

He wanders towards the street as I wipe the asphalt from my skin.

You need his money, keeps running through my head. Yeah, but am I willing to get close to him again?

Moving fast, I tug on my flowy t-shirt.

Just ask him for what I'm owed. Plus, his girlfriend is here; he won't be forcing me to my knees in front of her.

"Scott," I call out. "You got what we agreed to, so—"

His eyes thin as he looks at me from over his shoulder. "Get lost. You're not even that hot."

He turns away, adjusting his shirt and running both hands through his longish dirty-blond hair.

I stand there for a beat, then follow. When he reaches the edge of the alley, I catch up with him.

"I came out here with you. We made an agreement in the club. You said one private dance. I've never done that before. You owe me."

He scoffs. "For what? The pleasure of your company? Why would I pay for that? I don't owe you a damn thing."

"Scott!" a female voice cries in excitement from the

porch of the Kappa house. We've reached the end of the alleyway and houses sit on each side, all of them Greek at Hawthorne University.

Kappa is the biggest mansion, complete with imposing columns a la the White House. Our current dean of the university was a Kappa here. A sitting senator was a Kappa here. Whatever. Maybe those guys are okay, but now it's home to some of the biggest pricks on campus. Most of it because Parker is their leader.

I follow the female voice to a gathering of co-eds with perfect tans after Instagram-lake-life summers. They're drinking beers from Solo cups.

I look down at my pale skin from studying at the library and dancing inside a club with no windows.

It's the first party weekend of the fall semester at a small school, but these people feel like strangers.

The girl at the front, a petite girl with red corkscrews down to her shoulders, waves at him. With her hand cocked on her hip, she's dressed to kill in a strapless black dress and heels. "Pookie Bear, I've been waiting for you. What were you doing back there?" Her red lips make a pout.

Scott shrugs then jogs up the steps, meeting her on the porch. He kisses her on the mouth and I grimace.

A frat brother hands him a beer.

"Just coming back from the bars," he says cheerfully. "Closing time."

It's true; two is closing time for the bars, and it sends a wave of people to this side of campus where the parties go all night.

Platinum Nights, relatively new to Sparrow Lake, is also closed. My stripping career began at the Boobie Bungalow, a decent place I liked, plus my old roommate Sugar worked there as a bartender. Unfortunately, it's several miles off campus and requires a car. I had to sell mine for the cash. The Bungalow's clientele was mostly older men escaping their lives. Sometimes there would be a bachelor party that included some douchebags, but the regulars knew the drill. Watch the girls, then leave.

Platinum Nights is within walking distance of campus and has an entirely different animal: frat boys. This brand of douchebag doesn't follow any rules.

My head churns. My stomach rolls. I can't leave empty-handed.

I have to pay Connor so his goons don't take it out on me or my mom.

I feel eyes on me. Assessing. Mostly male. I stiffen as I smooth down my shirt. It's sleeveless but covers my ass, something I slipped on after my last set. There's a monarch butterfly on the front with the caption: *Give up being a caterpillar and fly.*

My throat tightens. I'm never going to fly at this rate.

"Hey, Scott," I call from the front lawn of the Kappa house, feigning confidence even though I keep plenty of space between us. The bass inside the house pumps hard, mirroring my own heartbeat.

Scott must have amnesia because he stares at me like he doesn't know who I am.

I cock my hip. "Yes, *you*. Asshole with the vomit on your shirt."

Red turns to look at him, a frown on her pretty brow. "Scott. Who is she?"

I laugh bitterly. She knows me. We used to party together sophomore year. I had no idea she was dating Scott now.

He drapes an arm around her. "No one," he says, glaring at me.

Challenge accepted. A grim smile flashes over my face.

He doesn't get it.

I owe none of these people.

I'm at the end of my rope.

And I sure as hell don't have a reputation to uphold.

"Who am I?" I scoff. "I'm the girl who was just dancing for your boyfriend. He wanted a little something extra in the alley. I gave it and he owes me."

The girl's jaw drops.

A low murmur picks up as several brothers laugh and razz Scott.

Red's lips twist. "You're one of those girls from Platinum Nights. What are you . . . some kind of whore?"

The word is like a fist in my gut.

"No" I want to scream. Never. How dare she?

What is the difference between me and her?

I've seen *her* dancing on a pool table in her underwear while frat boys cheered her on.

Another girl speaks, her gaze raking over me. "I think they prefer sex worker. Where are her shoes?"

The girls giggle.

"Maybe she's so poor she doesn't have any," Red says.

Another round of laughter.

"I took them off in case I had to run away from Scott," I say. "He tried to force me to do something I didn't want to."

"That's what you get when you put yourself in that position," a willowy brunette says. She was in one of my art classes freshman year, but that time period feels so distant now. "It's your own fault, honey," she continues. "When you act like a slut, guys don't know what to do. It's their hormones."

I shake my head as disbelief rises. "You, wow, you're *female* and excusing his behavior? Gross. Hormones have nothing to do with it. He has self-control; he just chose not to use it. He has zero respect for any of you." I tick off what happened on my fingers. "He asked for a private dance. I gave it. He went too far. Then he tried to run away without paying. Scott is scum. Scott is probably a rapist."

That gets their attention.

"She's a lying bitch," Scott sneers. "She came out of that strip place on Easton Street, and I just walked her back from the bars to be nice because she was alone. And this is the thanks I get?"

My blood boils.

That Strip Place Back on Easton Street is where he's been spending most of daddy's hefty allowance this summer.

I lift my hands in exasperation. "I just want to collect what's owed me."

He laughs. "You're owed jack. Get out of here."

"Yeah," his girlfriend mutters. "Before we call the cops and tell them you're soliciting."

"Go on, now," the brunette calls in a haughty voice. "We don't want your kind here. This is a decent place. Kappa doesn't tolerate sluts."

Frustration hits as my predicament slowly dawns. What cop is going to believe me over him? Over the girls?

Scott was easily tossing dollars at me in the club, but now I'll have to pry the money he promised me out of his slimy hands.

Connor is going to be livid.

And with that horrible realization, I panic. I rub the scar

on my wrist as my vision swims. A cold-sweat breaks out on my forehead. My anger ebbs into fear.

"Don't come back to my place of work, Scott," I yell as I back away. "The boys will toss you out."

I turn to leave and the second my bare feet hit the curb, a black, tricked out Toyota Tundra pulls right in front of me. It's one of those trucks with every upgrade and modification to make it look like it was used to cross the Sahara, but it's never been off-road. I stumble and reach out to steady myself against one of the big tires.

The driver's side door opens, and out steps a six-foot-four-inch wall of perfection—and he knows it. Eric Hansen.

He's clearly been hitting the gym during the offseason, but it doesn't look like he had time to shop. His arms burst against the gray Henley stretched across his chest, and his thighs strain against his black jeans. He truly is built like his nickname, Eric the Everest. He's broad-shouldered with a rugged face and wavy dark red hair. Long ago, I used to run my fingers through those unruly curls.

Whoa. His beard is gone. I'm able to see the chiseled lines of his jaw, the skyscraper cheekbones, the fullness of his lips.

I try to step around him but he stops, recognition sparking.

Fuck, fuck, fuck.

"Julia? Hey . . . I haven't seen you in a while. You going in? Looks like the party is in full swing."

This might be the most we've said to each other in years.

He tucks his big hand in the pocket of his jeans, a movement so smooth and sexy it appears choreographed. Confidence surrounds him. He's rich. Beautiful. Popular.

That's right.

He's charming up until the last moment, then he pulls your heart out and rips it to pieces.

He's speaking in that easygoing way of his, playing Mr. Nice now, but just wait...

"No, I was just leaving," I mumble, my voice drowned out by the music wafting out of the mansion.

"Are you okay?" he asks, pivoting with me as I move around his truck.

I cut a look at him, and I mean to glance away, but his topaz eyes hold mine. They aren't regular topaz; they're a brilliant gold with layers of gray, green, and blue as if his creator didn't know what color to give him. They're the softest part of him. I used to think they reflected a deep person, someone vulnerable, someone who had a side to him no one knew.

I was wrong.

He glances at my feet, and I lift my hands and heave out a sigh. "Nothing to see here. I lost my shoes."

"Ah." He frowns, looking back at the Kappa house, then again at me. "Did someone take them?"

"No." I huff out a laugh and shake my head. "They weren't worth stealing."

"You seem upset," he says and moves closer until there's only a foot between us.

The tension sizzles—or at least it does for me.

He's staring at me, hard, and I swallow thickly as the silence builds between us.

For three years, every time we've seen each other on campus, we've purposely avoided one another. He'd see me coming and turn the corner. I'd see him in the cafeteria and choose a table on the other side—behind a plant. Even when our roommates, Z and Sugar, started dating, we kept our distance.

You should keep it that way, a voice says.

I whirl to leave.

"Bye, slut," one of the girls from the porch calls behind me.

"If you ask me, Eric should've hit her with his truck," another says as they burst into laughter.

Tears sting my eyes.

If I don't get some money soon, I'll be in for a lot worse.

2

Eric

Julia's long mahogany hair flies behind her as she dashes away, the glitter on her shoulders sparkling as she runs under the streetlights. I guess she wears it when she strips.

Jesus. She hates me.

Do you blame her?

An emotional exhalation comes from my chest.

I push down the guilt I feel about her as I climb the steps of the frat house and take in this year's assortment of new frat girls. Most of them are doe-eyed girls in short dresses, clutching their beers as they smile.

"Who called her a slut?" I ask the group. Just for the hell of it. And because I know she isn't.

They glance away from me, like they've got no clue what I'm referencing.

Whatever.

They part like the Red Sea to let me pass. Another girl,

one who wasn't part of the group giving Julia the evil eye, chases after me. "Wait. You're the one they call Everest, right?"

"Yeah. That's me. And you are..."

"Fiona." She stands up straighter, smoothing out her skirt. "You're a Kappa?"

As I start to shake my head, one of the guys calls out, "He fucking wishes."

I give him the finger over the girl's shoulder. I could've been a Kappa, but that's ancient history. I got out. Or kicked out. Depends on who you ask. These days I only come to Kappa to check out the party scene or celebrate hockey victories. Long ago, tradition dictated that Kappa throw our parties for us. It's the biggest—and supposedly the best—frat on campus.

"Excuse me. I gotta go see someone," I tell her.

"Are you coming back?" she asks, pouting. She has round cheeks with dimples and pretty blonde hair that curls around her face.

"I might."

She gives me a bright smile, lashes batting. "Come find me later."

Fine. I'm game. She didn't call Julia a slut.

"Alright."

She giggles. "Promise?"

Her crop top is only covering half of her tits. I picture my hands around them.

All in good time.

For now, I touch her cheek, and a little of the darkness that swirls in my head abates. I hate going to bed alone. Sex releases endorphins I crave.

"Wait here for me?" I give her a wink and go inside the

house, which reeks of sweat and old beer. The music in the common room blasts as strobe lights dance.

That's when I see my target.

Parker Fucking Cavendish.

Quarterback of the football team, Kappa President—and a giant prick.

Reason number one of many why I'm not a brother.

He might as well be sitting on a throne in the room the way people look up at him. Really, he's standing on a stage at the head of the room, bookended by two girls, taking turns making out with them.

Probably naïve of me to think he'd fallen asleep and wouldn't be coming out of his suite at the top floor of the house for the rest of the night.

That's where he was when I left a few minutes ago. When I had to give a crying, drunken girl a ride home.

I found her wearing her bra and panties outside his door, trying to get back in. Her knuckles were bleeding because she'd been knocking on his door so long. I'd gone up there to use the head and ended up playing nursemaid to her.

She told me a slightly incoherent story about how she met Parker tonight. They went up to his room together and had what she thought was something great—until she left to use the bathroom down the hall. He wouldn't let her use his because it was dirty. Yeah, right.

Then, he unceremoniously locked her out without her clothes and ignored her.

I helped her wash up and found her a roomy sweatshirt from one of the bedrooms, then gave her a ride home. She's just a freshman. When her parents dropped her off at Hawthorne to start her college journey, she'd had hopes and dreams . . . but being locked out of a frat room, half-dressed, her first weekend away from home, wasn't one of them.

I make my way around the thrashing bodies and stalk over to him. He doesn't notice me until I'm at the bottom of the stage.

"Hey," I call over the music. "I took care of your *problem*."

He nudges the girls aside and gives me a superior look. "You think I have problems? Look around." He throws his head back and laughs.

Dude is what girls call "hot," I guess. Short dark hair, All-American chin, a footballer's athleticism.

I hate the fucker.

We pledged together freshman year and you'd think we'd be friends, but it never happened.

Instead, we competed for everything.

Who could get the most girls—me; who made the better grades—him; who won more intramural games—me. All in good fun, unless you grew up with him because your dads are business associates and he's always hated you. In the end, he had more friends in the pledge class since most of my friends were hockey players who hadn't pledged.

That freshman year is a blur to me. Too much alcohol. Too many mornings of waking up and hating myself because I wasn't someone else. I wasn't in a good place. Most days I think I'm past that emptiness, but I'd be fooling myself.

"You know what I'm talking about," I growl. "The girl."

"If you're talking about the girl upstairs . . ." He squints, his toothy smile already focused on a female across the room. "Or who-the-fuck-cares. She wasn't a problem."

I cross my arms. "I think she would have a different perspective."

He snorts. "What are you? Patron Saint of Drunken Girls? I didn't promise her anything. When it was over, it was time for her to leave. Simple as that." He lowers his lids. "She's lucky I didn't cuff her to my bed and go all night."

His bookends don't seem fazed by this at all. They're staring daggers at *me*, as if I'm the one who's going to fuck them over.

He smiles. "She was past her expiration date."

A song comes on that his bookends must like because they jump up and squeal and begin to sway seductively, pushing their tits up against him.

There's no point in giving him shit over this. He'll never have remorse. His frat brothers worship him like a god. The more terrible of a human he becomes, the more they idolize him.

My hands clench. I can't believe Julia dated this asshole.

Easing my way out of the sea of sweaty bodies, I step out into the night. The porch is empty; the girl gone. Ah, well.

Dragging my hands down my face, I decide to leave my truck parked on the street. It's a good spot, and if anyone messes with it, the alarm will blast their ears. Plus, I get satisfaction knowing Parker will see my truck parked in front of his house.

With a laugh, I launch myself over the railing and cut behind the fraternity house to the street behind where the houses are nowhere near as extravagant. They're privately owned older homes rented to college kids. Some are well kept, others, not so much. Our house is owned by Reece's dad and is somewhere in between.

Before I reach for the doorknob, the scent of cooked chicken from down the road hits me.

My stomach rumbles. I had double practice and a lifting session and haven't eaten much today.

Turning, I take in the lights of the food trucks lined up in the park down the street. There's a Korean BBQ place, a taco bar, and my new favorite is Burt's, the gyro place.

I jog to the park. As I'm fishing through my jeans for cash, I notice Julia.

She's sitting on the curb, her long legs stretched out in front of her. She counts dollar bills and puts them in piles. A lone tear falls down her cheek.

Is she trashed?

She stumbled around me earlier, but that could be because she didn't have shoes.

She's going to get herself in trouble if she keeps flashing cash.

Fuck it, I think, heading over to her. *Just call me the Patron Saint of Drunken Girls.*

It's only when I'm halfway there that I notice the kid in the black hoodie standing behind her.

3

Julia

It's not enough.

My hands clench as frustration rolls over me.

When I started at HU my freshman year, I had scholarships and a work-study that covered everything. Times were great. I was a normal girl and I felt free, as if I were on an exhilarating adventure. I went to class and soaked in knowledge, I joined clubs, I went to poetry readings, I went to art museums.

I loved the rolling hills, the ivy that grew up the old buildings, the trees. I'd sit on the grass in one of the parks and read or draw. I wasn't popular, I'm an introvert who often needs to decompress alone, but I made friends.

Everything changed when my mother got hurt my sophomore year. Suddenly, at nineteen, I was thrust into the role of caregiver while trying to go to class. I picked up a second job at the bookstore to help while she got back on her feet. When she got worse, I wrestled with how to balance it all. My grades dipped and I became reckless.

I needed to forget that my life was falling apart.

I partied. I slept with guys I never intended to see again. I lost my scholarship.

I missed seeing that my mom was in a deep pit of despair and pain.

Then life turned upside down when Connor appeared my junior year.

I quit my other jobs (that didn't pay well) and turned to stripping to try and stop the spiral. It worked—for a while.

But summer arrived and the clientele disappeared.

And tonight...

I swallow down anger. I hate that I followed Scott to the alley. It was stupid and naïve. He could have hurt me. Most of all, I despise that he enjoyed his power over me.

Just like Connor.

Whatever I do, it's *never* enough. I'm just picking up speed on this downward slide, hoping I can survive until graduation.

And who knows how deep the hole will be when I get there?

Or what my mental state will be?

Every time a man sticks money under my bikini brief, there's a heaviness inside of me as the girl I was before slips further and further away.

I'm just about done counting it out—for the third time—and the number hasn't changed. Two hundred and fifty dollars.

I promised Connor five hundred.

I look around at the college kids forking over money for

giant hoagies they'll regret devouring tomorrow morning. Paying off a loan shark is not on any of their minds.

Suddenly, a hand swoops down and grabs the pile of money off the curb.

"Hey! Stop!" I jump up, too shocked to move for the moment.

People at the food trucks turn and watch as a guy in a black hoodie launches himself over the bushes and heads to the far end of the park where there are no lights.

"He stole my money!" I shout, but no one seems to care.

All right. I'll save myself. As usual. I take off running in my bare feet as a blur passes me, racing after the thief. He catches up with him before he reaches the end of the lot and grabs his hood. The thief swings back like he's on a yo-yo, legs flying in the air as he thuds to the pavement.

I rush up to the guy on the ground. My money pours out of the kangaroo pocket of his sweatshirt. I reach down to take it back.

"What do you think you're doing?" I call out. "I need this!"

The skinny kid—and he's just a kid, maybe fourteen—looks terrified. He scrambles to his feet.

"I'm sorry!" he says and rushes off, his sneakers making squishing noises on the pavement.

"You should be," I yell.

My savior takes a step to follow, and I reach out and put a hand on his arm. Or I should say huge bicep. Tingles of awareness zip over me. Eric.

He bends over with his hands on his knees as he catches his breath. "You don't want me to chase him down?"

"No. All of it seems to be here. He's probably desperate."

Just like me.

I shake my head as a realization hits me. Every loser leaves high school hoping they'll make something of themselves. I had that hope, however distant, that I could go to my high school reunion a changed person. Successful. Powerful. Boy, was I going to show Eric that I was way out of his league.

But Sparkly-Golden-Boy Eric has always been a success since he came out of the womb.

"What were you doing? Leaving your money out like that? Really dumb, Julia." There's judgment in his voice, tinged with haughtiness.

There's the Eric I know.

I'm sort of relieved this version of him showed up.

I glance around and find people holding their phones up, recording the incident. None of them offered to help, but they love to catch things on video. I imagine he'll be heralded as a hero in the captions.

I turn to go, but he stays close on my ass. I can almost feel him breathing down my neck. "A thank you might be in order."

If my only way to lose Eric is by thanking him, I'd *definitely* rather die.

I pick up the pace, meandering around trucks and people as I walk toward the street that leads to my house.

Pushing the theft attempt behind me, my mind races. I'm out of time. And what will I do, anyway, if I do somehow get the money? I'll be in this situation again next month.

Okay. Here's what has to happen. I have a few guys on my contacts list I've gone out with. Some are super nice. I tend to end my brief relationships amicably—except for Parker. Some I talk to on a regular basis since they aren't

Kappas. I'll just text a few and see if any of them can loan me the money. It's something I haven't tried yet.

It's a plan. I pick up the pace.

"Where are you going?" Eric snaps.

"My house. It's two streets over."

"And you're walking? It's late. Weirdos are trolling. Don't be careless."

A bitter laugh comes from me. Poor Eric. He's built like he can level mountains, but he's so bubble-wrap-protected that he's afraid of my part of town.

He was the wealthiest kid at our private prep school about an hour from here in Bellemeade, where we both lived. He walked those hallowed halls like he owned them, and I guess he did since his family was a huge donor.

Girls swarmed him. Guys collected around him to be his friend.

And me? I was the scholarship kid that came along senior year. They had an amazing art department, and my public school counselor arranged for me to nab a scholarship to bulk up my portfolio for college. It felt like a dream come true. My mom dropped me off every day in an old Chevrolet, a few times with the muffler dragging the ground.

He and I may have been at the same school, but we lived in different worlds.

Until our poetry class when we sat next to each other.

Our worlds collided as he led me down a path of desire and passion and lust.

My body throbbed for him. I ached, wanted, needed.

I worshipped him. I followed him around like a puppy dog. Gah, it's so embarrassing.

I march to the path in front of my house and wheel on

him. His eyes try to hold mine, but I look away. I just can't. Even now, after so much time has passed, each time I look at him I feel the rawness of betrayal.

"This is where I get off," I tell him, pointing up at the crumbling Tudor-style home that might have been quaint and charming about a hundred years ago but now needs a lot of attention.

The façade is a faded red brick accented with cracked timbers around the doors and windows. The roofline is pitched and complex with black tarps over the spots where it needs to be replaced. The crown jewel of the house is a beautiful stone chimney off to the side with orange and red roses scaling up to the sky. The weeds are out of control in the landscaping. The trees need to be trimmed back. It looks a little crazy.

I freaking love it. To me it looks like it belongs in the English countryside, a fairytale house.

In another world, if I were wealthy, I'd restore it to its former grandeur.

I cross my arms. "Thanks for getting my money." He does deserve a thank you, but I can't stop the sharpness of my voice.

He eyes the place like it's a horror house. "You live *here*? I thought it was condemned."

I glance up at it. "Well, it does give that impression with some of the boarded-up windows. To be honest, it probably helps keep the place from being robbed."

Poppy's parents bought it in April as an investment opportunity. It was supposed to be fixed up by the end of the summer, but they're busy people, and they've been sluggish with renovations. The bottom floor is done, but not upstairs where the bedrooms are. I don't mind. Having no working HVAC knocked a hundred bucks off the rent. Plus, this is Minnesota; not everyone has air conditioning.

It's the coming winter that scares me. Note to self: buy an electric blanket. Or two.

He crosses his arms, his face flat. I think he might have planted roots.

"What?"

He grimaces as he waves a hand at me. "Why were you crying?"

I start at the question. Why does he fucking care? "Me? Never happened."

He points at my cheek.

I wipe at it. Mascara. Shit, okay. My eyes are probably red, too. "None of your business."

"You need money?"

Pride rears up immediately and forces me to glare at him. There's no way in hell I'd ever admit my predicament to him. I made the mistake of fucking him once, but I learned from the experience. Even at my lowest, the payback he'd expect is far more than I'd be willing to sacrifice. "No."

"Liar."

I huff at him. Of course, it's a lie. I wasn't desperately counting money on a street with tears streaming down my face for nothing. "I've got to go. I'm not your problem, Eric."

This time, he doesn't stop me, but I feel his eyes on my ass as I climb the steps to the front porch. I don't look back until I'm in the house, and when I do, he's gone.

Good.

The house is dark, and it's a good bet my roommates, Poppy and Taylor, are asleep. I'm the one who keeps vampire hours. I rush up the stairs, fingers working my cell, seeking out Arnim, a wealthy lacrosse player I hooked up with last year before things went to shit.

I text: *Hey. What's going on? How was your summer?*

No response.

I scroll to Brendan, a rugby player. Another text: *Hey. How's the knee?*

Nothing.

They're probably partying or sleeping.

I sigh and scroll some more, my fingers stopping on a name. Parker Cavendish. My heart clenches. Oh, boy, is he a memory I want to forget.

I hooked up with him once and cut him loose. But he was persistent in chasing me and I enjoyed the attention. He hated that I stripped and would show up where I worked and glare at anyone who tucked bills under my bikini. Once he started a fight at Boobie Bungalow over me. I know, I know, I should have seen the signs that our relationship wasn't healthy—but I ignored them.

Still, I thought we had something special. Ugh. The truth is, I'd never dated a guy for real and assumed everything was rosy.

I mean, why the gifts if he didn't care?

Why the hand-holding and dates to nice restaurants?

Why the long drives out in the country with the top down on his Mercedes for a picnic?

My jaw pops. A few months into our relationship, I caught him in bed with two girls at a Kappa party. He was trashed and begged my forgiveness.

It's like masturbating with other girls, a means to an end, he told me. *People expect it of me. I get off and it's over. It's not like I'm dating them. You dance half-naked for men. How is this different, Ju-Ju?*

I shove thoughts of him away.

Sears. A basketball player. That could work. *Hey. How's your sister?*

Nothing.

I stop at the next name and stare at the Tennessee area code. Sugar, my old roommate. After graduation, she moved to Nashville with her boyfriend Zack—or Z—Morgan. She'd help, but prickles clog my throat at the thought of explaining all of this to her. I just can't. She'd be so disappointed in this awfulness I've gotten myself into.

"I'm doing the best I can," I whisper to myself as I head to my room at the end of the hall. Inside is my bed, a full-length mirror leaning against the wall, and an old dresser. My textbooks are piled on the nightstand. On the walls is a faded blue and gold butterfly damask wallpaper, a throwback from a different era. It's actually beautiful and as soon as I saw it, I knew this was my room. Over my bed are hundreds of drawings painted with watercolor. Butterflies, roses, peonies, and rabbits. I adore rabbits. "It's the long ears," I say to no one.

Little quotes accompany my art, written above or below.

I stare at my latest, a Painted Lady butterfly, one of the most common in the world with its orange and black wings.

A butterfly is proof that you can become something new.

It's rebirth and transformation.

Something beautiful.

Ethereal.

Someday that will be me.

Off to the side of my bedroom is a small bathroom that must have been added about fifty years ago. There's pink tile on the floor, an aqua colored pedestal sink, and a rusty clawfoot tub with a shower added into the wall.

I throw my phone on the bed, grab underwear, then hop in the shower to get rid of as much of Scott as possible. I scrub up, paying extra attention to the places where he touched me. My eyes close as hopelessness attempts to take over. I fight the emotion, pushing it down deep.

When I get back to my room, feeling almost human, I thought I'd have at least one message, but no one has replied.

I check the time. It's getting close to four.

With wet hair, I throw on a bra, a pair of gray joggers, and an oversized shirt. When dealing with Connor, it's best to look unattractive.

I kneel at the basket of dirty laundry and check pockets for cash I might have forgotten. Nothing. Heaving a sigh, I pull open the top drawer of the dresser and grab a diamond ring.

My mother's engagement ring, a solitaire with sapphires around it.

My dad died in a car accident before my parents' wedding, but he left her a lovely parting gift—me.

I had it appraised, once. Just in case. It's worth a thousand dollars.

I cling to it, remorse washing over me at what I'm thinking.

Gathering the cash together, I tiptoe out of the house. The streets are empty as I put my head down and walk to the seediest part of Sparrow Lake, in the opposite direction of campus.

After half an hour, I turn into an alley between two buildings that don't have any obvious businesses or tenants. Near the end is a lone light above a set of stairs leading up to a door on the second floor. At the bottom of the stairs is a heavy-set man wearing a blue suit with a crisp white shirt. It's unbuttoned at his collar, revealing wiry silver chest hair and a thick gold St. Christopher's medal. His brown hair is slicked back as he leans against the railing smoking a cigar.

My heart thumps. Coming to his part of town, not to mention seeing him, brings dread and fear roaring to the surface like a storm. Scott was a blip compared to Connor.

Just to look at him, you might think he's just a regular middle-aged businessman with a wife, kids, and a minivan, but he runs a flourishing drug and loan shark business out of his decaying, twenty-four-hour laundromat. He drives a blacked-out Range Rover. I have no clue if he's married, but he wears a wedding band.

I stare at the lit tip of his cigar and rub the scar on my wrist. He burned me last month when I was short.

Everyone thinks he's killed people. Once, when I came to pay early, I watched him pistol-whip a man into a bloody mess.

I cross the street to the small storefront and head to the back of the alley.

"I was just thinking about you," he says, flicking the cigar away. "You have my money, sweet thing?"

I let out an uneasy breath and nod.

"Good girl."

I pull the stash out from my pocket, already bracing myself. "N-Not all of it. But most of it."

One dark eyebrow shoots up. He grabs the money and starts to count. Dark eyes meet mine as a flicker of a smile crosses his face. "This is half. Can't you count?"

"I know, I—" I pull out the ring. "I have this. If you just—"

Another smile that stops my words. Cold. Deadly. "You know the rules. Cash only."

"Fine. Fine," I say, teeth chattering. "I-I'll go to the pawn shop when it opens and—"

"It's due now."

"T-The shop opens at nine. Just give me a few hours to—"

He laughs. "Sure, but every hour past six, you owe me twenty dollars more."

I gape. "What? But I—"

He reaches out, grabbing the hair at the nape of my neck. I feel the pop-pop-pop of it ripping from my scalp. Pain screams up my neck as he draws me to his face. The smell of smoke on his breath makes my eyes water.

"Connor, please..."

His finger traces down the center of my chest. "So pretty. I like you a lot. I don't want to hurt you." He gazes at my wrist. "How's the burn, sweet thing? Still hurt?"

I shake my head as my heart pounds so loud that it's deafening in my ears. "D-don't—"

"I'm a kind man. I told you how you can work the debt off." He dips his head to my neck and inhales. He bites my earlobe so hard I yelp.

"Why go through this every month? I can put you up in a nice place, take you out. You like Vegas?" He tugs on my nipple and I rear back, struggling.

His girlfriends end up cast aside, usually struggling with addiction.

Like my mom.

I should be used to his offers, immune to the horror since I've been here so many times, but the fear never subsides. "Never been," I say shakily.

He smiles. "Ah, you'll like how I treat you. Real good."

Never. Never. Never.

I shake my head. "Connor—"

Just like that, he's gone.

Someone jerked him away from me and slammed him to the ground.

I blink as I see Eric standing over Connor. He brings his fist down on Connor's stomach with a sickening sound, like slapping wet sand.

"Hands off her," Eric snaps as he rubs his knuckles. "This one's taken."

What?

"No—no—don't—" I rush over and try to shove Eric away.

He doesn't budge as he gives me an assessing look, eyes flashing as he takes me in. "I thought you were going to bed," he yells. "And you come here? What the fuck is wrong with you?"

He says it as if he's in charge of me.

"You want to talk about that now?" I shriek.

Connor lurches to his feet, roaring angrily, and lunges at Eric. Caught off-guard, Eric stumbles back, and the two of them careen into a random shopping cart.

"Stop!" I shout. "He has a g—"

I bite my tongue. The last thing I need to do is remind Connor of his weapon.

Eric delivers a punch to the side of Connor's head, and he falls to the pavement, moaning and disoriented.

Eric grabs my hand, gasping. "Fuck me, he's a big dude. Come on. Run!"

I take Eric's lead and we tear off back down the alley. All that's running through my head is that when Connor comes to, or worse when his morning-shift people arrive, he's going to kill me.

When we're a block away, I twirl to face him. "Eric. Where did you come from? Did you follow me? Why did you do that?"

He flashes me that same astonished expression he had back when he did his Superman act before. "I just saved you from that man. He was feeling you up!"

My hands squeeze his as my words rush out, trying to make him understand. What he did was dangerous. And stupid. "I know it looked bad, but I had it under control. He wouldn't have hurt me."

His jaw tightens. "I saw him!"

I lick my lips. "Look, okay, yes, he is an awful person, b-but you don't have a clue what you've gotten yourself involved in—" I stop and tremble, the terror dawning more and more. "H-he could have shot you. You could be dead and it would be all my fault!"

His brow wrinkles as his eyes hold mine. "Julia, no . . ."

"Don't you understand? This is my life, and it's messed up, and I can't have any more people I'm responsible for. I can barely take care of myself. He won't forget this, you know. I-I'll have to face him sooner or later and pay for what happened."

"Julia—"

"Connor doesn't care who you are. He doesn't care if you have money or that you play hockey." My lashes flutter. "Eric, please. You can't . . . you can't be my knight in shining armor. Just. Don't."

"Julia!" he calls as I dash away.

"I'm not worth it" dances in my head as I flee, but I stop that line of thinking.

I am worth something and I can't forget it.

Hitting the sidewalk on my street, I kick in what little energy I have left and hurry up the steps to the front door. I slam it behind me, shoving the deadbolt into place.

I sink to the floor and replay the scene in my head.

Eric slamming him down, Eric taking up for me.

My hands cover my face. God knows I'm so sick of weeping.

Of the knowing looks I get on campus.

Of the worry that gnaws at me like a dog with a bone. It never leaves.

I'm sick of this half-life, of being paralyzed with fear and anxiety as I push friends and emotions to the side. I'm just trying to be strong. To power through.

Why does each day seem like a battle just to stay alive?

I curl into a ball on the hardwood as I try to stop the tears, I really do, but they come, hot and wet against my cheeks. Perhaps I need this cry. It's not like before at the park when I wept out of frustration. I need to let this doubt and uncertainty go. They rain down, a release from the adrenaline from a night that feels as if it lasted years.

My face presses against the cool floor as my shoulders shudder. A wounded sound comes from my throat as I try to keep it quiet.

I remember the shy young girl I was freshman year, the stars I had in my eyes.

The rose-colored glasses I wore.

Somedays I wake up and forget for a moment that I'm not her anymore.

Maybe the butterfly inside of me has already emerged and a storm has broken her wings.

What do I do now?

4

Eric

That's the thanks I get?

She's lucky I saw her when I went out for a jog. I needed to wear myself out so I could sleep. I noticed her from across the street, her face pale, her steps hurried as if someone were after her.

Most of all, I hated the slump in her shoulders.

It niggled. Pricked like a goddamn needle under my skin.

Yes, I followed her. Because I was worried.

And when I came around the corner and saw that guy with his hands on her, my body went from zero to kill.

It's not hard to piece it together.

She was counting her money and crying for a reason. She owes him. But for what?

He's a super bad guy, yeah, I get that, but what Julia doesn't know is that I've been in this predicament before with someone else, even though I didn't know until it was too late.

It cost me everything.

I keep picturing his hands on Julia, and my own tighten into fists as I walk back to the alley we came from.

The place is empty except for a yellow cat with matted fur. It licks its paw and watches me warily as I check between the trash cans. Dude is gone. There's a light coming from the door at the top of the stairs, but I'm not going up there.

I look around for anywhere else Tons-of-Fun could be.

I'm about to leave when I see something glinting in the moonlight in the puddle at my feet. I stoop and pick it up.

A ring.

I came into things late, but I'm pretty sure I wasn't interrupting a marriage proposal. Slipping it into my pocket, I turn and start when I see him in front of a store with a sign that reads *Fresh Set Laundry*. His nose is bleeding and he holds a paper towel to it.

"Ha, the tough boy comes back. Surprise, surprise."

The door opens and another guy walks out. He's got tattoos on his neck and is short, but definitely has a look of someone that can handle himself in a fight. The new guy pulls up both sleeves and smiles as he assesses me.

I raise my hands in a placating manner. "Look. I don't want any trouble. I just want to straighten this out. Obviously, I lost my head. What can I do to make it right?"

The big guy smooths his hair back. "Okay, college boy, how much you got?"

The short guy has never stopped moving. He slowly circles me, never getting closer, but ready to jump in.

"First, what's the deal with you and Julia?"

He smiles, his teeth damn near perfect. White. Shiny. He could be in a toothpaste commercial.

He looks me up and down, evaluating, then brushes gravel off his sleeve. "My business."

I stiffen, my eyes narrowing. I have fifty pounds on the little guy, and I've already knocked around the other one. I've had my share of hockey scrapes on and off the ice. I even trained with some wrestlers at an MMA place. I'm not scared of throwing gloves, even if it is two on one.

The big guy cocks his head at me. "Do I know you?"

"Nope."

He wags his finger. "Nah, you look familiar. I've seen you before."

"Maybe around town," I say. "What does she owe you?"

He rears back and laughs. "I get it. You're that hockey player. Winger on the Hawthorne team. Everest."

I think about denying it but... "Yeah."

He holds his hand up at his friend, then points at me. "Bobby. He's a celebrity."

"I fucking hate hockey," Bobby mutters, beady eyes on me.

"Fine by me," I say.

"Yeah. She owes me money," the big guy tells me with a smirk. "So, you gonna front her the cash?"

"How much?"

"It was five hundred she owed today. But now?" He wipes his nose with his hand and stares at the blood. "Consider it double. Pain and suffering for me."

Jesus. "That's a grand."

He pulls out a pack of cigarettes and lights one up. "Yep."

My teeth grit as I pull out my phone. "What's your Venmo?"

He chuckles and looks over at Bobby. "This guy. Cash only."

I let out a breath. "You think I carry that kind of money on me?"

He rakes his eyes over me, taking in my expensive sneakers, the designer clothes. He shrugs. "Do you?"

I reach for my wallet and pull out six hundred. I'd hit the bank earlier for cash for the first week of class. "This is all I've got. Take it and call it even. Plus, I know she gave you some already."

He stares at me for a long time, then snatches the money. "Tell Julia that if she pulls this shit next month, she's dead."

My stomach pitches. *She goes through this every month.*

What the hell is going on?

He continues. "Keep out of it next time. Or you'll regret it, feel me?"

I back away but can't let it go. My hand rubs at my jaw. "How much to settle her debt for good?"

"She's under your skin, huh? I can see that. That innocent look. Big tits and long legs. I'd like a taste of that."

My back ripples with tension as I resist the urge to clock him. Julia's more than just her body. She's smart. Sweet. Funny when you get to know her.

Or she used to be those things.

I don't know who she is anymore.

"How much?" I plant my feet in a defensive stance.

Surprise moves over his face as he raises his eyebrows. "Well, the exact math is a little complicated, but let's call it six grand."

My eyes thin as I stare at him. I bet it's less than that.

Most of my money is in a trust fund, but I have a healthy

bank account my mother drops a check in each month. Sometimes I barely use it, usually during hockey season, and the amount piles up.

"I never have that kind of cash, but I'll give it to you through Venmo. I'll add an extra thousand if you do something for me," I say.

"What?"

"You have to leave her alone from now on. I want your word." I'm sure his honor isn't worth shit, but it's the only thing I can think of.

He considers this as he dabs at his nose. "Why? Guy like you—you look like you're going places. She's a throwaway. Who is she to you? Girlfriend? She a good fuck?"

I dip my head, hiding the anger on my face.

Who is she to me?

Yeah, that's a story.

She's someone I used and never looked back.

I raise my eyes. "After I pay you, if she comes to you for drugs, for anything, you need to walk away. She's off-limits. We have a deal?"

There's confusion on his face—I don't think anyone's tried to make a deal like this with him. He nods. "Alright. Bobby has the Venmo. He's into crypto and all that. Ain't ya, Bobby?"

"Block chain . . . the future." Bobby holds up his phone with a QR code.

I pull out mine and scan his. Venmo pops up and we both hear a whoosh sound.

Seven thousand out of my account and on its way to a lowlife scumbag.

Bobby glances down at his phone then holds it up to his boss and they both nod their heads.

I head home to what Reece and Boone, my roommates, call Hockey House.

My stomach growls as I go inside. In the kitchen, I open the cabinet and grab a box of cereal and reach in a hand. Empty. I grab another box. Same thing. The kitchen clears out of food within seconds after one of us makes a supermarket run. I curse, wishing once again that Z still lived here. He kept things organized—and clean. I glare at the overflowing trash can.

I yell out to no one in particular. "Who keeps putting empty cereal boxes back in the cabinet?"

A voice from the couch responds. "Stop putting your dirty hands in the box and we'll stop putting empty boxes on the shelf."

I find Boone in the den on the couch, wearing nothing but plaid boxers and playing video games. Oddly enough, that's the exact same position I left him in six hours ago. There's cheese dip drizzled on his chest and two empty bags of chips next to him. A grease-stained McDonald's bag and an empty two-liter Mountain Dew are on the coffee table. He's chewing on a Snickers bar as dark brown hair falls in his face. He's a good guy. Kind of innocent.

"Jesus, Boone. Have you been up all night?"

He gives me an irreverent grin as he chews. A sophomore center on the hockey team, he was on the second line last year. He was Z's back-up and took his place when he graduated.

"We're lifting today at one instead of ten this morning. Got it?" I tap him on his forehead. "One o'clock. Workout. As your captain, I'm commanding you to get some sleep."

"Uh-huh."

I sigh. The kid keeps telling me that he's the first O'Brien to go to college, but I've never seen him crack a book. Lean with a muscular build, he's not the biggest guy on the ice, but what he lacks in size, he makes up for in cunning and hustle. I've seen him take down players no one else could and come out on top.

Trouble is, he thinks he knows everything already.

"This conversation has been fulfilling. I'm off to get some sleep." I turn to go up the stairs.

"Wait, one o'clock?"

"Yeah, that's what I said. I have to be somewhere this morning."

He shoves floppy hair out of his face. "Yeah? Where?"

"The LSATs. Again." Sure, I get decent grades to stay eligible to play hockey, but my brain chokes on tests.

He pops an eyebrow.

I shrug. "I have to get into the right law school. My brother went to Harvard. Big shoes to fill."

He squints. "I don't see why you have to be a lawyer to work at your dad's hedge fund."

"My dad expects me to be a lawyer." The words feel like sawdust in my mouth.

Reece comes into the den, rolling his neck as he stalks around wearing tiger print bikini bottoms. Dude looks shredded from all his workouts. With broad shoulders and a stocky build like his brother Z, he's a brick wall you don't want to run into.

I lean on the banister, glad for the distraction. "Morning, precious. Did we wake you?"

"My bedroom is right off the den, and you two won't shut the fuck up." He gives a casual stretch, then darts up the stairs fast as lightning, puts his hand on my head and rubs it vigorously.

"I pass the puck!" he calls then dashes away.

"Fucker," I say as I rear back and fix my hair. "Was that puck in your hand the whole time?"

I checked but didn't see it. I always check when we're all in the house together.

You never know when one of them will jump you.

Reece laughs as he holds up a puck that has *The Best Puck* written on it in white paint. "This is yours now, bro. It was in my hand."

The puck is from a game last season where we kicked ass. Of course, we saved it and created a game of tag with it. The holder of the puck can only force it on another player if they're touching his head and saying, "I pass the puck". The three of us must be in the same room to witness the pass, and there's no passing while someone is sleeping or trashed.

I come back down the stairs and take it out of his hand. It's mine now. "You could've done that to Boone at any time. He's a sloth. He's literally on the couch, eating his way through junk food. He'd trip before he got past the trash."

Reece grins. "But it was more fun waiting on you. No passing it for forty-eight hours. The puck belongs to Eric."

"Concur!" we say together.

Maybe it's a stupid game, but it builds brotherhood. One night, Reece and I waited in Boone's closet for an hour while he got ready to go on a date. He had his hair perfectly gelled and styled when he opened his closet and I jumped him. He actually fell to the floor and screamed like a girl. He said he peed a little. The memory makes me chuckle.

Glancing around, I notice a familiar red flier stuck to the refrigerator. I've seen them posted all over fraternity row. *Rush Kappa*, it says with a pic of the frat house with all the brothers in suits on the porch. My jaw clenches.

"What's this?" I ask Boone. I know it's not Recce's. He's been around me long enough to know how I feel about Kappa.

Boone shrugs. "Just considering..."

I frown. "Hockey players don't pledge. The team is all you need."

He gives me a look. "There's no official rule against it. And why wouldn't I?"

"Because—"

He cuts me off. "You might not want to be a Kappa. You don't need to be. You're gonna be the next billionaire hedge funder. The rest of us..."

I sigh. "Yeah, but—"

"Being a Kappa opens doors in the business world. Even our dean is Kappa." He turns back on his video game, ending the discussion.

Yeah. And so were my brother and dad. Without Kappa, my father wouldn't be where he is today. And if Boone wants to get into a good business school, there's probably no better way than to use Kappa connections.

Fuck it. It's been a long night and I still haven't slept.

I trudge up the stairs, concrete on my chest. I should have stayed home last night and crammed. I planned to. The angel on my shoulder said it was the right thing to do because my scores from this summer were dismal. But the devil on the other shoulder decided to take a break and have a beer, maybe find a hook-up. Next thing you know, I'm your friendly neighborhood dude saving damsels from drunken embarrassment, thieves, and mobsters.

My stomach swirls. This is my last chance to salvage those hopes of going to law school.

Which is what I want.

I think.

I used to want to fulfill that family dream, but the closer it gets, the more I want to punch a wall.

After we won the championship and Z went pro, I floated the idea of pursuing the NHL to my dad.

Don't be stupid, he said. *You have the potential to make the kind of green Wayne Gretzky would shit on a Canadian flag for.*

My hands clench. Whatever. I was passed over for three years in the hockey draft.

It's not even an option.

At the top of the steps, I find Lucifer, the house ferret, a freaky thing Reece bought this summer because he thought Hockey House needed a mascot. He said it was just like a cat. It would use a litter box and catch mice.

I'm convinced he mostly shits in Boone's room.

"I don't have any food for you," I mumble, wondering why the animal has taken a liking to me. It's usually curled up with its furry tail in front of my door. I haven't been nice to it since the day it made me do a nut-plant over the railing when I was moving in boxes.

The thing just stares at me, head tilted.

"Go on!" I motion it away.

Not even a twitch from the thing.

Stepping over it, I open my door.

It slips in with me.

Fucker.

"A cat would eat you in one bite!" I yell as it disappears under my bed.

My LSAT prep books are sitting on my night table, uncracked. I stare at them, then collapse onto my mattress and stare at the ceiling, rubbing my eyes with the palms of my hands.

Then I reach into my pocket and pull out the ring.

I study it, then turn on my bedside lamp and hold it underneath. My eyes are bleary from lack of sleep, but I can make out the inscription: *NL + LL Forever.*

L for Lauren, Julia's last name? Who does the ring belong to?

Holding it in my fist, I close my eyes and see the fear on her heart-shaped face as we ran from the scene. Her whiskey-colored eyes glittered with unshed tears, her bee-stung lips tight and compressed.

I flip over and beat my pillow.

Focus.

You need to ace this test.

Go to law school.

Be like your brother Kurt.

The one who isn't here to carry on the family name anymore.

5

Julia

I open my eyes and realize I'm leaning against my headboard. My neck is bent at an unnatural angle with my cheek resting on my shoulder. I rub it to soothe the tension there, but it isn't the only muscle that hurts. My knees are scabbed and my leg muscles are sore. Even my spine aches. That's what I get for going to the alley with Scott, chasing a guy in the park, then running like hell from Connor.

Poppy, my roommate, calls through the door, "Julia? You in there?"

"Yeah!" I crawl out of bed and grab an olive green tank top and slip on some denim shorts.

"Hurray!" she calls, too cheery for morning, but that's Poppy. A quick glance at my phone tells me it's eight.

I stagger in my bathroom and stare at myself in the mirror as the night before plays through my head.

The ring. I need to pawn it today.

I grimace then wash my face and brush my teeth.

After I pawn it, I'll need to go back to the laundromat and beg Connor to forgive Eric.

I reach into my pocket from last night and my stomach drops. The ring! I remember holding it out to Connor—then Eric showed up. Shit, shit, shit. I've lost it.

"Julia? You going to be long? You have a visitor."

A visitor? I push down the despair of losing the ring and take a deep breath.

"You could have started with that," I say with a grin as I open the door. I take in her ladybug pjs and fuzzy slippers. I'm surprised she isn't wearing her pearls. "You look adorable. Who is it?"

"I wouldn't have let him in, but my dad said he was sending someone to install the HVAC. I assumed it was him and opened the door. Oh, it's Eric. I put him in that little foyer room. So, he's in the house, but not technically."

I groan. "Why didn't you warn me?"

"I did. Just now. Eric Hansen is here. Hockey player. Hottie. Whatever. Catch up." She smiles, and with Poppy, it's endearingly kind.

I've only known Poppy and Taylor for a year. They were really Sugar's friends and sort of adopted me.

I sigh. "Great. Thanks."

She tucks a piece of her shoulder-length black hair behind her ear. "Want me to stall him? I could say you're still sleeping?"

"No," I say. "The man refuses to listen. I'll deal with it."

"Rough night at the club?"

"Nah, it was fine." I ease past her and paste on a smile, hoping she doesn't notice the scrapes on my knees. Sure, I could have asked Poppy for the money this month, and I did a few months back. She gave me what she could spare, but her family keeps most of her funds in a trust.

I don't want to be that friend, the one who begs for money. I hate putting them in that position. I want to do this on my own without involving people I care about. I need to. It's my problem, and yes, it's humiliating to admit the situation that is my mother.

I open the beveled-glass doors that lead to the foyer. It used to be a greeting room for visitors to the house to leave their calling cards. The only furniture in the room is a lime green buffet table that Taylor redid with chalk paint. On top is a pretty blue vase with boho-style beige plumes inside.

Eric's large frame and rugged handsomeness takes the air from my lungs. His hair is pulled back in a man-bun, my fav look on him.

No. I do *not* have a favorite look for him, but it does show off his ridiculous cheekbones and aristocratic, slightly bent nose.

He's wearing jeans, gold Converse, and a HU shirt. The lion on the front seems to glare at me—much like he is now.

I lean against the doorjamb. Be cool, be cool. "Howdy, partner."

He doesn't smile. "That guy at the laundromat is scary. Stay away from him. I mean it."

I huff. The nerve of him to tell me what to do.

"That's what I told you. I repeat, you could have been hurt. Let me handle Connor."

His arms cross. "How did you get involved with him? Are you on drugs?"

I tuck my hands in my pockets and dip my head so he can't see how much his words hurt. I know I strip, no one has to remind me, but in prep school, I was the goody-two shoes who never wavered. I had to keep my grades up to keep my scholarship—not that I was ever invited to parties. I wrote poetry. I drew. I daydreamed about him. "Do I look like an addict?"

His golden eyes roam over me. Assessing. "Maybe."

My throat tingles with words I want to say but know I shouldn't.

The less he knows, the better.

His nose flares. "I'm trying to help you and you're giving me the cold shoulder. What's wrong with you?"

I swallow thickly as I gaze at him. "Eric. Please. Being around me will only smear your good name—"

"Stop," he calls out, then rubs his face, his anger seeming to deflate like a popped tire. "Don't put yourself down like that. You're a person, Julia. One that people care about."

And I want to protect those people.

I chew on my bottom lip. "You shouldn't have interfered."

He lets out a long sigh, gives me a searching look, goes to leave, then stops. He reaches into his pocket and holds something up. "This is yours, I assume."

I stare at the ring, my lips parting. "How did you...?"

But he's already out the door.

I turn to find Poppy and Taylor with their faces pressed against the glass, clearly eavesdropping. Taylor has his robe on, a flowy orange and pink kimono silk with cherry blossoms on it. He's tall with silky dark hair, brown skin, and a lilting British accent. Lash extensions adorn his warm eyes.

"What was *that* about?" he asks as I come back into the den. "You've been keeping secrets?"

I grunt.

"I didn't realize you guys were hanging out." He follows me in the kitchen.

"We're not."

I think back to freshman year at HU, the first time I'd seen him since prep school.

It was about a month in and I got the nerve up to attend a frat party. Just as promised, the brothers at Kappa were hot. I dressed up, wore tons of makeup, and made my way to Frat Row.

I thought it would be hard to mingle. It wasn't after a few drinks. I was approached on all sides, guys asking me questions in rapid succession. *And who do we have here? What are you studying? Where are you from? Are you in a sorority?*

Then I saw Eric and all my happiness crashed.

I knew he was playing hockey at Hawthorne, but I wasn't prepared to run into him.

That night, the first thing I noticed was that he was under a light bulb, and he was so tall that it cast a supernatural aura over the hard lines of his face. The only thing on him that didn't scream *man* was his lips, full and lush with an indentation line that went down the center of the lower one. Back then, he only had a field of stubble, a shade darker than the hair on his head.

My breath hitched, those old insecurities rising up as he brought harsh reality back into focus.

I'll never be able to escape the girl from prep school who wanted the unattainable hockey star.

Then, I realized there was something different about him.

The Golden Boy looked . . . troubled. Was that even possible?

I nudged off the other guys, craning my neck to see him

as he stared at a blank wall.

He looked almost sad.

And with liquid courage coursing through my veins, I decided I'd let bygones be bygones. This was the new me; it might be the new him. We could start fresh.

I stalked up to him, formulating some line in my head, but another Kappa guy stepped between us and asked if I wanted a beer but I shook my head, craning to look over his shoulder.

"I was just trying to see..."

He followed my line of vision and laughed. "Oh, forget the pledge. He's in one of his moods."

Since when did our prep school star have moods? "What do you mean?"

He grinned. "Look. I'll show you."

He snapped his finger in Eric's face, and Eric blinked, his eyebrows furrowing in annoyance as he caught sight of me. His gaze was hot, a punch to the gut.

Arcs of electricity raced between us.

For about two seconds.

His upper lip curled in a snarl. "Fuck off," he growled and stalked away.

I was sucked back to prep school, to the day when he told me he didn't stick around for seconds.

Eric Hansen wasn't different; he was the same privileged jock.

I shake off the past as I face Taylor. "In British words, Eric Hansen is a bloody wanker."

Still...

He thought he was helping me last night. I can't be angry at that.

"I take it you declined his marriage proposal?" Taylor

asks.

I follow their line of vision to the glinting diamond I slipped on my finger. *Oh.*

"It was my mom's. I lost it last night. I guess he found it. Long story."

Taylor's mouth makes the shape of an O but he doesn't say anything, just trades a glance with Poppy, a worried one. I've seen that furtive look between them more than once, but I don't address it because addressing it means I'll have to explain about my mother.

"We're here for long stories, Julia," he murmurs.

"That we are," Poppy says brightly. "All you have to do is talk."

I shrug, keeping my eyes down. "Hmm."

He heads past me to the antique white stove. "Fine. Breakfast it is. I'm making kippers!"

Poppy laughs. "No one in here eats kippers, Taylor. Where do you even get those smelly things?"

It's entirely possible he gets them from Sparrow Lake. He's just crazy enough to attempt to go fishing there. Probably in his silk robe. But there's also a chance that his family sent them to him in their care packages, which consist of Cadbury Twirls, Marmite, Quavers Crisps and shortbread biscuits. I'm thankful he shares it with me, because usually all I buy is ramen. He can keep the kippers, though.

He also loaned me money. I still haven't paid him back. I rub my forehead. The list of people I owe makes my stomach hurt.

I pour a big cup of coffee, douse it with creamer, then make one for Taylor and hand it to him as he moves from the stove to the fridge, pulling things out and generally playing host. Sure enough, he has a mason jar of some oily, amorphous things which he throws on a hot pan. The smell hits me halfway across the room.

Poppy sips her hot tea. "I saw Eric a lot last spring. He was in my theater appreciation class. Everyone flocked to him. You'd think he was giving away free candy."

I snort. "I'll bet."

"He's very sexy," she continues dreamily, then looks at me and clears her throat. "Well, to everyone but you. You never have liked him."

Taylor pokes the sizzling fish in the pan. "I'd like to flock all over him."

I pop open a window to get fresh air in the kitchen. "Believe me, he's totally overrated."

Poppy gives me an inquiring look. "There's always been this, I don't know, energy between you two. What happened?"

I'm not giving them the R-rated version. That story is dead to me. "We went to prep school together."

Poppy gasps. "Julia! You were school friends with him and you never told us?"

I sigh. In her world, everyone is a friend. A stranger is a friend you haven't met yet. She's an all-the-woodland-creatures-follow-me-around-the-forest-and-isn't-life-just-awesome kind of girl.

I wince. I used to be like her.

I take a sip of my coffee. "Sorry."

"Okay, so he was mean to you in high school and now you want to hate-fuck him?" Taylor asks.

I glare. "No."

Poppy nods vigorously as if his theory makes sense. "Do you fancy him, Julia?"

I smirk. Taylor's British has a way of rubbing off on us.

"Was he one of your clients at Platinum Nights?" Taylor asks.

"He's not like that," I say, frowning. Someone like Eric doesn't need to feed women dollar bills to make them go crazy over him. "I'm not his type, and there are plenty of ready females that are. Not to mention he's not *my* type." I stick a bite of scrambled eggs in my mouth and chew to cover the lie. He's exactly my kind of poison.

Tall, built, and protective to the point of stupidity.

"Were you hurt by him?" Taylor asks.

I exhale gustily. "I shouldn't have said anything. Eric was not proposing to me. Never, ever, ever. I don't like him; he doesn't like me. We hate each other. The end."

Taylor sets a plate of little fish in front of me. They've been split open in a butterfly fashion from head to toe, salted, smoked, then fried. The briny, woody scent assails my nose and I swallow.

"Can I tempt you, love?" He waves the flowy arms of his kimono.

My stomach rolls. "You're, um, sweet, to make breakfast. Are there any more eggs?"

He nudges the plate closer to me. "You've lost weight. Come on, get some real protein. They're high in Omega fatty acids."

There's an edge to his voice, and I get it, I do. They haven't seen me much this summer, both of them out of town, and I've lost weight since May. My hip bones protrude and my face is thinner.

"Try it, please," he begs and I groan because I can't resist his puppy dog eyes.

I grab my fork, pointing it at him as he takes the seat across from me. "Fine, but I'm not promising I'll like it."

He watches me with excitement as I poke the brown fish, get a tiny bit on my fork, stick it in my mouth, then wash it down with a sip of coffee.

"Well?" he asks.

Poppy stares at me intently, her hands clasped on the table as she leans over. "If you like it, I'll try them."

I gaze at them and emotion tugs at me, expanding more at the concern I read in their eyes. I've missed them this summer. The silence in the house ate at me greedily, especially when I came home from work filled with self-hate and loneliness. I really don't have a family. I can't depend on my mom anymore.

I take another bite and smile. "Sort of like sardines but milder."

Poppy gags delicately.

I toss a fish at her and she shrieks.

"Your turn," I say with a smirk. "Eat 'em up, love."

She picks it up by the tail and stares at it like it's a bug. Then sniffs it delicately.

"Boo!" Taylor says, and she starts and throws it up in the air. It plops back down on her cheek. Horror flits over her face as she shoves it to the floor, then looks at us and starts giggling.

I chuck it in the trash as Taylor gets her a new one to try.

We hover over her as she puts a microscopic piece in her mouth and chews.

She immediately hops up and spits it in the trash.

Taylor exhales dramatically. "I guess it's an acquired taste."

We laugh, and for the moment, I feel light, like everything is going to work out, but I know the big bad is coming.

Sooner or later, I'll have to face Connor.

6

Eric

"Yeah, I think I did good," I say to my dad as I drive back to campus. My head bangs like a monkey is inside clanging cymbals.

"You do?"

I clench the phone to stop from saying what I really think. *That test might as well have been in Chinese.* "Definitely. Why?"

My father lets out the standard sigh of disappointment. I've heard it so many times you'd think I'd be immune, but it cuts deep. "You said that last time. And you bombed it."

"I know, I know."

I hear the tapping of his pen against his desk, his tell that he's irritated and wants to dig at me more. He used to do it when I was little and would pop by his home office to say hi. He'd tap his pen and tell me to go find Mom.

There's an empty hole inside of me, and I keep thinking

that if I try harder to be like Kurt, if I'm smarter, if I'm a lawyer, then maybe my parents will love me as much as they loved him.

Sure, I had basic needs met growing up, but my likes and dislikes? I bet my dad doesn't even know my favorite meal. Brisket and roasted potatoes with olive oil. The cook knew. She made it for me all the time.

My parents rarely acknowledged my hockey achievements. They were irrelevant compared to Kurt's GPA or his acceptance into Harvard Law.

Growing up like that is almost like rejection. It's as if getting their love and attention was almost attainable, only to be yanked out from under you when you bring home a D on your report card.

Kurt came first. His needs. His wants.

I loved him. I was jealous of him.

"Curtis said that Parker aced his LSAT. He studied with the frat apparently. I'm sure he'll be accepted anywhere he applies."

Parker is a sonofabitch and can rot in hell. "Good for him," I mutter.

He rustles papers around. "Did you ask the frat for help?"

My gut twists and the monkey bangs a little harder.

"Yep." I don't like to lie to my father. But he's left me no other choice. Needs must.

He thinks I'm a Kappa. He was stoked when I pledged. Proud. The pats on the shoulder he gave me felt almost alien. Of course, Kurt was dead by then and I was all that was left.

I never told him I left the frat. In the three years I've

been at Hawthorne, through luck and serendipity, I've managed to keep up the façade. That first fall semester when I was pledging, he visited the Kappa house a few times, but hasn't returned. I have Kurt's pin in my room. If worse comes to worse, I can wear it in front of him.

"This time I have a much better feeling. I knew what to expect." More lies.

I need to tell him *something*. He sank a thousand dollars into a fancy LSAT prep class that was supposed to make me into a genius.

I did go to those meetings.

Did it work? Hell, no. I felt just as lost this time.

But the scores won't be in for a few weeks. That will buy me some time.

"Tell me the second you get those scores, Eric."

"Sure. How's Mom doing—"

He hangs up without a goodbye.

I stare at the display long after the line goes dead, until I see my face scowling in the reflection on the glass.

I miss my turn and need to cut back on a side street. It takes me past Julia's house, and my head goes back to seeing her this morning.

Her insistence that she doesn't need help.

What is it about her that pricks at me?

She isn't the kind of pretty that's flashy or takes your breath, no, her prettiness is quiet, almost regal. She has this aloof quality—until those caramel eyes capture your gaze. They positively glow with every emotion inside her. They're hard to look away from.

She's got freckles across her perfect nose.

Her lips are overly full, pink, and soft.

Thick black lashes—

Nope. Not my monkey, not my circus . . .

Yeah?

So why did I fork over seven grand—plus the six hundred in cash?

Whatever. I can't think about her.

I park in the alley behind our place and see several Kappa brothers on the rooftop porch of their house in cheap lounge chairs. Looks like they're drinking and getting sun.

Assholes.

"If it isn't Robin Hood," a loud voice calls out.

It's Scott, otherwise known as Kappa Douche number two after Parker.

I'm assuming he means the freshman I took home last night. Ignoring him, I go to the door of my house, which faces the back of theirs.

As I'm fishing for my keys, Scott calls out, "Hope she gave you a freebie, Hansen. Was it good?"

This isn't about the freshman. This is about Julia.

I saw Scott on the porch last night—or this morning—watching me talk to Julia after she bumped into my tire. Something happened between them. Was he the reason they called her a slut?

I put my keys back in my pocket, turn, and stalk toward the Kappa house. "Was *what* good?" I growl up at the roof.

"Don't make me say it out loud . . ." He chuckles as he looks back at his friends, smirking.

I gesture with my hands, an angry motion. "Please. Say it."

"That whore you talked to last night. Julia? The one you saved at the food trucks? She had to be grateful."

It's becoming clearer. During a test break, Reece texted

me the video of me tackling the thief by the food trucks. I guess everyone on campus saw it.

My hands twitch like a live wire, aching to hit something. Anger rises in my throat with unsaid words as I stare at them for a long, hard moment.

I'm on edge. Skating on thin ice.

Maybe it's because I bombed that test.

Maybe it's because my dad mentioned Parker.

Maybe it's because I'm living life in a pressure cooker.

He lazily runs a hand through his dirty-blond hair. There's a gloating expression on his face. "Yeah, she likes to go the extra mile for her best clients, if you know what I mean. Her lips around my cock?" He pumps his pelvis. "Oh, man, she sucks like a porn star."

An image of Julia and Scott together pops in my head and my teeth clench.

He's pushing your buttons, I tell myself. *He wants a reaction.*

And God knows I want to give him one, right in the face.

Deep breaths. In. Out. Again.

Never in a million years would Julia suck him off. I know this in my gut.

Whipping around, I stalk back to the house, go inside, and slam the door.

Boone is still on the couch in his underwear. There's a new Mountain Dew bottle on the floor and more candy bar wrappers. Another McDonald's bag has been added to the mix, and a milkshake container has spilled over onto the coffee table.

"Boone? What the hell?" I survey the carnage.

"Sorry," he murmurs as he leans to the side, flying a spaceship on the TV.

"Do we have a vacuum?" I ask Reece when he waltzes into the den. "Boone has some cleaning to do."

"What am I, Martha Stewart?" Reece asks.

I grimace as I wave my hand at Boone. "The sophomore is a pig. All he does is eat and play games. We're gonna get roaches with this kind of mess."

Boone pops up, dropping his smirk and his controller. "Did you say ... roaches?"

"Yeah. Big ass crawlers. Six inches long," I tell him.

He shudders from head to toe.

I huff. "That got your attention, huh?"

He nods. "I hate those fuckers. They've got laser eyeballs and razor teeth, well, not real teeth like we do, but they bite. My mom put one in a jar with no food or water and it lived for three whole months. She told me if one bit me and sucked my blood, I'd turn into one. I believed her until I was like, ten. I legit have nightmares about them crawling on my junk." He cups his groin. "You sound like my mom, bro, asking me to clean up. I miss her."

Boone has three settings: hockey, video games, or chatterbox.

He shakes his head as he kicks the McDonald's bag. "I guess I got a little out of control this weekend. Summer camp was great, but now I'm nervous. Taking Z's place on the line? Man, that's a lot."

"I get it." There's a feeling of responsibility on all of us since we won the championship.

"I'll just, um, pick all this up and take out the trash, yeah?" he says as he snatches one of the candy wrappers and sucks out the extra chocolate.

"Good idea. Glad you thought of it," I reply dryly.

He looks between us. "Anything crazy ya'll are scared of?"

Reece shrugs. "Bugs don't bother me, but I don't care for thunderstorms."

Boone picks up the Mountain Dew, opens the cap, and sucks down a drink. "Serial killers bother me. I've watched too many documentaries, and those Ted Bundy types are so random. My uncle lived out on a farm in the seventies and someone stabbed him inside his house. The police think it was Bundy. A man fitting his description was camping nearby. Have you noticed that most serial killers live in rural places? I mean, Sparrow Lake is sort of isolated. Lots of woods, farmland, and lakes. Perfect places to dump a body."

I chuckle. "*Rural Minnesota Killer*. Sounds like a good show idea."

"Dude. Don't even," Boone replies with a wince.

Reece pops me on the arm. "Eric here has a thing about bananas. Called them the demon of the fruit world."

I start. "What? When?"

He nods. "You said it one night when you were trashed. Something about your brother and you."

I lift my shoulders in a shrug.

Boone narrows his eyes at me. "Come on, spill. Did you choke on a banana as a kid? Did it get stuck in your throat? Was it that mushy feeling, like a slug?"

My lips twitch. "You've had too much Mountain Dew."

Boone cocks his head and gives me a knowing look. "The smell, right? The freaky strings?"

"No."

"Are you intimidated by their girth because your dick is small?" Reece tosses in.

"No," I say, exasperated.

They cross their arms.

"Tell us the truth," Reece says.

I throw my hands up. "Fine. When I was five or so, I went to bed and there was a long curvy thing under my covers. I screamed and Kurt came in and said it was a python, that he'd seen it outside earlier. Then he pushed me on top of it, and I could feel it moving under me on the bed. Turned out it was a bunch of bananas he'd put under my covers." I can still see his lanky form bent over laughing in my room. "He was crazy like that. Fun. Anyway, I hate bananas. I'm not scared of them."

"Demon of the fruit world," Reece reminds me and I chuckle.

A few minutes later, Boone has taken out the trash and is loading the dishwasher with green, fuzz-covered dishes. I've vacuumed, and I'm about to head upstairs when Reece catches me by the arm.

"Hey, how was the test?"

"Not good," I say on a sigh.

His brow furrows. "I knew you were tense when I walked in. Since when do you care about cleaning, right?" He nudges his head at Boone who's singing as he works. "He's a good kid. He's just anxious. And the Kappa thing? Hopefully he'll figure it out on his own."

"I hope so." I went through hell when I pledged. Forced to drink, play stupid games, run errands for the brothers. The alpha in me rebelled from the beginning.

Reece holds my gaze. "And tell your dad to ease up. It's your senior year. You aren't perfect. No one is."

I nod, but...

He doesn't know my family history.

Everyone must be perfect—or they pretend to be.

My dad.

My mom.

And me?

I took the place of my perfect, dead brother.

7

Julia

I walk to the city center four blocks away and find the local pawn shop.

A man with too much aftershave looks the ring over with one of those jeweler's loupes while I stare at the big TVs on the wall.

Desperation fills me as I mull about Connor. He's been known to rough up a few of the girls that used to dance at the club because of their debts . . . or worse. One of them, Minnie, quit to go "work" for him, fell into his heroin trap and overdosed a year later. Another, Gina, slapped him one night at the club when he groped her.

There are still missing posters of her on light poles around town.

The other girls told me not to mess with him, but the warning came too late.

My mother had already started buying from him.

She wasn't always an addict. When I was growing up,

she was a manager at an upscale restaurant called Spinelli's. The clientele and staff loved her. It didn't have great health insurance, but she assumed it was enough.

One night after working late, she fell asleep at the wheel and ended up upside down in a ditch. She somehow walked away from the wreck but had cracked three vertebrae in her neck.

It hurt to walk. It hurt to sit. It hurt to breathe.

I remember tears streaming down her face when she stormed out of an orthopedics office after finding out how much her surgery was. She finally had the surgery—what choice did she have—then another one. Her pain got better but never went away.

Connor offered her a never-ending supply of painkillers. Of course, they weren't free. When her bill became several thousand dollars, he cut her off, then came to me for the money.

The pawn shop owner frowns. "Three hundred for this."

Nausea swirls. I've seen enough pawn-shop scenes in movies to know he'd try to undercut me, but I didn't realize he'd do it by that much. "It's worth more."

"No one's gonna want it—it's already inscribed."

"Yes, but can't you buff it out—"

He shoves it to me. "Sell it to one of those places that pays cash for gold. They might give you more."

I can't deal with the thought of it being disassembled and melted down. At least if I pawn it, I'll know that someone else will use it.

He lets out a resigned sigh. "I see that look in your eye. It means something to you. You're going to try to buy it back. So just pawn it. Three hundred."

"Will you sell it to one of those gold places?"

He leans in over the counter. "I won't trade it unless it doesn't sell in three months."

That's actually . . . nice. Oh, wait. "How much would it cost to buy it back?"

He shrugs. "I'll sell it back to you at twenty-five percent interest."

I gaze at it in despair. I don't want to part with it, any more than I want to part with my own heart.

But I need to let it go.

There's no point trying to buy it back.

One by one, I'm losing everything we once owned. First it was our house, then the furniture, my car, and now this.

"Four hundred," I counter.

"I don't make deals."

"Three-seventy-five."

He blows out a breath, his gaze softening a hair. "Okay. I'm in a good mood today. Deal."

My chest relaxes. With the other money I gave Connor, that's enough to pay him the rest of what I owe plus get a start on other bills I need to pay. I still have rent, utilities, school supplies, and food. I'd love to buy something besides ramen and soup.

I leave the pawn store and pull out my phone to make the call I've been dreading.

Connor answers with a grouchy, "Yeah?"

"It's Julia," I say as I cross the street, heading toward the laundromat. "I'm sorry about earlier. I don't know who that guy was."

"Interesting."

"Really, I have no clue. Anyway, he spooked me so much, I ran. But I have the rest of your money for the month."

He cackles. "Yeah, right, my money. Leave it under the doormat."

I frown, unease rising. I thought for sure he'd be more pissed. "What?"

"You heard me. Leave it."

I hesitate, wondering what this means. "All right..."

"Later," he says, and there's nothing but dead air.

I pocket my phone as I head to the laundromat, checking behind me every two steps. He's not just going to let this go. What if he has guys waiting on me?

I might even wind up like Gina—gone forever, part-myth, part cautionary tale.

When I reach the laundromat, I look around, but the area's empty except for a few people gathering in the shadows of the sidewalk. A long set of metal stairs on the side of the building looms like a one-way street to danger.

My head flashes to an image of me in a ditch.

Eyes open, staring at nothing.

I push it away and take the stairs, trying to be quiet, but my sneakers ping against each tread. When I reach the doormat, I half-expect a gun to be pointed in my face.

I lift the *Wipe Your Paws* doormat and stick the cash underneath. I descend the staircase like I have wings and point myself toward home, checking behind me every few seconds.

My phone pings with a text. From Parker. *What r u up to? Wanna fuck?*

Seriously?

I scroll back over his previous texts, ones he sends every week.

Just checkin' in.

Miss ur tight pussy.

Saw u today. Fuckin' hot.

My cock is calling ur name.

Ju-Ju, where u at? Coffee? Lunch? Dinner?

At the lake. Without u. Whore. Gonna fuck this girl in the ass and say ur name when I cum.

My jaw tics.

He can't understand why I broke up with him. Does he think I *like* these messages? Should I be scared of him? I don't know. I thought I knew him, but this is over the top.

Pushing it aside,

I text my mother to check in. *R u okay?*

My throat tightens when she doesn't reply.

I'm worried about u, I send.

It's been a few days since we talked, and I need to give her a heads up about Connor. He might take what happened out on her.

By the time I get home, there's still no reply from her. Exhaustion takes its toll as I trudge up the stairs. Maybe I can borrow Taylor's car and drive around town and look for Mom. She stays with friends on and off. I can check in with them and the usual bars she likes.

I fall into my bed, lashes fluttering closed.

I should do that . . .

I'm asleep before I realize it.

8

Eric

"Hansen. Thumb up your ass?" Boone snarks as he sails past me on the ice.

Yeah, I missed the puck. It sailed between my legs.

Falcon, one of our reserve defensemen, snatches it and shoots it into the other goal.

Perfect.

That's the third pass from Boone I've missed.

He arcs around and slides to a stop in front of me. "What's your deal?"

I slap my helmet. "Didn't get much sleep last night."

Reece skates up to us, ice spraying as he looks at me. "You're never this off."

I move toward the face-off spot. "Whatever. Yeah. Let's run it again."

We do, and it's as if I have chunks of lead in my body. My legs are heavy like molasses. I can't stop running LSAT questions through my head and wondering if my father will call the board to see if he can get the scores early.

If he has time. Which he doesn't.

I used to hate that my father was never around, but now it might be my saving grace.

Why didn't I study?

The puck connects with my stick, and I go through the motions from muscle memory, take it up the ice, doing the footwork to avoid the defensive trap. I fake right and go left, leaving the defenseman panting in the icy mist of my skates. I assess the goalie's weakness, the spot over his right shoulder. I get in position, ready to shoot, and . . .

Julia...

Why didn't I tell her I paid off her goon?

Was it because I didn't want to admit that I spent that kind of money on a girl who hates me?

Falcon slips in behind me and scoops the puck off my stick. He spins, crosses the center line, making it past the blue even before I turn around.

He shoots, scores.

My shoulders twitch with anger. It's just a scrimmage, yeah, but in my head, I hear the buzzer go off, see the crowd cheering for the other team. I see fans, the ones who depend on me, glowering.

The hat-trick I pulled off in the playoffs last year feels like ancient history.

"Maybe Falcon should be on the first line," Boone snarks, gliding in next to me.

"Fuck off," I reply, skating toward the benches.

"Whoa," Boone calls after me. "You can't take the heat, Everest? You're always talking trash and I can't?"

I don't reply but imagine they're exchanging looks behind me.

Coach Swearingen shakes his head. "We should have just all gone to the beach instead of summer camp because I can't see a damn thing you guys learned. Do you love this fucking game or not?"

"Yeah!" We shake our sticks.

"Good! Then you better come better prepared tomorrow!" He tucks his clipboard under his arm and blows his whistle. "Let's call it a day."

Boone slaps me on the back. "I was just joking, you know. Falcon doesn't have shit on you."

"Yeah." I head to the locker room, jerk off my helmet, and sweep a hand through my hair. I love the ice. It's the one thing I'm actually good at—only I'm feeling haunted by the specter of my dad—and Julia.

I rub my neck as I recall our poetry class in prep school. I took it for an easy A, then found that I liked it. I especially liked staring at her in class, her shiny, sleek brown hair, the shy looks she sent my way. She'd walk by my desk in her plaid skirt and I'd groan with want.

Too sweet. Too innocent. And I wanted to taste it—to see if she'd rub off on me.

On the bench, I unlace my skates as Coach stops in front of me.

"Hansen. In my office," he murmurs.

Shit. I like him better when he yells.

I trudge into his office, not even sitting. My hands clench at my side. "Sir?"

"What the hell was that? You looked like my nephew's team. And he's in fourth grade."

"School just started. Our mojo is off," I say, shifting on my feet.

"You've been off for the past few practices. Is something going on? Do you want to talk?"

Yes, there is, and no... I can't.

He leans back in his chair. "Look, you still have a shot at the NHL. The scouts were here for Z last year and saw you. They liked you, Eric."

My heart thuds. Yeah, sure, but it's like being told you won the lottery but lost your ticket. I'm too old to be drafted. A team could sign me after the season, but it's rare. If they weren't interested the last three years, they aren't interested now.

"I'll try harder, sir."

"You have to lead, Eric. Get the others to fall in line and focus. That's when the scouts notice." He pauses as he leans in. "Do you *want* to play in the NHL?"

I shrug.

A long sigh comes from him. "If anyone else played like shit at practice like you have this week, I'd demote them. Prove me wrong, okay? Do better."

I take my time getting out of my clothes so that when I hit the showers, the rest of the guys are gone. I spend most of the time staring at the tile wall, letting the water ping my face.

When I'm changed into my street clothes, I gather my duffle and walk out of the arena. Thunder rumbles in the darkness and the air smells like rain.

"Yo, Hansen!" Reece calls from the parking lot as he leans against my truck.

I walk his way. "Hey. Why are you waiting?" I honestly didn't want to see anyone. My head needs to decompress.

"Let's get a beer."

I stick my hands in my jeans. "You're worried about me. I'm cool, man. I've got no issues, just a bad day."

"Come on. I just wanna hang." He slaps me on the back.

I sigh. I haven't slept well in over thirty-six hours, but do I really want to go home alone?

"Alright. Where's Boone?"

He pauses, then gives me a wry smile. "He's rushing Kappa tonight."

A long exhale comes from me. "Dammit. We need to drink just for that. He's not going to be the same anymore."

"I wish there was another frat on campus with some power, but there isn't. They're the best."

"At being motherfuckers," I add.

"And parties."

Right. I get in my truck and we head to the Tipsy Moose, an off-campus bar we frequent. Rustic with a wood-beamed ceiling, it's lowkey with pool tables, dart boards, and booths.

We're walking up the sidewalk to the entrance when I catch sight of something farther down the alley.

A sign in pink neon. Platinum Nights.

I was there, once, the night I turned twenty-one, and as a result of those twenty-one shots, I can't remember a thing except some big-chested, older woman pressing her boobs in my face. Other than that, it's not my scene.

"Hey," I say, backing up. "What if we go someplace different?" I point to the sign.

Reece raises an eyebrow. "Really?"

"Change of pace."

He cocks his head at me. "Any reason you want to go there? Julia? That video of you chasing down that thief was crazy. Anything going on between you two?"

"Nah."

But part of me wants to see her.

To talk to her.

As a friend. Of course.

He smirks. "Whatever makes you happy, yeah? You wanna feed some dollar bills to a girl's thong, I'm here. I've got cash. Let's do this."

It's hazy in the club as a cloud of fake smoke wafts around us. The air feels thick and sticky, bristling with anticipation and lust. The room is dark except for a few dim lamps and the colorful flashes of neon lights behind the long bar.

On the stage, a woman gyrates to "Runnin' with the Devil" by Van Halen. Her shoulders and stomach glisten with sweat. She's a brunette, curvy, and older than Julia. She's wearing glittery red pasties on her nipples and a black thong. Devil horns are on her head and she carries a sizeable pitchfork. The crowd of men cheer as she whips her hair around and shakes her hips. They tuck bills under her thong when she gets close.

I scan the room—mostly college boys. A few businessmen.

One of the college guys puts his knee on the stage as if to reach the girl to hand her money, and a bouncer appears out of nowhere and yanks him back to his seat. His companions laugh and slap him on the back, then hand him a beer.

Reece lets out a low whistle. "Damn. This place is on fire. Maybe we should have our hockey parties here."

"Hmm."

Reece heads to the bar to grab us some beers while I find a seat. I grab a booth near the right of the raised stage and look for Julia. It's possible she isn't working tonight.

I find her on a small stage to the left, sliding around a pole.

How the fuck did I miss that?

She's wearing a white lace bodysuit that barely covers her tits. Fluttery wings move behind her as she dances. My lips twitch when I see the halo tiara. An angel.

She undulates her body and struts out to the edge of the stage. Her hair cascades down her back, and she flicks it over her shoulder and smiles into the crowd. Her lips purse as she blows a kiss. She eases off the straps of her bodysuit in teasing little gestures, and I shift uncomfortably in my seat as my cock thickens.

She's flawless. Her skin perfect.

She unsnaps the bodysuit and whisks it off and twirls it in the air. Gold pasties are on her tits. She bends over seductively and shows us her ass in her bikini briefs. I groan. Shit. I didn't come here for this. No way.

She shimmies to a guy who tucks a twenty under the waistband of her briefs.

I grit my teeth.

This was the wide-eyed girl from high school.

And now...

This wasn't her plan. No way. She couldn't wait to get to college.

Am I somehow responsible for this?

Did I hurt her that bad?

No, she's too strong for that. Too fierce.

There's a wolf underneath the lamb she appears to be.

Yeah.

The only person I ruined was my brother.

I don't know where the thought comes from. I thought

I'd stuffed them so far down they'd never come up, but they do.

Anguish ripples over me like a tsunami.

I squeeze my eyes closed to shut it out, but it rises higher and higher.

Kurt was the real deal.

Valedictorian, Kappa, athletic.

His hair was blond, his eyes blue, like my mother's.

At fifteen, I didn't know the demons that haunted him. No, the whole truth would come out after his death. The night he was killed, he was home for Christmas and wanted to make a stop before we went to the movies. We drove to a small dingy trailer on the outskirts of town and I sat in the car while he went inside. Sure, I noticed he seemed different. Moodier. Thinner.

After half an hour passed, I got worried we'd miss the movie, so I got out of the car and walked in the house without knocking.

Shadowy images flash in my mind.

My perfect brother sitting on a couch as he shot up heroin. A wiry guy yanking out a gun and pointing it at me. The bang that made my ears ring. Kurt on the floor with blood blooming on his chest. He'd jumped in front of me and taken the bullet.

A shuddery breath comes from me.

I shouldn't have walked in.

He's gone and I'm still here—dealing with it.

It's why I paid off that man for Julia.

It's why I'm worried about her. Well, not the only reason. I feel as if I might owe her something? Jesus. It's confusing.

I get up and move toward the stage. Weaving through tables and dodging waitresses, I reach the edge and stop.

"Julia," I say, loud enough to be heard over the music.

When she focuses on me, a wrinkle appears on her forehead and she loses a step. She moves to the other side of the stage and mouths, *Go away.*

"I need to talk to you," I say, following her. Some guy is waving cash at her and she reaches down and swipes it from his hand as the song ends.

Wobbling in her heels, she heads for the back of the stage.

"Wait a minute," I call, but she's already gone.

I scan the area and see a door that must lead to the back where the girls change. I stalk over to it, but two beefy men on either side grab me by the arm.

"Where do you think you're going?" one of them says as he eyes me up and down.

I point to the back. "Julia. I just wanted to—"

"Not tonight, Loverboy." He puts a hand on my chest as he backs me up. He grins behind a bushy brown beard. "If you want a private dance, check in with the bouncer at the bar."

"I don't want a private dance." I shove his hand away.

"Hey, no touching us, asshole." The other guy grabs me from behind, and I rear back to push him off, but it doesn't work. They pick me up like I'm a sack of feathers, carry me down the hall, then toss me out the back into an alley. I stumble onto my hands and knees in a puddle.

The door slams shut.

"Fuck!"

As I'm getting to my feet, a girl says, "Are you drunk, Hansen?"

Julia. She must have come out here before me.

She leans against the brick wall, practically swimming

in a black raincoat that she hugs around her body. "You didn't have to get thrown out, you know. I would have talked to you." A low chuckle comes from her. "Have to admit, I kind of enjoyed that."

I brush the gravel off my jeans. "Sorry, I don't know the rules in this place. Apparently, I need a private dance to talk to you."

Her eyes flash with something—excitement? Not likely. She hates me.

"I guess you got lucky, then. Here I am. Don't expect a show."

"I don't," I mutter.

"Who crawled up your ass?"

I shrug. "I just got tossed out of a club that I paid twenty bucks to get into. I lasted for one song."

She watches me fix my man-bun, amusement on her face.

"What?" I grouse. "Am I your entertainment now? You gonna toss me some dollars?"

She waves a five at me. "Dance for me. Show me what you've got."

"No," I say.

She laughs. "Sorry. I'm just not used to seeing you being towed around like a bag of potatoes."

I grunt.

She tucks her money away. "The big question is, why are you here?"

Rain pelts my face, and I move to stand under a small overhang with her. I stare at the sparkly eyeshadow on her lids. It's gold. "I guess . . . I wanted to know you're okay."

A vulnerable expression crosses her face before she quickly tucks it away. "I'm okay."

I put my hands in my jeans and study her features. "How do you know Connor? Will you tell me?"

A sigh comes from her. "Eric..."

"I went back to the laundromat after you went home. I paid off your debt. The whole thing."

Her eyes widen to saucers. Shock colors her voice. "W-What do you mean, *you* paid off my debt?"

"I paid him. You need help for your addiction, Julia. It ruins people. It ruined my brother."

Her mouth gapes as she shakes her head in disbelief. "You went back? After I told you how dangerous he is? Are you insane?"

"Apparently."

"He could have hurt you! I wouldn't have been able to forgive myself if..." A breathy exhale comes from her. "How much did you give him?"

"Seven thousand." I don't admit to paying him the six hundred.

Her jaw drops. "Oh my God. He conned you. I only owed him five. That bastard."

"I'm not surprised. Don't even care about it. I just didn't want him on your ass anymore. You shouldn't have to go through that every month."

Her face seems to crumble as she grapples with the idea. "Eric, t-this doesn't make sense... Why would you..."

Before I can stop, my hands brush her cheek. The touch sizzles and brings back memories of the past. God, how I wanted her.

I pull back. "I gave him extra hoping he'd forget about you. He swore he'd leave you alone."

"Why would you pay so much?"

I lift my shoulders. "I have the money. You don't."

There's a long silence. Her chest rises rapidly, and she chews her lips so hard I'm afraid they might bleed. "Did it put you in a bind?"

"My parents never check my accounts." Hopefully.

"Not funny, but I went back today and paid for the rest of the month. No wonder he didn't have someone waiting for me. Because of you."

She pauses, her throat moving as she swallows. "I hate that you think . . . that you believe . . ." She dips her head. "I don't do drugs, Eric. I hardly even drink these days."

Oh.

Then . . .

"I-I don't know what to say. I don't want to discuss the reasons why I owed him, but thank you, and I'll pay you back like I was with him."

"You don't have to worry—"

A wry smile appears as she cuts me off. "I do. I'm a proud person and that money is yours. I'll return it bit by bit, just not as much as I was giving him, if that's okay?"

"Sure. Anything."

"Congratulations, you're now a loan shark."

"No interest needed on your loan."

"I pawned my mom's ring—the one you returned—to help cover the cost this month."

Remorse hits. "I should have told you—"

"No, no, don't worry, please. I can't complain. I'm okay and it was bound to happen. I've been giving him so much that I'm behind on everything."

She moves around in the small space between us and her scent washes over me. She smells like lemons and sugar. Citrusy. Fresh.

She gazes up at me, her eyes searching mine. "What you did was... crazy."

It was.

A song blares as the door opens, and one of the girls appears and sticks her head out. She's the brunette from earlier and she's wearing what I think is a bird outfit. "You're up, honey." She glances at me and smiles. "Hiya, handsome. I'm Marcia."

"Hi."

She shakes the feathers attached to her bottom. "We've got a four girl peacock show coming next. You wanna watch?"

"They tossed me out," I say dryly.

Julia rolls her eyes and tries to push her back inside. "Stop flirting with him."

Marcia winks at me, then nudges her head at Julia. "She's my favorite. Mess her up and I'll come after you with my pitchfork."

I huff out a laugh as she prisses away.

Julia looks back at me, a sheepish expression on her face. "Sorry. Stripping isn't all bad. I've made friends with some sweet girls."

"I see." I don't really. I'm sure Marcia is fine, but Julia needs to get out of this environment.

She gives me a long look, then takes my hand and laces our fingers together.

Tingles race up my arm.

My body flares to sexual awareness.

And I'm sucked back to prep school.

Us in class, the sound of her voice, her lips against mine in the drama room, the gym, the yearbook room. Her cream as I fingered her. Her small cries when she came.

That afternoon in the Aston Martin when we put the top down and drove out to the lake—that was the best.

I took her panties off with my teeth. I kissed every inch of her. I sucked her clit until she screamed my name.

I recall her breathy gasps, the desperate way she kissed me when I broke through her innocence.

Stop.

Helping her isn't about the connection we once shared.

It's about me wanting to help, maybe repent for dumping her afterwards.

"I don't know what to say except thank you. A million times. It was brave and really stupid . . ." She tries to hide it, but I see a glimmer of wetness in her eyes.

"Julia?"

"Yeah?"

"I'm sorry for prep school. You were a virgin, and I should have known you'd get hurt. I didn't want attachments. It wasn't me, I mean, it was, but I was different then. I had issues. I still do, but . . ." I'm babbling.

She blinks rapidly. "Okay."

"Julia, you're up," says the guy with the beard who tossed me out. He's opened the door and glares at me like I'm scum.

"You alright, Julia?" He checks her out from head to toe in a businesslike way. "This guy giving you trouble?"

"No. I'm fine, Eddie. He's a . . . friend." She looks back at me and gives me a little smile. "See you around."

She slips through the door and leaves.

I stand there for several moments, feeling winded by her abrupt departure.

I circle back to the entrance and find Reece waiting

outside as he thumbs his phone. My phone buzzes from him. *Where u at?*

He looks up and laughs. "Dude! Were you the guy they *escorted* out?"

"Me? No way."

He smirks. "Good thing I videoed it. What the hell happened?"

I push out a laugh and consider explaining the Julia situation but decide to let it go. She's a private person.

I feel relief. In telling her. Hoping it helps.

9

Julia

The *buzz, buzz, buzz* of the alarm stirs me from a nightmare where I raced down the alleys of Sparrow Lake trying to catch up with my mother. She laughed, then darted into the laundromat.

I rub my temple and sigh as I get out of the bed. I barely slept last night from worry about her not replying to my texts. My morbid mind goes to the worst-case scenario. My mother dead in a ditch. Overdosed.

I grimace when I see a text that came in last night.

U r so hot. I want to pull your hair back and fuck you until you scream.

Parker. Drunk texting. Again. Bye, Douchebag. I press the block button. Should have done it ages ago.

After I take a quick shower, I change into frayed shorts and a tank top, scuff into my flip-flops, and scrape my wet hair back into a bun. I shove my school-issued laptop into my backpack and head out.

My early morning class is a seminar in the history of Sparrow Lake, an elective for my degree in art. My steps are light as I make the trek to campus. Some of the chaos that's usually in my head is defeated. The fear that's haunted me for a year feels snuffed out.

Now that the pressure is off to pay back Connor five hundred a month, I can cut my hours at the club and focus on looking for a new job. Sure, it won't pay as much, but it will be enough to pay back Eric a little at a time, cover bills, and maybe sock away money for next semester.

I still owe Poppy and Taylor. And Marcia. I need those burdens lifted too.

A side of me wants to dash to the pawn shop and get the ring back, but that feels impossible. I need to put other things first.

I think about Eric showing up at the club and a bittersweet feeling washes over me. His act of kindness was surprising. And not at all something I imagined him doing.

My mind races with thoughts of us in prep school. His lingering looks. The little notes he'd slip me when he walked by my desk. The way his leg felt pressed against mine when we did a project together. We each had to write a poem, then read it and take critiques. I have it saved on my phone and bring it up.

I'm angry at the world
For taking you away from me.
I'm angry at God
For not saving you.
I'm angry at fate
For being so cruel.
I'm angry at you

For leaving me behind.
Most of all, I'm angry at myself
For stepping in that house.
I'm sorry I'm not you.

I'd been stunned at his emotional words, at the hesitant way he waited for me to tell him my thoughts.

"It's beautiful," I told him.

I didn't care that he had a reputation.

I believed he was as crazy about me as I was him.

I remember the day we had sex. After it was over, his eyes were far, far away.

And when I texted him the next day, and the next, and the next, he blew me off with *I'm busy. Can't talk.*

I saw him kissing another girl later in the week, and when I confronted him, he told me that he played around and he was sorry if it hurt my feelings and perhaps it was best if we didn't mess around.

I was devastated. I felt used. So. Much. Pain.

I thought Eric was mine, but he didn't do girlfriends—especially one like me.

Just as that thought flies through my head, I see him on the quad with Boone and Reece. They're standing under a big elm tree with a group of girls around them. Not surprising. Eric is gorgeous, Reece is built with blond hair, and Boone has a chiseled jaw and a mischievous smile.

The sun is shining. Birds are chirping. Life feels different.

Maybe this is the moment when we can be friends for real.

I'd like that. I mean, he did something awesome for me.

I walk to them with a bit of hope mixed with wariness.

A tall blonde girl, I think her name is Tillie, has her hand on Eric's arm and laughs up at him. She's pretty. Athletic. A volleyball player. Just his type.

"Hey," I say as I reach them. There's a big smile pasted on my face.

Eric turns to me and blinks as if he didn't expect to see me on campus.

"Hey," Boone and Reece reply, then ask me about classes. We chit-chat for a few minutes and I keep glancing at Eric, meeting his stare.

I fidget as I turn to him. He's wearing jeans and a white HU shirt that stretches across his muscled chest. His hair falls around his face in dark red waves. There's scruff on his jawline.

"Um, it was good to see you the other night," I say.

"Where did ya'll go?" Tillie asks as she sizes me up. I can tell she finds me wanting by the way she sniffs.

"Platinum Nights." I smile without warmth, giving her the same level of greeting she gave me.

She grimaces. "Oh. Gross. You went together?" Her eyes dart between us.

I ignore her and direct my question to him. "Maybe we could get coffee later?"

Oh, hell. Why did I say that?

Tillie twines her arm through his and gazes up at him adoringly. "He's busy."

Ah. She's staking a claim.

I wait for him to reply, to maybe say he *isn't* busy, but Eric just looks at me, his expression blank.

Use your words, jerk.

I'm not the innocent girl from before.

My armor is thick, built of solid steel, impenetrable from a year of living on the edge.

Rejection bounces off the fortress that is my heart.

There are no cracks. No flaws.

I can handle your rejection—even in front of your friends.

Tillie breaks the moment by tapping Boone on the arm playfully as if she's been part of their group for a while. "We should go to that new pizza place on Brooks Lane tonight. They've been getting rave reviews."

Reece throws an arm around me and gives me a squeeze. He's always been a great guy. "I'm up for coffee. Text me. You have our digits?"

Yeah. Sugar made sure I had all the numbers once she and Z got serious.

I nod at Reece, wave bye to them, then walk off.

Heat rushes up my face. Eric basically ignored me. Why?

Is he ashamed to be seen with me?

Steel walls, remember?

"His loss," I mutter as I trudge up a hill to class. "It was just freaking coffee, not a prom date."

I wind up ten minutes late. When I pull open the door and try to sneak in, it makes a horrible screeching noise, the sound echoing in the packed auditorium. Every eye turns to look, and the professor, who according to my schedule is Dr. Fillmore, stops mid-sentence and glares.

Wincing, I close the door as quietly as possible, but it makes another terrible screech.

"Sorry," I whisper, hoping the professor will continue on, but she doesn't.

She—and two hundred other students—watch as I look for an empty seat.

I take the first one I see in the back, which, unfortunately means I have to climb over a girl at the end of the aisle. I step on her toe.

"Sorry," I whisper again, slipping into the seat next to her.

She's typing notes on her laptop and already has a page of them. What are the chances I can make friends and we can share?

From the way she shifts her body away from me, I'm guessing that's a big nope.

I pull out my laptop and get situated. As I follow along with the syllabus, I hear whispering a few rows ahead.

I look up to see a few familiar faces.

I see Scott's red-haired girlfriend and her brunette friend. They look gorgeous and fresh-faced, as if they spent hours getting ready for class. Sitting with them are a couple of familiar looking guys with backwards Kappa hats.

Red looks over her shoulder at me and mouths, *Whore.*

I glare right back. Then I catch sight of one of the guys. Channing. I've seen him around. He's not smirking like I expected. Instead, he frowns and nudges Red with his elbow. She looks a little embarrassed and turns back around.

Sorry, he mouths to me.

A few moments later, a phone dings in the auditorium.

Then it starts to ring, and I realize the sound is coming from my bag.

As mortified as I am, that drains away the second I read the message on the display.

I NEED YOUR HELP

Mom.

I close up my laptop and shove it in my backpack and ease my way around my none-too-happy neighbor.

The professor pauses mid-sentence as I rush to the doors, typing out a message to my mom.

Where r u?

When I'm out in the lobby, I pace the tile floor, waiting for her to respond. I press my fingers to my forehead. She could be in Tahiti, for all I know.

The double doors swing open and out pops Channing.

"Hey. I noticed you rushed out. I hope it wasn't because of Samantha."

Scott's girl.

"No."

"You okay?" he asks.

I eye him cautiously, searching his face. We've never spoken before, but I know he knows I'm the girl who dumped their president. It didn't matter that he cheated; I was the one in the wrong.

"I'm fine," I say quietly.

He approaches me, lugging his backpack, and another smaller one, a camera bag. With spikey dark hair and glittering sapphire eyes, he's handsome, yet there's always been an unapproachable vibe about him.

Quiet. Serious. He's the type to sit back at parties and take it all in.

I've never seen him in the strip club. A point for that.

"You looked a little rattled when you ran out." He glances at my phone. "Anything I can help you with?"

"Just a little family issue. I can handle it."

"Cool." He turns to leave but stops. "Are you planning on going back in there?"

I shake my head.

A rueful laugh comes from him. "Same. I was going to go to the lake and take some pics. This is my only class today. You want to, um, come with?"

I blink.

He grimaces in a self-deprecating way. "Of course, you don't. You have classes and you don't know me and that sort of came out of nowhere. Hi, I'm Channing, and you're Julia. Sorry to be weird."

"I remember you. You used to run the bar in the basement last year at Kappa. You're a junior, right?"

"Yeah."

"So, you take photos?"

He lifts the camera bag. "Photography is my major."

My smile is wide. Photography is art. Getting the right composition, playing with the colors, adding filters. "Thanks for the invite, but I . . ." I point at my phone. "I'm waiting for a text from someone."

He hoists the bag higher on his broad shoulders like he hasn't a care in the world. "So. Boyfriend?"

I feel a blush creeping up my face. "No."

"Good. Raincheck? Maybe tomorrow? We can go after classes?"

I sigh. "Is that really a good idea? You know, with Parker . . ."

He looks away, then back at me. "We're not all assholes. Have you ever seen me being a jerk?"

"No." But given time, his colors will shine through.

I stop that thought and exhale. Is it right to paint them all with the same brush?

He shrugs. "It was an impulse to ask you. I like company when I take photos. It can get lonely at the lake."

I know what he means. I feel lonely in my bones.

"Sure. Maybe we can chat sometime." I'm not going out to a deserted lake with some rando but talking through text is doable.

I rattle off my number as he enters it in his phone.

As he saunters away, I feel something I haven't felt in a long time.

Fuzzy and warm.

Meeting a nice guy. Texting.

Eric. He's the one who's made me feel as if I can breathe again.

But those feelings are mixed with him ignoring me.

My phone dings.

My mother has finally responded: 3rd *and Chestnut.*

That's on the other side of town, so I call an Uber and find her old Chevy parked half in a no-parking zone, the front tires scraping the curb. There's a ticket under the windshield wiper. I pluck it out and realize it's been there four days.

An accordion sunshade rests on the dashboard for privacy. A wall of her belongings in the back does the same.

Frustration gnaws at me. I hate that she lives in her car, and I've tried to get her to move in at the house. There's a small room on the third floor. It's old and dusty and doesn't have a bathroom, but it's a place to sleep. Taylor and Poppy were fine with it, but she refused.

She rolls down the window and stagnant air hits me, old food and unwashed clothes.

"Hey," she says lightly as she rubs her eyes.

"What's wrong? You sent me the text that said you needed help. Are you okay?"

She pats at her oily hair, tucking it behind her ears. You

have to understand, my mother used to be a beautiful woman. Long, honey colored hair, pretty skin, a killer body.

She looks ancient now. "I'm okay now," she says. "I haven't felt good lately. My head hurts."

"You have a headache?" I dig around in my purse for Tylenol and hand it over to her.

She takes it. "Your face is red."

"Because I rushed over here from class. You didn't text me all weekend, and I thought something happened to you."

"My phone was dead, and I didn't have the money to pay for minutes."

My hands clench.

I can't tell if she's hungover or sick. "Is everything else okay?"

Her face contorts with confusion, then she nods in a distracted manner. "I was looking for that cardigan, the yellow one with rabbits on it? I think you borrowed it."

I know the cardigan because she's owned it since I was a kid. She used to wear it on winter mornings when she drank her coffee and cooked breakfast.

But I never borrow her clothes. And it's too warm for a sweater.

"I don't have it. Are you staying cool in the heat?"

She picks at the vinyl material on the door. "I think I'm getting a fever."

"Let me see." I feel her forehead and tell her it feels fine. I hold up the ticket. "You have to move the car."

She grabs it, gives it a look, then tosses it over her shoulder. "Solved that problem."

I sigh. "Why don't we go somewhere and get breakfast?" I want to get a good meal in her.

"I've got somewhere to be."

"Where?"

"Anita wants me to cut her hair." Mom used to cut hair before she worked at the restaurant. She was never licensed, but she wasn't bad at it.

But Anita?

Mom stays on her couch on and off. I've been to her house before. It's covered in vodka bottles—and cats. About twenty of them. I shudder. Cats are cool, but not that many, plus the smell is horrible.

She shrugs. "Not sure I'll make it out to her house. You got any money for gas? I'm on fumes."

I pull out the stack of bills I'd put aside for groceries. "Yeah. Don't spend this on alcohol. Okay? Get your gas and buy some food."

She palms it. "I promise. Anita said she'd give me some cash for the haircut."

I take her hand, gearing up for the most important thing I need to tell her. "Mom. Connor is all paid up. If you keep going back to him, then paying him off will start all over again—"

A long blink comes from her. "How did you pay him off?"

"A friend."

She swallows, looking uncomfortable as she glances away from me. "I won't. I mean, I'm trying. I haven't seen him in weeks."

She's just as scared of him as I am.

She licks her lips. "It's just vodka for now. It numbs things, you know."

I sigh as I lean in. "Okay, but I can't do this again with

him. I won't. If you rack up any more debts, and we can't pay, he'll hurt me. Maybe you."

She climbs over the console into the front seat. "Just concentrate on your college classes. Get that degree, then you'll be set. Don't worry about me."

"But I do." My jaw clenches as she starts the car, gives me a wave, and drives off.

I hug myself, unease dancing down my spine.

Maybe I do need to walk away from all of it. Her.

Emotion clogs my throat and I look up at the sky to make it stop.

I can't do that.

She isn't a bad person.

I recall my thirteenth birthday when she surprised me with a road trip to the beach. She took off from work and planned the entire thing. Our car sputtered twenty hours to Gulf Shores, Florida. We stopped in every state and bought a magnet to remember it by. We rented a small house by the ocean, wore bikinis, and held hands as we splashed in the waves, laughing and shrieking. She helped me build a sandcastle shaped like a butterfly. She bought me ice-cream every day.

When I asked for her special tea cookies instead of a birthday cake, she taught me how to make them, letting me do the measuring and mixing. The kitchen filled with the smell of vanilla and sugar, and with the sound of the waves right outside, I felt like I was in a fairytale. It was a moment of pure happiness.

I've not had enough of those memories with her.

Instead of calling another Uber, I decide to save that money and start the long walk back to campus.

She is and isn't my mom.

She's only half of the person I once knew.

Addiction has her in its grasp. She didn't choose to be an addict. She didn't choose to be homeless. Somewhere inside her is the woman I knew.

And me? I'm trying to hold on to her as hard as I can.

10

Eric

There's a movie playing, a thriller about a woman who's convinced her neighbor was murdered, but for the life of me, I couldn't tell you anything else about the show. It's a blur.

I squint at the girl on the screen. She reminds me of Julia with her brown hair. She asked me to get coffee a month ago, but the way I've dwelled on it, you'd think it was yesterday.

Not agreeing was the right thing to do. I paid her debt. End of.

Tillie eases off the couch as the credits roll on the movie. "I need to get going—unless you want to go upstairs?" She gives me a sly smile as her hand trails through my hair. "I can think of a few things we could do . . ."

I click off the movie and stretch out my arms. Tillie and I haven't done the deed, which is weird for me. Usually by now, I've fucked girls left and right.

"Nah, I've got some research to do."

She gives me an odd look, then huffs. "Fine. I'm headed home tomorrow and need to pack."

Home. Sounds like a death sentence to me.

"My condolences."

"I like my home," she says.

"I forgot people did that. You're going to miss our first game." I say it more to tease her than anything else. We've had some good times. She likes to drink. She likes to hang out with hockey guys.

So why haven't I fucked her?

"When is it?" she asks.

"Tomorrow."

"Oh, well, if it's really important, I could come . . ." her words trail off as she picks up her purse.

"Don't worry about it. I'll see you when I see you."

She pouts. "Maybe I'll see you at the Kappa house soon?"

"Maybe."

I swat her on the ass as she heads for the door. Grinning, she opens it then lets out a little squeal. "Eric! What is that thing?"

Lucifer has climbed up my pant leg. I meet his beady eyes. I vaguely remember tripping over him early this morning when I went to piss. I'm surprised she hasn't seen him when she's popped over, but he mostly stays in my room.

"He's a ferret." I tug him off my pants, and he curls around my forearm.

"A pet?"

"*Pet* would imply I like the thing."

"He's licking your hand."

"Yes, he does that. Annoying as hell." But I don't stop him and I think he grins at me.

"Hmm. Bye, Eric." She closes the door behind her.

After she's gone, I change into running shorts and head outside for a run. I put in my earbuds and fire up some music. I cut through the backyard toward campus. Fall leaves crunch under my feet. I'm coming around the student center when my steps falter.

Julia walks with Channing as they exit one of the coffee shops. I slow and pull out my earbuds and stare, trying to get the lay of the land.

Is she seeing him?

As they head across the road to the library, they playfully nudge against each other.

My jaw tics.

Channing. He's a Kappa. He isn't the worst of them, but . . .

Anger swirls inside of me.

At what?

I don't own her.

We aren't a thing.

Clenching my fists, I shove down the emotion and take off in the other direction. I have my own problems to deal with.

After a five-mile run, I come back to the house soaked in sweat and breathing hard. I fish my phone out of my pocket and find a text from my dad. *Call ASAP.*

And there goes the day.

Dammit. I got my LSAT scores last week but haven't told him.

I sit on the steps to the house as I punch in the call and dip my head.

My father answers at once. "Eric."

"Dad." I try to match his hard tone, but to my chagrin, my voice wavers.

"I called the board and had your test scores sent over to me. You bombed it." I hear his pen tapping against his desk. *Thump, thump, thump.*

My lashes flutter.

I got a one-forty-six. The twenty-ninth percentile.

Kurt got a one-seventy-nine. The ninety-ninth percentile.

My father couldn't stop bragging to his friends about Kurt. If he could've rented a plane to fly a banner over town, he would have.

"Yes."

His words chop at me. "This is an embarrassment. You did *worse* this time. What the hell happened?"

What happened?

Besides me not being Kurt, I didn't study, oh, and I got in a fight with a drug dealer and got tossed out of a strip club. I'm struggling each day to focus. I'm not the carefree guy I was last year. One of my players is pledging Kappa. And Julia is seeing Channing. WTF.

I can't tell him any of that.

"Do you know how hard it is to get into law school with those scores? Even with the most glowing recommendations—"

"I know."

"What do you have to say for yourself? Is hockey distracting you?"

Anxiety spikes.

Dad was fine with me playing hockey when Kurt was alive. I was the second son of royalty—free to do stupid shit.

I wasn't the basket my parents put their eggs in.

Now, I'm the basket.

My hands clench the phone. "Hockey is *not* a distraction. I'm not good with tests. I'm not... maybe I'm not..."

Maybe I'm not cut out for law school.

"You're a Hansen, for God's sake. You're better than this. You've disappointed me, Eric."

"Yeah. What else is new? How's Mom?" She's been in therapy since Kurt died. She has these bouts where she forgets he's dead.

There's a pause and I picture him gnashing his teeth. Maybe throwing his pen across the room. He doesn't want to talk about her.

She isn't perfect. Not anymore.

"I'll call Margorie on the board of trustees at Hawthorne Law. It's not a top school, but it will do. No promises."

I rub my eyes. "Okay."

"Another thing, why did you take seven grand out of your account?"

My mouth dries. He's never checked how much I spent before. Mostly because I'm not one to splurge and he doesn't have the time, but since my scores are shit...

"Checking up on me?"

"Are you buying drugs?"

"No," I snap. "It was for a friend. She's paying me back, so don't worry."

"It's a lot of cash. Why did she need it?"

"None of your business," I mutter.

His pen taps on his desk over and over. My head starts to clang. Welcome back, monkey.

"Don't worry," I bite out. "I'll keep my spending low for the rest of the year."

More silence.

I sigh. "Are you coming to the game—"

The line goes dead.

"I'll take that as a no," I mutter.

Reece comes out and sits down on the steps next to me. "You ready for the game?"

I've gotten hockey together since August, thank goodness, but I still feel uneasy. "Yeah."

Reece nods. "Where's Boone? I checked his room and he wasn't there."

"Guess," I say as I glance at Kappa House. I haven't found him playing video games in two weeks. He spends most of his time next door.

"Is he even going to be upright tomorrow?" Reece says.

"He has time," I say, but I'm recalling being a pledge and the hazing I went through. Either it was too much fun or not fun at all. "I'll check in on him."

He stretches out his legs. "My dad is coming. First game and all. Yours?"

"Nah."

"You tell him about the scores?"

"He already knew."

He nods, giving me a commiserating look. "You wanna talk about it?"

I shake my head. Z was my best friend, but he isn't around anymore.

A sigh comes from him as he slaps me on the back. "I'm your friend, yeah? If you need me, I'm around."

11

Eric

A few days later, after our first hockey win, I watch in the hallway as Boone fixes his hair in the mirror.

"You can't rush perfection. Almost done." He pulls at one strand, sliding it into place on top of his head.

I take a sip of my beer, then tip it at him. "I'm glad you're hanging with us. Did you have to get permission from Kappa to go tonight?"

He throws me a look. "No. It's not like that."

I smile even though I bet it's a lie. "Good. Let's have fun, then."

"Why did you quit Kappa anyway?" he asks as I head toward the stairs.

"Lots of reasons. Mainly because it interfered with hockey." And your president is a dick.

I go downstairs ahead of him, slip on my leather jacket,

and find Reece in the den. I nudge him and waggle my brows. "You wanna pass the puck on Boone?"

"Hell yeah. What's the play? The picket fence?"

"Nah, I was thinking the ole lookey-loo," I say.

We hear Boone coming down the stairs, and Reece rushes over to the front window and pulls back the curtains.

Boone hits the landing as I glance over at Reece.

"Yo. What's going on at the window?" Boone asks as he follows my gaze.

Reece looks over at us. Eyes lit. "Guys, you won't believe this. This girl is jogging topless down the street. Big jugs. Prettiest ones I've ever seen."

Boone bolts to the window and nearly falls, steadies himself, then peers out the window. "Where? I don't see her."

I dart over and place my hand on his head, rubbing it. "I pass the puck!"

He struggles and tries to push my hand off, then lets loose with a long stream of curses, then grunts. "Jesus Christ on a bike! You've got to be kidding me. I invented the lookey-loo. That's low down."

"Boone has the puck," I announce with glee as I shimmy across the den.

"Concur," we all say.

A few minutes later, I pull my truck into a spot outside an escape room called Get Out or Die.

Boone frowns as we exit the vehicle. "I heard there was an ambulance here the day it opened. Hopefully they got that issue fixed."

I smirk. "They probably paid the city to have the EMTs park out front and make a scene."

We walk inside, and his face puckers as he takes in an

Egyptian mummy tomb on one side of the room and a dungeon scene on the other. "Um, whose idea was this?"

"Mine," I say. "Don't shit on it."

Reece shrugs. "I'm just along for the thrills."

Three girls come out crying from one of the hallways. "Don't do it," they tell us. "It's so scary!"

I smirk.

"I sense bad juju," Boone mutters under his breath, watching as the girls exit and run to their car.

"Pussy," Reece tells him.

Boone shrugs. "Look, I'm from Chicago, and when we sense bad vibes, it's real. Say what you want, but small-town folk do weird shit. Ever watch *Mind Hunters*? It's all gravel roads, corn fields, quarries, and lakes."

"We're in a shopping center," I say with an eyebrow arch.

A man with black hair and pale skin rises from behind the desk. He's wearing a tux with a red lined cape.

"Good evening," he drawls in a bad Transylvanian accent.

Reece bursts out laughing, then reins it in at the seriousness on the man's face.

Boone glares at the fake vampire, and I have to bite my lip to keep in the mirth. I can add vampires to the list of things Boone doesn't like.

"Hansen, party of three," I say.

He swishes his cape. "Of course. You will be paired with the Fab party. My assistant will be—"

"Wait, we're with another group?" I ask.

He nods. "Our rooms are difficult and require at least six participants. My assistant will be—"

"Hello, darlings!" says a familiar accented voice. "Looks like you're with us. We're the Fab party."

I turn and it's Taylor and Poppy, which means...

The mummy case opens and Julia's inside, her red lips curled in a smile as she pops out at Poppy—who screams.

Julia bends over giggling, her face lit with happiness. She's wearing black leggings and a pink oversized sweater with yellow Converse. Her mink-colored hair swings around her face as she smiles.

Something twinges in my chest.

Relief. Joy.

Fuck, she looks gorgeous.

"Oh, hi," she says uncertainly when she sees me.

"Hi."

She glances at Taylor. "Are we with them?"

Taylor nods, then waves his hand dramatically at the vampire behind the desk. "Carry on, sir. We're ready to go."

"Igor, there you are! Please show our guests to their room," the vampire says as a tall man limps in from a back hallway. He's dressed in dirty brown clothes with a hunch on his back. He drags one foot behind him.

"They go all out, huh?" I say to Boone and he narrows his eyes.

"I don't like this freaky shit."

I slap him on the back. "Come on, it'll be fun."

"Says every person right before they do something stupid," he mutters. "If there are roaches in here, I'm out."

We stop to leave our phones in a basket as Igor leads us to a room. He pulls out a key ring, runs through the rules, and says other stuff, but I'm barely listening as I watch Julia.

She's gazing around at the hallway, a half-smile on her face.

My throat thickens, prickling with feelings I don't understand.

Igor unlocks our door with a key shaped like a bat.

We peer inside the dark room.

"Please enter," he orders when we just stand there.

"Let's do this." I clap my hands and hoot.

They all blink at me—except for Julia who pumps her fist with me. Clearly, she gets it.

My eyes adjust and make out what looks like a bench in the middle and horizontal metal bars on the other side of the room. The rest appears empty.

Bang.

The door slams behind us and locks.

Boone grabs the handle and tries to open it. He stalks to the other side and checks out the bars. "What if this place *is* a front for murderers?"

No one replies since a clock eerily appears on the wall and glows into the darkness. It starts to tick down.

Boone huffs. "What if I have to piss?"

Taylor pats the bench he's sitting on. "Just have a seat and calm down, love."

"The bars need a combination of four letters to be opened," Reece calls out as he messes with them. "It's our first thing to solve. Obviously."

I nod at him. I should be helping, but...

I nudge Julia. "So, Channing. I saw you guys on campus. Is that a thing?"

She arches a brow. "Are we friends who chat about our love lives now?"

"Yeah. Can't a friend ask about another friend?"

"Not while the second friend is trying to escape from a cage. Find a clue." She taps me on the nose. "Boop."

I'm shocked by the touch, then laugh as she dances away from me.

Okay, okay. Things aren't weird between us.

Taylor speaks up. "The hunchback didn't say *I hope you like THE dark*. He said *I hope you like DARK*. Try DARK as the combination."

I didn't hear a word Igor said.

Reece tries the four letters and we hear a click. The bars squeak as he swings them open.

We rush out of the cage to continue the search while Taylor stays on the bench.

I flick on a light switch and the room fills with a purple glow.

"Another fucking door," Boone says faintly. "With words written on it."

> GOOD TO 5EE YOU MADE IT THIS FAR,
> BUT ABANDON HoPE.
> IF YOU WANT TO AVOID BEING DiNNER,
> DON'T CHoKE.

I MOTION THEM INTO A HUDDLE. "Alright, team, we've got a poem and we need a key to open the door. Look for puzzles, maps, anything you find could be important."

A few minutes later, I find a key under the rug, but it doesn't fit any of the doors.

"None of you searched this bench," Taylor murmurs.

Julia rushes over to the bench, feels around the legs, and finds a small drawer underneath. A box falls out with a four-digit combination lock.

"We need four digits to open this," she says, looking at me.

Several minutes pass as we go over the current clues we have, then—

"5010!" yells Julia. "The poem has a 5 instead of an S on the first line. Some letters are actually numbers. 5010."

She uses the combination and squeals as the box opens. "A key!" She hands the key to me and I open the new door.

We enter a room with chainsaws, sledgehammers, handcuffs, knives, and chains on the wall.

"Serial killer shit," Boone grouses.

"Keep searching," Julia and I call at the same time, then look at each other and laugh.

I slide in next to her. "We seem to have the same sense of team spirit."

She smirks. "Good thing. One of your guys is terrified and one of mine is sitting out."

"I knew the first clue!" Taylor shouts, obviously listening to us.

Reece works a puzzle box but can't get it to open, Poppy examines old news clippings about missing college students while Julia and I do a crossword.

"Fun?" I ask her.

"Less talking, more puzzle solving," she says tartly.

"Seven minutes on the clock, loves," Taylor calls out.

"We're not gonna make it," Poppy cries.

"Fine, I'll help." Taylor sways into the dungeon room and glances down at the crossword. He scoffs. "Two across is *CUR*. And nine down is a seven-letter word for *Banal*. The answer is *TEDIOUS*. Just like this puzzle."

Julia shouts in victory. "Good job, Tay. Okay, guys, the

word in the puzzle is *ICHTHYOLOGY*." She throws a wild look around. "Does anyone know what that means?"

We stare at each other.

"It's the study of fish," Boone says and we stare at him. "What? I know things," he adds grouchily.

"There's a bookshelf on the wall. Mostly anatomy books, but I saw one about fish," Poppy says.

We rush to it, and inside are more news articles. We place them together, revealing four shapes in order: a square, triangle, circle, and hexagon.

"Use it for this," Julia calls out as she holds up a lock box with another combination.

"The sides of the shapes. Square has four, triangle three, circle one, and hexagon six," I call out. "Four, three, one, six."

We hoot as we open the box.

"It's a bat key!" Poppy exclaims. "It's the way out! Go, go, go!"

Julia takes the key and rushes to the door.

"Thirty seconds," Reece calls out.

Julia fumbles with the key in the lock. "It won't turn!"

I grab her hand and we jiggle it.

"Sometimes you just need to wiggle it in just right," I say.

Julia laughs. "Oh, hockey player, you slay me."

I snort. "I wasn't being sexual."

"Sure," Reece calls. "Now shut up and try it again."

It finally clicks. We swing the door open and rush out into the hallway.

I call out, swoop Julia up in my arms, and swing her around while she bats at my shoulders, laughing.

"You're crazy," she calls as her hands rest on my shoulders.

"No one's going to swing me around?" Taylor says with a pout, and Reece sweeps him up like a bride and lets out a big victory yell.

Taylor fans himself. "Just keep carrying me, darling. I feel faint."

I let Julia down and our eyes cling until she looks away, a slow blush working up her throat to her face.

"Boop. That was fun." I touch her nose.

"Hmm," she murmurs.

"Worst experience of my life," Boone calls, but he's laughing.

"You're the first group to solve that room since we opened," the vampire says as we exit to the front.

Boone walks to the counter and leans on it. "Liam Neeson has the old man ability to kill lots of human traffickers in movies, and my skill is having friends who enjoy escape rooms. We wouldn't have gotten out if I hadn't known that last thing," he reminds us. "Hey, Fake Dracula, you guys sell T-shirts?"

He buys a shirt, then tosses an arm around Poppy. "You ever come to Kappa parties?"

Julia tugs her away from Boone and gives him a mock-stern look. "Hands off the girl, Kappa."

He grouses as we head outside.

A cold gust of wind blows in and Julia's crew dashes for Taylor's sedan. Before Julia goes, she grabs my hand.

"What?" I say, smiling like a fool.

Her whiskey eyes shine up at me. "Nothing. Just . . . it was good to see you."

My hands itch to pull her to me. Stupid. "Yeah, same."

All at once, her breasts are pressed against my jacket as she gives me a tight hug. My nose dips to her hair and she smells so fucking good.

She pulls back, a shy smile on her face. "Bye."

Don't go...

"Bye."

I watch her as she climbs into the car. I watch until they pull out of the parking lot.

It's not until I get home that I find an envelope in the pocket of my jacket. Inside is two hundred dollars with a note.

More to come.

Love, Julia

Maybe she's been carrying it around. Waiting.

I don't know. I type out a text.

I found ur cash. U don't have 2 pay me back.

I delete it and fall back on my bed.

It wouldn't do any good. She wants to pay me back.

Lucifer jumps on my chest, his claws digging into my flesh. I flinch then gently toss him over to his side of the bed.

"No snuggling, motherfucker."

He blinks at me and curls up his tail.

A text comes in on my phone. Julia. I bolt up and snatch it off my nightstand to read.

I put money in ur pocket, Everest. I'll give u more. Little at a time.

Whatever u want. U haven't seen Connor?

Nope. I had fun tonight.

Same. U in bed?

I wonder if she's alone. If she's fucking Channing.

Yeah. I'm going to quit my job soon. U did that for me. Thank you.

I send another one before I think too hard about it.
Wanna grab coffee sometime?

A few minutes pass before the next text comes in.

Yeah. Night.

I flop back down on the pillows and stare up at my ceiling fan. I imagine Julia and I having coffee, then me kissing her, then—

No.

Sleep. That's what I need.

And I try, I do, but my head keeps circling back.

Her laugh, her silliness, the way she felt in my arms.

Refocus.

Right, right.

Instead, I think about being a lawyer.

I picture Dad proud of me.

I picture Mom sane and whole.

I picture me doing Kurt proud.

12

Julia

My eyes dart from the red dress to the yellow one. Both give off different vibes. One is sexy, one innocent. I snatch up the demure yellow one, then put on low-heeled brown boots. I swish from side to side in the mirror.

Perfect for a day date with Channing. Our first *real* date.

Taylor opens my door and plops down on my bed. "Your guy is downstairs."

A long exhale comes as nerves hit me. Channing and I have been hanging out as friends for a while, but last week he kissed me in the library. He asked for more from me. He asked if I'd give him a chance.

My gut twists. "He isn't Parker," I say mostly to myself as I rub on a pale pink lip gloss.

"Thank God," Poppy muses from where she's sitting on my bed. "He's a freak."

"I like Channing. He's sweet. He walks me to class and

takes me to lunch." I color in my brows.

"Are you trying to convince yourself?" Poppy asks with a wry grin.

I wince. Maybe.

Taylor grunts. "I've said it before, but I'll say it again, you're fishing in the same asshole pond Parker came from. I'd just hate for you to forget that."

I brush out my hair, then turn to take them in. Both look back at me with serious expressions. "Are you saying I can't trust my instincts? I haven't lost my grit, guys. I just want to have fun with a normal guy for once. He's the only one interested."

Taylor gives me a sly smile. "Not Eric?"

I chew my lips. Sure, I've thought about him, especially since the escape room. "We're just friends."

Taylor shrugs. "I'm just saying, Parker was the perfect guy—then he screwed around. It runs in Kappa blood."

I stiffen. "You can't paint all men with the same brush, plus Channing never talks about Parker. It's apples and oranges. I won't let myself be fooled again."

Leaving them there, I smile at Channing as I come down the stairs. He looks handsome, his dark hair swept back, his face clean shaven. Only he's wearing faded jeans and a Kappa shirt.

"Gorgeous," he murmurs when I give him a hug.

I grab my purse. "So, what's the surprise date? Where are we going?"

He winces. "I have to cancel. I would have texted but wanted to see you in person."

My shoulders slump with disappointment. "What happened?"

He sighs. "I've got that Soc paper to do. I tried to finish

last night, but it sucks and I need to get my grade up. But, to make it up to you, I brought you my old camera to use. You've been talking about snapping pics of the town, so I thought you might do that today instead." He unzips the bag and shows me the camera. "It's older than my new one but still in great shape."

"Or I can just wait until you finish your paper? Better yet, we can hit the library and I'll hang out while you work on it. I don't mind." I glance down at my dress. "I can change."

"No. That won't work. Besides the paper, there's a hockey game tonight and we're hosting the after-party. You know how it is. The guys have asked me to run the bar."

"A pledge can do that."

He rubs his face. "Parker asked me to be there. It's not like you're free tonight. You're working at the club."

"Right," I say, my eyes narrowed.

He tucks a piece of hair behind my ear. "I can stop by after you get off and walk you home."

My voice is tight. "Sure. Sounds good."

He steps in and kisses me on the lips. "Just text me when you're done and I'll wait out back."

"Fine."

"It's a date."

"No, today was a date," I say.

"We'll do it again."

Mm-hmm.

As he walks outside and gets in his Mercedes, my body prickles with Parker memories, the times he said he was busy with Kappa.

If I have misjudged Channing, how can I ever trust my instincts again?

13

Julia

When I get off-stage, I go to Eddie to see if anyone's asked for a lap dance. I sigh in relief when he tells me no. I've only made fifty in tips, which is terrible for a Saturday.

Eddie tells me I can take off after my next set and I whoop in excitement.

I text Channing. *Leaving early, can u meet me in an hour?*

After my routine with Marcia, I head to the changing rooms where I remove my makeup and change into a short athletic skirt and a hoodie. I brush my hair up into a high ponytail, then check my phone, but there's no reply from Channing.

I sigh and scroll on Instagram, stopping when I see that Hawthorne blew out Boston College, 5 to 0. Eric scored four of the goals. A slow smile curls my lips as I text him.

U have a new nickname. They're calling u The Miracle on Twitter. Don't let it go 2 ur head.

His reply is immediate. *U r welcome. I'm awesome.*

I snort, then send him a selfie of me smirking at him with a thumb's up sign.

We had coffee together in the student center last week. It was awkward at first but lessened the more we chatted. We talked about hockey, law school, and my seminar about Sparrow Lake. Light and easy. He bought me a cinnamon bun I swore I didn't want, but he insisted I have it.

Before we realized it, two hours had passed, and we'd missed our next classes.

He sends me a pic of him in the locker room, sans shirt.

Holy shit. Alrighty then.

I blink at the bulging pecs, the defined six-pack, the luscious golden skin of his chest. As a redhead, you think he'd be pale, but he isn't. Nope. He's tawny like the Lion he is.

There's a low-lidded, sexy look in his eyes as he looks at the camera.

I let out a soft whistle.

U got a puck bunny waiting 4 u? Tillie?

Three dots appear, then disappear, until a text comes through. *No.*

Interesting.

I send him a row of sad emojis.

My phone rings, startling me, and I answer it. "Eric? Hey!" Laughter comes from me as a thrill zips down my spine.

"Yeah, hey." I hear the muffled sound of male voices in the background, yelling and talking over each other.

"Congrats on the win. Did your parents come in?"

"Nah, my dad is out of town and Mom isn't feeling well."

I hear the disappointment in his voice, and my heart does a fluttering thing, hurting for him.

"You're the first non-hockey person to congratulate me," he continues. "I just wanted to call and say I appreciate it."

"Well, I'm going to catch the game on ESPN later. You scored 4 points!"

"Yeah, I'm in a groove. I feel focused. For once." He laughs.

"Your mind is all kittens and unicorns, huh?"

"Hardly." He pauses. "So, you're working tonight?"

I guess he saw where I was in the pic I sent. "I'm getting off early. We're dead because of the game."

Marcia starts to change for her next routine. She's been sitting next to me doing her makeup. "Tell college boy hello for me," she says. "Also he's sexy. You banging him?"

"No," I whisper to her under my breath. "Stop."

"Mm-hmm," she replies.

Eric laughs. "I heard her. Tell her hi. We could do something if you're free."

I chew my lips, wishing I hadn't already texted Channing. "Oh, dang. I have plans."

"Ah. Not surprised. Maybe next time, yeah?"

I clench the phone tight, not wanting to let him go. "Yeah. For sure."

We say goodbye and get off.

Later, I'm mulling about missing out on seeing Eric as I sit in the kitchen area for the staff at the club. The TV is on and I watch highlights of the game as I eat pizza one of the cooks made. Earlier, I gabbed with Eddie and talked to Marcia when she took her break. When I check the time, I gasp. It's been two hours since I texted Channing.

I step outside in my Converse, shivering in the autumn

chill. It's a little before midnight, which means the Kappas are waist-deep in beer and women.

I head down the street and type out a text to Channing.

R u okay? Never mind getting me.

I walk the few blocks to Frat Row and head to the Kappa house, stopping in front of it.

Hovering on the sidewalk, I weigh my options. There's nothing stopping me from going in. Sure, it'll suck, because most of them don't like me. Plus, I might see Parker or Scott. They might toss me out.

A prickle tiptoes down my spine. A tug, or an inkling, tells me to go inside.

I flip up the hoodie and keep my head low as I take the steps up to the porch and enter the house.

The first floor of the mansion is beautiful with mahogany paneling and a dust-covered chandelier that looks like something out of Victorian England—except for the drunk partiers dancing beneath it.

A fog machine puffs out smoke, reminding me of the strip club. A strobe light flashes, and I squint between each mad blink to check out the people. The party has dissolved into chaos. I catch a guy in the corner, eyes rolling back as some girl bobs her mouth on his cock. Another girl dances in her bra and panties, Red's brunette friend. My mouth compresses.

Oh, the irony.

I catch sight of Parker near a stage, lording over it like a king surveying his domain.

It's when I hit the bottom of the staircase that my real reason for being here solidifies in my head.

I need to know if Channing is in this for real or if I'm just a girl on a Kappa's string.

And a party is the best way to find out.

At the top of the stairs, two lofty gatekeepers leer and step aside, as if giving me entrance to some magical kingdom.

As I walk down the hallway, I hear rhythmic banging and people moaning. I dated Parker long enough to know that's normal background noise.

At a door at the end of the hall, I see a sign that says *Channing*. I stop and knock.

"Go away," he mutters in a low voice.

Nope. I turn the doorknob and push the door open a sliver.

The light from the doorway illuminates the bed and the woman lying on it, her legs spread.

Channing is between her, his naked backside on display. He doesn't stop fucking her, just turns and glares at me as he slurs his words. "I told you—" He blinks, then stops, his mouth opening and closing like a fish. "Julia! Shit! Shit!" He tries to scramble away from the girl but ends up falling off the bed.

I'm winded, a punch to the gut, some of it hurt, some of it anger. Mostly at myself.

How did I let myself believe for one minute that he was any different from Parker?

No, we weren't in a committed relationship, but he led me on for weeks and for what? Just to throw it all away?

The girl pushes up in the bed, tugging the covers with her. "Are you his girlfriend?"

I laugh darkly. "Oh, he wishes."

I walk to where he is, still prone on the floor. He sits up, leaning against the wall as he rubs his head. "Julia. I can explain."

"I'm sure you can and I've heard it all before." I crouch down and rake my eyes over him, taking in his flushed, sweaty skin. I gag at the lack of a condom.

I hold his blue eyes, the ones I thought were kind. "Listen good, Channing. Don't call me, text me, think of me, look at me, or drive past my house. Whenever you see me, walk the other way. I'll cut your dick off if you try to contact me."

He licks his lips. "It was the tequila. I never should have had that last one. It wasn't my fault. She flirted with me. She followed me up here—"

"Shhh, stop that." I tap him on the cheek, not quite a slap, but I hope it stings. "There's no excuse for lying just so you could get laid. I don't need jack-offs like you in my life, okay?"

I glance over at the girl who's hurriedly putting her clothes on. "No need to rush on my account."

"Julia, wait . . ." comes from Channing as I leave the room and dart into a bathroom to calm myself. My hands clench in and out and my face is lobster red. I splash cold water on my skin, then look up at myself in the mirror.

I keep doing the same things, expecting different results. I let him in through the chinks in my armor. Why? I just wanted normal. A guy to date.

I point a finger at myself, my chest heaving. "That is the last time a man ever does you wrong."

Downstairs, the place is clearing out. The music has stopped, and the chandelier glitters with light.

The second I hit the foyer, a broad-shouldered Kappa brother steps in my way. "Where you going? Come downstairs to the basement and let's get you a beer."

I sidestep him and go for the door. "No thanks."

I try to move past him, but his hand latches on my wrist. "What's your name, gorgeous?"

"Let me go—"

"Cute thing like you, you're too serious. Come on, the after-party is more fun."

"*No.*" I try to tear my hand away, but he's too strong.

Someone behind me speaks, the tone full of wonder. "Julia."

I know that voice. Too well.

Parker. I jerk away from the guy and turn to him.

He's a gorgeous guy, tall and broad-shouldered with a big smile and dark hair that frames his All-American face.

He gives me a wolfish, drunken look. "I've been texting you, baby. Where've you been?"

I ease closer to the door. "Well—"

"You blocked me, didn't you?" He crushes a Solo cup in his hand, letting the beer slosh on his hand.

"Parker. You and me. We've been over for a long time—"

"You're wrong about that," he says as he reaches out and touches my hair. "You don't get to say when it's over. You never gave us a shot, Ju-Ju. I would have been really good to you. I mean, come on, you're a stripper. A guy like me is the chance of a lifetime."

I nod, agreeing just to agree.

A couple of his brothers gather around us.

"She says she doesn't drink," the original one says.

"Oh, yeah?" Parker says. "She's just an *angel*, aren't you?"

He's referring to one of my routines. I smile nervously. "And you're a little devil."

Parker wipes his hand over his mouth, his bleary gaze roaming my body lasciviously. "I miss you, Ju-Ju."

Someone snickers and Parker throws his cup at him. The guy apologizes profusely, then darts away.

Parker barely notices. He's got a glint in his eyes. One that makes fear skitter up my spine.

It's fine. There's no reason to be afraid. There are plenty of people around. This is just a bunch of drunken guys playing around.

"I have to go. Have a great night," I say and give him a small wave, trying to pretend like we're civil.

Parker shakes his head. "I say when you leave."

Goosebumps raise on my skin. I back away but wind up hitting a wall. And now I'm farther away from the door.

"I think you should come downstairs and give us a show," one of them says. "I've got some dollars on me."

"Really not interested, okay?" I snap.

Parker gets up in his face and scowls at him. "No one is looking at her. She's mine."

Normally, I'd say, "No, I'm not," but the faster I leave, the better. I can rant at him outside the house, not where the testosterone addled frat boys have me in their hunting grounds.

I'm inching around them when Parker grabs me, tugging me back against his chest. He smells like beer and expensive aftershave, the same scent I remember when I dated him. I used to love it.

Breath whooshes out of me as I struggle. His grip tightens, pushing down on my arms. I squirm and kick back at him, but nothing lands.

"Parker! Let me go. Now!"

One of the guys—maybe the only decent man at Kappa—rears back and watches him with uncertainty. "Uh, I don't think she likes you. Maybe you should let her go."

It's the wrong thing to say. Mostly because Parker can't stand it when someone tells him what to do.

"You don't know anything. Get lost," he barks at them. "All of you. Go downstairs."

I watch them turn and walk away, the one rather hesitantly, but my gut tells me he won't be getting help. Parker has them under his thumb, and if they don't obey, then they'll be next on his list.

His head bends to my neck, where he inhales deep. "Oh, Ju-Ju. How I've waited for you to walk in this house all semester—"

"Let me go—" I scream out, but his hand clamps over my mouth.

Grunts come from me as my blood pumps faster.

"I hate it when you interrupt me." His breath fans against my ear, and I shudder. Sure, I knew he was a guy on the edge, someone who had mood swings, but I never believed he would resort to physical violence.

My teeth bite down on the meaty part of his palm and he hisses and jerks it away.

I'm free and run for the door, but he catches me by the hem of my hoodie.

I try to talk reason. "Stop this. You're the king of Kappa. This isn't you. There are a hundred girls here who you can have—"

My words are cut off as his shoulders hit me in the gut. I think I'm going to fly across the room, but instead the world is hurled upside-down as I'm thrown over his shoulder and marched up the stairs. He weaves precariously on the top steps as I beat against his back and yell for help.

But everyone's vanished, either out of the house or to the basement.

He opens his door and carries me inside. My hands pummel him, aiming for his spine, and he grunts in pain when I land a good one. But I'm running out of steam, my head swimming from dizziness as black dots dance in front of my eyes. My head churns with how to escape him. There's a window, maybe a fire escape, I can't remember. There's a small bathroom. I can lock myself in it.

Half-formed thoughts whirl in my head as the panic reaches a crescendo.

He tosses me down on the bed and looks at me with wild eyes as he holds my hands above my head.

"You just had to go and date Channing, didn't you? To rub it in my face, yeah? To let me know that he was fucking you."

"No!" I shout. "We barely even kissed. I caught him with someone else."

He laughs bitterly. "Good. I sent the hottest girls after him. See, we're all the same, Julia, only I cared about you. I really did. You were different. Sweet." He presses his forehead to mine. "I'd give anything to fuck you again. I beat the shit out of Scott, did you know that? For talking shit about you and saying you sucked his cock. I even told his girlfriend." He laughs. "Did you blow him?"

"No." I wiggle underneath him. "Let me go!"

"Stop struggling." He runs his nose up the middle of my chest to my face. "I smell your fear. I hate that, I really do, 'cause you're brave and that mouth on you, Jesus, you don't know when to stop, but no one leaves me . . ." He pauses, his tone hardening. "Especially a piece of trash that strips."

I swallow thickly. I try to appear calm. "That's right. I'm not worth the trouble. I'm done with Channing. You got what you wanted. Scott is a loser. I'm glad you beat him up."

He kisses me hard, his teeth grinding into my lips as I wrestle to get him off me. His hands fumble with something above me, and I have a three second reprieve from the pressure of his grip, and I use it for all it's worth. I squirm and buck to shove him off me, but he easily overpowers me. He pulls me to the top of the bed, and I feel something cold and hard click around my wrist. Then he stretches out my other arm and does the same. He stares down at me, and everything I ever thought was handsome about him is replaced by something deranged.

"I've got you now," he says.

Forget being calm. I spit at him as I jerk against the hold. "You're insane!"

He stands up, breathing heavily. Blood drips down his arm to the floor from where I bit him, and he studies it thoughtfully.

He squeezes one of my breasts through my hoodie and I growl, arching my back to shove it away.

He smiles. "I like your fire, Ju-Ju. We're gonna have fun now."

He goes over to his phone and cranks up loud music.

14

Eric

After the game, I tag along with Reece and Boone to the Kappa house.

At the moment, we're in the basement as Boone pounds on the table and chants our fight song. Beer is getting sloshed everywhere, girls are hanging on us, and we're yelling like Vikings back from a victorious battle.

Boone tips his glass at me and I smile, and yeah, the love and congrats we get from the fans is cool, but it's still Kappa and my mood is off. There's not a girl here I look at for longer than a second.

Hooking up with randoms feels empty.

Lonely.

Depressing.

It kept me satisfied for years, but there has to be more than this. In the past, I've never wanted more than sex because making myself vulnerable to someone meant the possibility of getting hurt, and no one needs that shit in college.

I'm buzzing from a couple of beers, and part of me wants to go to Julia's place while the other side of me knows I shouldn't. I can't show up like some fool.

The lights come on, the music dies, and Kappa guys motion for people to leave.

Since I left my jacket on the main floor, we head that way instead of exiting through the basement. I'm just grabbing it out of a closet when I hear a scream from upstairs. It's hard to tell with Boone's drunken singing.

I look up the stairs and see a couple guys, but they disappear out of view.

I snap my fingers at Boone, who breaks from his group and staggers over to me.

"Hey, did you hear something?"

"Hear what?" he says, weaving on his feet. "Lighten up. We're super stars here."

I glance upstairs. "No, it's not that. You didn't hear—"

"I'm going to find this girl I was talking to," he says, then walks to a group of college girls.

All right. Fuck it. I'm out of here.

As I reach the threshold, there's another sound, a thump. Maybe I'm not thinking clearly, but considering the fact that Parker is missing, my gut tells me to check it out.

"Hold on," I tell Reece, who's been standing at the front door waiting for me.

"You go ahead. I'm walking home," he says, then heads out.

"Fine."

I take the staircase two steps at a time. I'm not sure why

I'm doing this. Could be the beer. Could be that freshman at the beginning of the semester.

At the top landing, I stop and listen, but all I hear are the sounds of rap music from Parker's room.

A Kappa appears next to me, frowning. "Hey. Parker says he's busy. No visitors."

I size him up. "I'm pretty sure you aren't going to stop me from doing whatever I want."

He puffs up his chest, thinks for a moment as he assesses me, then steps aside.

The door isn't locked and I shove it open to a dim room.

Parker stands at the foot of his bed, staring down at a girl handcuffed to the headboard.

A roaring sound echoes in my head. Anger rushes in so fast, I get dizzy.

"Julia?" I breathe, the air sucked from my lungs.

Parker turns to me, his mouth gaping, incredulity on his face. His shirt is off as he weaves on his feet. "What the hell? What are you doing in my room?"

My entire body tightens, every muscle ready to pounce. To destroy.

He holds his hands up. "Whoa, simmer down. It's not what it looks like. I just wanted to talk. She never lets me talk. Nothing happened."

"Eric," Julia croaks. Her voice sounds raw as tears stream down her face. "Help me. Please."

Parker glances down at her, then back to me. "Hey. I'd never hurt her. I care about her."

His version of caring for her is sick.

I lunge for him without warning, my fist connecting, twice, rapid fire, square on his jaw. He stumbles back against his desk, books and papers flying.

He slides down to the floor, curses falling out of his mouth.

"Get up!" I loom over him.

Last time I laid Parker out like this, we were freshmen. His older Kappa friends stuck up for him (and not me). It was the perfect reason to ditch Kappa.

"This place is fucked up," I say as I bend and get in his face. "And you're the reason."

He struggles to his feet and clings to the edge of his desk to steady himself.

Footsteps pound up the stairs as brothers call to each other, asking what's going on.

Hands grab me from behind, trying to pull me back. "Hey!" a guy says. "You can't do that—"

"That was nothing," I growl as I shake him off, then stalk to Julia.

"Are you okay?"

She nudges her head at the end table, a small whimper coming from her. "He put the keys in there."

I unlock the cuffs, and she jumps off the bed and weaves on her feet, her face ashen. She rubs the red marks around her wrists. "Eric..." Her throat bobs.

"I've got you," I say in a gentle tone as I reach in to pull her into a brief hug. Staring down at her, I search her face. "Did he rape you?" I rub my thumb over one of her tears.

She shakes her head. "H-he dragged me up here and locked the cuffs on me. I screamed, but no one heard me."

"I heard you."

"Hansen, get out of this house," Parker mutters, climbing to his feet. He moves forward, making a play for Julia. "This is none of your business."

Jesus. I can't believe he wants more.

I shove him back to the floor. "Don't come near her," I say, then lace her fingers with mine.

Parker gazes at our hands, his nose flaring. His lips open and close. "Wait? Are you and her..."

"What if we are?" Julia yells at him, regaining some of her equilibrium—and anger. "You can't do anything about who I'm with, Parker!"

"Come on, we're walking out of here," I say to her.

She leans into me, nodding. "Okay, okay."

"Do you want to die tonight? Because I will end you," I tell another Kappa who appears at the door. I shove our way between all of them.

I maneuver Julia in front of me, my hands around her waist to keep her steady. The stairs are full of brothers as we walk down. They shoot eye-daggers at us, but no one moves.

I catch sight of the photograph of Kurt in the composite from his senior class before he went to Harvard, and my lips twist. The fraternity was good then; it had people like him to lead by example. If Kurt were here, he'd do the same thing I'm doing right now.

We reach the main floor and walk out the door. The porch is mostly deserted as we descend and head to the back alley that leads to my house.

"Hang on," I tell her as she stumbles.

"I feel weird," she murmurs faintly. "Like I can't breathe."

I sweep her in my arms, and she goes limp as her cheek rests on my chest.

"It's the adrenaline. You're crashing. You're safe. No one will hurt you now."

I sit on my steps with her in my arms as she shudders,

then weeps softly into my shirt. I rub her hair, smoothing it back into where she had it in a ponytail.

"I got you, let it out, all of it."

"I felt so powerless. And scared. Not one of those brothers helped me. I mean, Connor frightened me too, but I expected it. I prepared for it. But Parker never got so rough with me. I thought they'd just give me a hard time, and I'd leave, but..." She sniffs and wipes her face.

"You broke up with him. Everyone knows it. And he can't let that go."

My gaze goes back to the Kappa house, anger amplifying now that I've gotten her out. Later.

I focus on her and murmur softly to her as I rest my chin on her head. "You must have broken his black heart."

She huffs out a laugh, just like I was hoping. Her fingers rub at the collar of my shirt. "Eric, you're always saving me. How does that even happen? You're always there when I need you."

"Lucky you."

Another small laugh.

I take her hand and turn her wrist over, exposing a small round scar, pink and raised. It looks irritated from the cuffs. "Did Parker do this?"

Her head shakes. "Connor burned me with a cigar after I missed a payment. I seem to attract the wrong kind of men in my life. I always thought Kappas were your friends, but tonight..."

"They're not. Even if they were, I'd never support that kind of mentality."

"Why are you always hanging out there?"

"Hockey fans come to their house, but trust me, I'm *done* with that frat."

"Because of me?"

I stare into her eyes. "You are the final straw, yes." I pause, recalling Channing making out with a girl at the party. "Hey. Are you and Channing..."

She presses her face into my neck and sighs. Little tingles skate down my body.

"I don't even know what that was. Me trying to be normal, I guess. Doesn't matter. Same story, different guy. He was with someone. Apparently, Parker set him up, but still..."

"Monogamy really isn't in the Kappa dictionary."

"Yeah."

My hands tighten around her waist. "Fuck them. I'll drive you to the police if you want to press charges."

"No," she says immediately, her body stiffening.

"Why not? They—"

"You don't get it. You're you. You're rich. You have power. I'm a stripper. My mom is, well, let's just say the police know who she is. I'd say one thing happened and every one of those guys would back Parker. They'd say I went up those stairs on my own. It's a man's world. Everyone else is just paying rent."

"I'd back you."

She looks stricken. "You've been so good to me. I'd never want to drag you into this mess."

"I don't care what people think about me."

"You should. You're a hockey star. People adore you. I won't bring you down." She chews on her bottom lip. "I shouldn't have gone in there. I just wanted to check on Channing. He said he'd walk me home and he didn't, so I went inside to see if he was with anyone."

"Hey. It's not your fault."

"I know. I do. I just want to forget it. It's funny—or not—but I thought men putting money in my underwear was awful, but Parker, he's so much worse..."

My voice is gruff as I stroke her wrists. "I'm going to kill him."

"No," she says. "Don't say those things."

"Why not?"

"Because you can't get in trouble for me! And I don't want you to go to jail."

He's the one that should be in jail.

A long exhalation comes from me and I pull her closer. "Sorry. I won't kill him." Today.

"You wanna come inside?" I ask a few minutes later.

She shakes her head. "I should go home. I need a shower."

A sound comes from my stomach and a little smile curls her lips. It takes my breath I'm so thankful.

"You're hungry, aren't you?"

I grimace sheepishly. My eyes go to the park where the street trucks are. "I wouldn't mind a sandwich. How about you? My treat."

"There's no way I can eat, but a hot chocolate sounds good. My shower can wait until afterwards." She dips her head, almost shy as her hands play with the ends of my hair. "Can we wait a minute and just sit here? I-I don't want to let you go just yet."

My heart skips a beat. We've turned a corner somewhere.

I sense it.

She senses it.

If the blush on her face is anything to go by.

"Then don't," I say softly.

15

Julia

A few minutes later, we head to the food trucks, our hands laced.

Seeing Eric march into Parker's room and push everyone aside plays through my head like a movie reel. I should probably go home, but I don't want to be alone.

I keep seeing his fierce, pissed off face, his big fists, then his gentleness with me.

Part of me wants to report the incident to the police. I do. (I couldn't report Connor, not without him putting me or my mom in a ditch.)

But Parker... I'd love to see him get what's coming.

Then I think about the notoriety that will fly at me from all directions.

The school, the media.

People will have opinions about how I'm a stripper and that I don't really matter. They might not say it to my face, but they're thinking it, even the authorities. Plus, a part of me has been told to keep silent my entire life, starting all the way back to grade school when they teach you not to tattle.

Is Johnny pulling your hair? He's just playing. Go back to your seat.

I recall a teacher who required us to stand in front of the class if we wanted to tattle. I made sure I was never one of the ones who went up to tell on another student. Because afterward? Everyone is mad at you.

The only person who can support my story is Eric. And how can I drag him into a tawdry police investigation when he's who he is? And after everything he's done for me. No. I just can't do that to him.

I push those thoughts away as people call out to him as we make our way to the parking lot of the food trucks. He nods and smiles, soaking in the accolades from the game. You'd never believe he was livid earlier.

People in line to order food step aside to let him go first. He gets his sandwich and we find a table.

"So, tell me about yourself," he murmurs around a huge bite.

"I went to prep school with you for a year, dork."

"Yeah, about that . . ." He sets his sandwich down. "This isn't an excuse for what I did, but I was dealing with my brother's death. My mom had gone to a psych ward and my dad was on my ass to bring my grades up. I pushed people away."

I knew he'd lost a brother but . . .

"What happened? Ugh, I'm sorry. It's none of my business."

He looks away from me and swallows. "Kurt had a secret life with heroin. None of us knew because he was in Boston.

He was home for the holidays and went to make a buy. I interrupted them and he got shot. Died at the scene." He rubs his face. "I blame myself."

His hands fist and I loosen them.

"I get it," I say. "I want to tell you something. It's big. And I don't want you to think differently of me."

His eyes lift to mine. "Okay."

"The reason I started stripping was because . . ." I pause, digging deep for the nerve to tell him. "My mom's the reason I owed Connor. She's an addict. And homeless." Stammering, I rush through the story of her car accident and her spiral into prescription pills. I explain how we lost our house. How she lives with friends or in her car.

His gaze is soft. "I'm sorry, Julia. If I can help out in any way, let me know. Wait. That ring you pawned? Was it hers?"

I nod. "I was afraid she'd sell it and took it. She pawned or sold everything after we lost our house. Silverware, candlesticks, jewelry."

"Shit. You've been through hell, Julia."

I grimace, wanting to move on. "I'm sorry about your brother. Addiction is vicious."

His shoulders seem to cave in. "Back then, I handled everything in my life like it didn't matter. At the time, nothing did. I went through the motions. Girls were a way to distract myself from what was going on." He pauses. "You were one of them."

"I guess your life isn't as perfect as I thought."

He laughs harshly, then sobers. "Uh, no."

I retell him the story of the party freshman year, how I saw him staring at a wall.

His face reddens. "I don't remember seeing you. I was probably trashed. They made us go days without sleep and

I'd been kissing Kappa ass all week." He smirks. "Not anymore."

"What happened between you and Parker before? Why do you not like each other?"

"Well, he's Parker. Our dads do business together, and we grew up around each other, even though we went to different schools. Honestly, I think our dads encouraged us to compete. Who was the better athlete, who made the best grades, who had the best car."

I wince. "That doesn't sound fun."

"It wasn't." He ruffles my hair. "Come on, I'll walk you home. I need to sober up and work off this sandwich."

We walk through the park and down the street to my house. We aren't holding hands anymore, but they brush against each other.

We stop in front of my house.

He rakes his hair off his face. "So. You wanna go to brunch tomorrow?"

I laugh nervously. "Is food all you ever think about?"

"Athlete."

"Actually, I was thinking of going to the lake and taking some photos at sunrise. It's a good time. There's never anyone there, plus I don't think I can sleep for a while—not after Parker."

His lips tighten as he heaves out an exhale, getting that pissy, angry look on his face again, so I change the topic.

"Taking photos has become a little hobby of mine." At least Channing was good for one thing.

He nods. "Want some company? I could use the time away from campus to clear my head." His face hardens. "I really want to go back to Kappa and beat the shit out of Parker."

"And it would solve nothing and get you in trouble."

"Right. So? Can I come with? We can take my truck and you can drive."

Yes. A million times. I can tell myself that I don't want to be alone, but the truth is, I want him with me for other reasons.

I go up to my door and let him in, putting my finger to my lips. "Wait down here. I need to grab the equipment."

He doesn't argue as I tiptoe up the stairs. In my room, I change into jeans and a sweatshirt and grab Channing's camera bag. I can't say I feel guilty about using it.

Twenty minutes later, we're at the lake.

He sits on a park bench. "What's so great about this place?"

I catch a couple of ducks drifting on the water under the purple, pre-dawn sky and snap the pic. "It's pretty. I love nature. There's no artifice. Everything you see is true."

"Ever go to Bell Mountain?"

I snap another photograph of the trees, the sky glowing behind their brightly-colored fall leaves. "No car. I had to sell it to pay Connor months ago."

"I have one."

I snap another photo, my nerves zinging. Does that mean he wants to do this again? This night has been one of a lot of surprises, good and bad, shifting my world in big ways, and I'm not sure I can take it shifting anymore.

The lighter the sky gets, the better I feel.

I shove the ugliness from earlier away.

Nothing Kappa can touch me here.

Parker doesn't matter.

Someday his actions will slap him in the face.

Karma will get him.

And I'll be waiting for it.

When the sun has fully risen, I find Eric asleep on the park bench, his mouth parted as he lightly snores. I stare at his face, the way the sunlight makes his reddish hair glint with golden lights. My gaze traces his bent nose, the curve of his lips.

"Eric?" I whisper, shaking him slightly.

He opens his eyes sleepily. "Yeah?"

"How many times have you broken your nose?"

He gives me a squinty, confused look. "Uh, three or four. I lost count."

I laugh. "Okay, it was just something I had to know."

"Glad to help." He yawns widely. "Where are we going for brunch?"

I tap him on the shoulder teasingly. "Stop that. I have to go. I have to check on my mom today."

"All right," he says, sitting up and stretching.

I start to move backward to let him stand, but I forget where we are, on the edge of the water, and nearly topple over. At the last second, he reaches forward and grabs me, pulling me flush against him so that all the breath leaves my body.

"I've got you," he murmurs as his hand caresses down my spine. "Every time."

16

Eric

I wake up, stretch, turn my head—and stare at the eyes that greet me. Lucifer is curled up with part of his tail in my hair. "Beat it," I growl.

He gets up and prisses to the other pillow.

After my shower, he's moved back to mine. "You aren't sleeping in here all day," I mutter as I throw on some jeans and a Hawthorne sweatshirt.

"Go bother Reece. He's your owner." I set him outside my room and close the door tight.

"Where you going?" Boone asks from the couch as I grab my jacket off the hook. He's still wearing his pledge shirt from last night. He rubs his forehead, and I'm guessing he just got home.

"Errands. Hey, I thought Kappa was doing black-out week for mid-terms, but you look rough. Are you guys still drinking every night?" It's been two weeks since the party where Parker handcuffed Julia. I told Boone about Parker and Julia, but he claims the brothers said she went into his room willingly.

Just like she said they would. Such bullshit.

"Every night. I have to be there." He lets out a heavy groan. "Once I get in, things will ease up."

Right. He's completely bought into the party-every-night lifestyle.

"Hope you know what you're doing."

He nods and looks away from me.

Instead of partying, I've been on the ice a lot. Studying. Running. Working out. I've met up with Julia several times. I've taken her to Bell Mountain, the lake, even a historic cabin on the outskirts of town.

Reece walks into the kitchen in an orange speedo and opens a kitchen cabinet and pulls out some cereal.

"Are you bringing breakfast in bed?" a female voice calls from his room.

I smirk at him and he shrugs. "I have a friend over. We may be loud."

I give Boone a slight head nod and he blinks, then catches on and moves to the bookcase. I chat with Reece, moving in closer to him as I block his view of Boone. I ask him who he's got in his room and how they hooked up. I must step in too close, because his eyes flare as he catches on and runs to the den to get away. His socks slip on the hardwood and he slams into the back of the couch. His feet fly over his head as he tumbles to the floor. Boone dives on top of him and puts his hand on his head.

"I pass the puck," Boone shouts.

"Fucking socks," Reece cries out in defeat.

"Belongs to you now," Boone says with relish.

"Concur," we say in unison.

Boone hands the puck to Reece and they climb to their feet.

Reece glares at me. "You were working with him? I thought we had a pact."

I laugh. "Classic prisoner's dilemma. I chose to turn you in and work with the jailer to save my own skin."

I leave them and head outside, a grin on my face. I'm not sure if it is the hijinks with the boys or hanging with Julia.

When I pull up to her house, she comes out smiling, and I wonder if it's for the photography or me. She's wearing flared jeans with daisies on them and a cropped pink sweater. Her hair is swept up in a high ponytail, her lips full and pink.

"Hey," I say when she slides in. She's wearing a new perfume, something floral and light. "Where to this Sunday?"

She packs her equipment on the floor. "I was thinking about doing something different. Somewhere inside?" She gazes out at the dark clouds. "It looks like rain. I haven't done much with indoor photography. Maybe I should start."

"Somewhere inside. Got it."

"You do?"

"Yep. Leave it to me."

Shifting gears, I drive us to the perfect place.

She wrinkles her nose when we arrive. "What is this?"

"My domain." I wink.

"An ice-skating rink?"

I scoff. "No. Hockey rink. Holy shit, you've never been?"

She laughs, the sound rather embarrassed. "No."

"I'm wounded. Come on. It'll be empty."

She wraps her fingers around the door handle but hesitates. "Yeah, but what do I take pictures of in there?"

"I don't know. Me?" I flex a bicep. "That is, if you can catch me with that lens of yours."

"I don't skate. I need to be close to a subject. Maybe the equipment? Hmmm." Her forehead furrows.

"Or . . . if you're more adventurous . . ."

"Skate? You want me to skate?" She shakes her head. "Nope. Big no. I had roller skates when I was seven and broke my arm."

"Don't be scared."

"I'm not," she mutters defensively.

I chuckle. "You're a chicken."

She opens the truck door. "You're trying to goad me."

"And it's working."

She smirks as we get out and head to the front door.

I use my captain's key to open the place up. Turning on all the lights, I lead her through the men's locker room, grab my skates, and head out to the home bench.

"You can put your stuff there." I lace up my skates.

She sets her things down, takes out the camera, and pulls out the lens. "When did you start skating?"

"I was born on skates. We have a lake on our property. Kurt used to take me out there. He was a better skater than I'll ever be."

Better at everything, actually. He never loved hockey, though. Academics was his ticket.

She gives me a soft look. "That sounds like a good memory to hang on to."

I grew up jealous of the attention my brother got, but most of the time I adored him. Memories of him teaching me to skate is one of those. "Yeah."

We reach the rink, and I back out slowly.

She watches me, her eyes big as saucers. "You're good."

I laugh. "This is nothing. You should see me with a stick and a puck."

She leans over the wall and aims her camera at me. "Which reminds me, when are you coming to a game?"

"Haven't considered it."

My hand goes to my heart. "Vicious girl."

She focuses the camera, a small smile on her lips.

I skate in a figure eight, drawing it out nice and slow. I haven't done this, skating for fun, in a while. It feels good. "If you come to a game, you might enjoy it."

"I don't know the rules."

"I can teach you the rules." I motion her forward. "Come on out here."

She stares at me, mouth slightly open. "No."

"Why?"

"I don't have skates."

"Don't need skates."

She looks around helplessly. "My seven-year-old self is seriously panicking right now. I'll fall."

"No, you won't. I'll keep you up." I open the door and beckon to her. She puts her camera down on the bench, and I take her hand and lead her out onto the ice.

Her feet slip out from under her a few times, but it doesn't matter because I keep my arm around her waist. As I walk her out to the center line, she clings close to me, and I can't say I mind.

"I've got you. See, that's not so bad, is it?"

"I guess it's okay."

We're nearly at the center and I slowly start to let her go.

"No," she cries, then lets out a sudden yelp as her feet slip out from under her.

I catch her. "Relax. We're in the neutral zone. Nothing bad happens here."

"Stop being funny and don't let me go again, Eric."

I chuckle but do as she says, holding onto her as I point down the ice. "This here, between the two blue lines, is the neutral zone. The red line is center ice. Every period, we start here with a face off."

"A face off?"

"Yep. It's just me, or Boone, or Reece . . . but usually Reece, because he's the best at them. The ref drops the puck and then it's game on. We try to get the puck in the opposing goal."

She studies the ice with concentration. It's fucking adorable. "What are the blue lines for?"

"Well . . . you have to be in the opposing team's zone, meaning past that blue line, in order to take a shot."

She squints down the ice, then her eyes skip to mine. "How? You've got to be really good to do that while skating. I can't even stand."

I shrug, feeling a flash of smug male pride because of the way she's looking at me. "It's kind of second-nature to me."

She shakes her head. "I still don't get how anyone—"

"I'll show you. Come to a game. Saturday. It's a big one. The Thunder are tied with us for first in our division."

"I'll think about it. I'm down to work, but I could ask one of the other girls to take my spot."

I begin to pull away and she lets out a chirpy little cry.

"Sorry, I was considering letting you drift on the ice until you agree, but I can't do it. You're too damn cute." I tug her back to me as our eyes cling.

Sparks heat under my skin.

Her tongue darts out as she wets her lips, and I track her movements.

Kiss her, my head says, but . . .

Her breath quickens.

Something plinks overhead, one of the lights going out.

She seems to shake herself. "Um, I need some action shots of you. Can you take me back to the wall?"

"Sure."

The rest of the time proceeds as normal. I skate, getting my exercise in as she works her magic.

After half an hour, I get back to the bench, and she's checking her phone.

"You have enough for your portfolio?" I ask.

She looks up. "Portfolio?"

"I saw a job listing in the student center for a job in town at the paper. I'll text it to you."

She puts her camera away. "Oh, wow, that sounds interesting. I'll check it out." She grimaces. "Sorry to cut this short, but my mom texted me. I need to go."

"Want me to go with you?"

"No," she blurts, almost before I get the question out. She tucks a fallen lock of hair behind her ear. "She'll just ask me a bunch of questions about you. I don't want to put you through that."

I unlace my skates and throw them in my locker, and we get back in my car. As I'm pulling up at her place, my phone buzzes with a text.

I plan on ignoring it, because I want to enjoy my last few minutes with Julia, but then I catch sight of the name on the display.

You're on. Thursday morning. Hawthorne Law building. 10 a.m.

I grab the phone. What the hell?

Dread and fear grip my chest like a vise.

"Eric? What's wrong?"

It must be written all over my face. "I just got a text from my dad. I got an interview for law school here at Hawthorne."

"Are you kidding? That's incredible!" She stops gushing. "Wait. Why do you look like you want to hurl?"

I'd been staring at the message, trying to think of how to respond to my dad. I glance up at her, part of me wanting to confess that I don't know if I can hack it or if it's what I even want.

She leans in and pokes me in the ribs. "Hey. You're good at everything. You're the Everest. You're The Miracle."

"That was just hockey. It doesn't apply to—"

She cocks her head. "What about hockey? Zack went to the NHL. He's playing for the Preds. Do you not want that?"

"That's not an option. See you later?"

She leaves the truck, and the air feels different without her.

Tense. Dark.

Another text from my dad comes through.

Don't screw this up.

I've never, not once, worried about the interview. I don't have the LSAT score, but when it comes to people, I can pour on the charm and get them on my side.

This is good news.

I should be on top of the world.

So why do I feel like it's ending?

17

Julia

"That's the most beautiful thing ever," Taylor squeals as he clutches at his heart. We're two of a handful of people in the library. I giggle.

"So, I should use that one?"

He leans closer to peer at the screen. He doesn't need to. The reason we're here instead of at home is because they have these lovely 28-inch screens. My photographs are practically life-size.

"All of them," he gushes. "Just . . . all of them. They're superb."

I wish he was saying that about my photography skills, but there's a little drool in the corner of his mouth. He didn't swoon over my panoramic photograph of the lake or the composition of the skies over Bell Mountain.

He's transfixed on one thing: Eric Hansen.

I nudge him. "Come on. Seriously. I need to know which one of Eric is best for my portfolio. One."

"I suppose if you're making me pick just one, I fancy that one." He points at one of Eric leaning against the boards with his hockey stick in his hands. His helmet is off and his hair is a mess around his face. It makes my heart twinge with excitement just to look at it.

"That one just makes him look hot. I need one that shows off my skills."

He tilts his head. "Okay, that one, where he's moving on the ice. I like how everything behind him is blurred out. The white of the rink is a nice contrast to his uniform. The effect is rather good."

I curl my lips. "I like that one, too."

He had his interview today. When I texted him this morning to wish him luck, he responded with a thumbs up and nothing else. Maybe he was nervous.

"Mmm," Taylor says, gazing at me with suspicion. "You like him."

"I don't," I protest, but it's a weak one.

I have squishy feelings about him. Ones I have to suppress.

He and I, we don't go together.

He's here as a pit stop on his way to his amazing life, and I'm careening around trying to take care of me and my mom.

Doubt practically drips off Taylor's tongue. "Why are you guys hanging out together, then?"

I avoid his gaze. "We're friends."

"Hmm. What's this portfolio for?"

"Oh . . ." I blush, not sure I want to tell anyone and jinx it. Eric sent me a link to the position he mentioned. "It's a photographer's job working for the paper. They need someone to take pictures for human interest stories. I probably won't get it. I don't have the experience."

"You're an artist, love. You have a real eye for this. If you show them those photos? You're gonna be a star."

His eyes catch on something behind me, and I notice a couple of other people staring as well, their eyes lighting up in wonder.

"He looks like a ginger James Bond," Taylor says.

I look over my shoulder at a tall man in a power suit. It was made for his body, stretching over his muscles. It's dark blue with a perfectly pressed white shirt and a purple paisley tie with a pocket square to match. His hair is slicked back into a tight bun at his neck. Shades cover his eyes.

I swallow.

Eric looks like a high-powered CEO. A sexy one.

He flips his shades up, swoops in, and hugs me. His breath tickles my ear. "Hey. Poppy told me you were here." He's wearing new cologne, something expensive and spicy.

"Ahrr . . ." I say. Only when it's out, I realize it's not actually a word.

Taylor gazes at me like I'm a complete weirdo and smiles, extending his hand. "Mr. Lawyer. You look fabulous."

"Thanks," he says, then focuses his attention back on me, staring directly into my eyes.

And I say nothing.

I want to punch myself in the face. I need to get it together and stop being a tongue-tied twelve-year-old.

I clear my throat and try to order my thoughts.

Taylor nudges me then, obviously not wanting to witness my imminent crash-and-burn. "I should leave. I've got a paper on Balzac calling my name."

"Good luck," Eric says as Taylor picks up his bicycle helmet and backpack, then sweeps out of the computer lab.

We watch him leave, and I'm glad for the interruption because it takes the focus off me long enough to collect myself. "How did things go?"

The few people in the lab watch him as he grabs the chair to the empty station next to me, turns it backwards, and straddles it, oblivious to his audience. "Good. I think. They pretty much said a space in next year's class is mine."

My jaw drops. "Good? That's awesome! Are you kidding me? This calls for celebration, Eric. You're going to law school!"

He nods in a distracted sort of way.

"You don't look excited."

He smiles. "I am. I just wanted to tell you. I've got to tell my dad. He'll be happy."

"Happier than you?"

He holds my gaze. "Yeah."

It all lines up.

This isn't for him. It's for his father.

I know something about family obligation.

He motions with his chin to the computer. "What's this about?"

I'm thankful I tucked away most of the photos of him. "I was just putting together my portfolio. You know, for that job."

"You're applying? That's good news."

I nod.

He jiggles the mouse and brings up the photo of himself. "Damn. That'll get you the job, right there."

I nudge him. "Are you sure? I thought this one was good." I pick out a photo that has him making a face like he's sucked lemons. It's one of the rare ones where he looks really goofy.

He laughs, then sobers when his phone pings with a text. "That's my dad."

"You guys can celebrate this weekend at the game."

He gives me a confused look. "With my father? My father doesn't give a shit about hockey."

"Really, with you playing—"

"No." He rubs the back of his neck, tugging on his collar, the first indication that the suit isn't nearly the second skin it looks to be.

I always took it for granted that because Eric had every luxury, he must've had perfect parents who were so proud of him. I mean, I grew up with nothing, but I had a mother who believed in me.

He mumbles something about going outside to talk to his dad, and I watch him go.

His shoulders twitch as he starts to talk on his cell.

I frown. Wondering about the relationship between them.

I pick up my phone and open a group text to Poppy and Taylor.

Hockey game with me on Saturday?

18

Eric

The doorbell rings and I open it up to greet Boone's parents, Will and Sylvia, and his younger brother, Mike.

Boone hit the jackpot when it comes to families. They aren't wealthy, but they have a nice apartment near the auto shop that Mr. O'Brien owns. At night, they drink beer, cook a big meal together, and talk about sports. They play dominoes and tease each other. They're the type of people who enjoy being together. I'm lucky by association—I've spent a couple weekends at their place in Chicago.

"Eric," Mrs. O'Brien exclaims, giving me a lipstick kiss on the cheek and hugging me tight. With short dark hair and a plump figure, she's the kind of woman that you immediately feel at home with. "How's my second favorite hockey player?"

"I'm good." I laugh as I give his little brother a high-five. "You guys ready for the game?"

"More importantly, are you?" Mr. O'Brien says, giving me a couple of fake punches in greeting. With graying hair, he's shorter than Boone, his frame solid and thick.

"I'm pumped," I say, smiling. In fact, things have been damn good. I'm going to law school. The Lions are kicking ass. Julia and I grow closer each day.

Sylvia looks up the staircase. "Where is our boy, anyway?"

"He's not here, but, um, let me check and see where he is." I'd been wondering the same thing myself. I dig my hand into the pockets of my jeans and pull out my phone. Reece has already left for the stadium to get some extra work in, and I plan on leaving in the next few minutes. Usually Boone is back from the Kappa house by now.

Where r u, I send, but he doesn't reply.

Worry niggles at me.

I haven't seen him since last night when he went to the Kappa house, but I don't want to rat him out to his parents. Sometimes he stays over at the house with a girl in one of the extra rooms.

I glance at his parents. "Maybe he's already at the stadium." It's a possibility, but his duffle is sitting in the kitchen.

His father nods. "Always nose to the grindstone, shooting for perfection. He's a good boy."

Shit. Yeah. I nod to them as I motion out the door. "Should we go? I'll drive you all if you'd like."

Mr. O'Brien shakes his head. "We'll head over ourselves. We're going to stop and grab something to eat first. See you there."

I watch them as they pile into their minivan and head out in the direction of the arena.

The second they leave, I jump into action, gathering my

stuff as I keep checking my phone. I double check with Reece to make sure he isn't at the arena and somehow missed getting his duffle. Reece replies back that he hasn't seen him in the locker room.

When I saw Boone last night, he said it was going to be a chill evening at Kappa. *We're gonna kick back with some beers and have a PlayStation tournament.* His exact words. He was loose and in good spirits.

But he missed our morning run.

I open another text to him: *Are u alive?*

Nothing.

The alarming thing is that the messages show as read. It's not like him to not respond.

I grab my keys and head out to the truck, that sinking feeling growing.

I drive around to the front of the Kappa house. There are empty kegs piled up on the porch, but that's par for the course. It looks deserted, which means the brothers are probably inside, recuperating from partying.

But it's after three.

I'm captain, and it's my responsibility to keep the team together. If he doesn't show up for this game, we'll struggle. We have a freshman, Donaldson, on the second line, and he's good, but not as skilled as Boone.

Slamming the door to my vehicle, I cross to the house and take the steps two at a time and bang on the door.

The door finally opens and Scott's there, scowling. There's a frozen bag of peas pressed to his forehead and his eyes are half-open. "What the hell do you want?"

"You look like shit. Where's Boone?"

He manages a smirk as he tosses the peas on a table by

the door. "Shouldn't you be at your game? Word on the street is, they can't live without you."

I stiffen, my fists clenching. I lean in the doorway and glance around. The smell of beer and sweat lingers in the air. Solo cups and pizza boxes litter the hallway, and I think I hear the sound of someone vomiting. "Where are the pledges?"

He leers. "The smart ones are home sleeping it off. The dumbasses ... who knows."

Is he calling Boone a dumbass?

Nah, nah.

I throw open the door and march him inside a few feet as I get in his face. His breath is rotten, like something crawled into his mouth and shit. I shove his chest and he skitters across the floor. "Answer my fucking question. Where? Is? Boone?"

He flinches, his face reddening, and I think he's going to talk, then several of his brothers stalk into the foyer and surround him, asking what's going on. They bump against me, their eyes stormy. Fine. I hold my hands up as I back out onto the porch.

"Boone has a game," I tell them.

Scott smirks as he pushes through his brothers. "Great, but it looks like he ain't gonna make this one." He slams the door.

Blood rushes through my veins. Is this on purpose?

Shit. *Where is Boone?*

I want to charge the house again, but fans have appeared on the street as they walk to the arena. The last thing I need is a viral video.

I pace on the curb, raking both hands through my hair, trying to think.

I've got to start considering Donaldson on the line.

I send a text to him and Reece: *Can't find Boone. Donaldson, b ready 2 start. Reece—run sets with him.*

As I'm throwing open the door to my truck, someone comes down the Kappa steps. It's a preppy looking kid in a hockey jersey and a cap. He starts to walk past me, and I'm set to ignore him, when he coughs to get my attention.

"Hey," he whispers in stealth-mode. "You looking for O'Brien?"

"Yeah."

He glances back at the house but keeps walking, slowly. At first, I think he's going to pull an asshole Kappa practical joke, but then he mumbles. "They took the pledges down to the cornfields."

My stomach drops.

There's a giant cornfield outside of town. Supposedly, it's haunted by a little girl that was murdered there over a hundred years ago. Locals say she wears a white dress and chases people through the stalks of corn with an axe.

It's exactly the kind of thing that would make Boone's skin crawl.

The property is owned by a Kappa alumnus. Every fall, he cuts it into a giant maze and charges admission. Adults only. The place is too eerie for a kid. The corn is around seven feet high and it's easy to get turned around and lost.

But it's three in the afternoon. Something's not adding up. "Is he still there?"

He shrugs and jogs away.

Dammit. This means I have to make a pit stop at the fields, which happens to be nowhere near the arena.

Unease grips me. I'm going to be cutting the game close.

I speed off. Saturday traffic is shit with everyone trying

to get in for the game, so it's a crawl. By the time I make it to the fields, the sun is low in the sky, giving an orange glow to the brown stalks. I speed up the long dirt road and pull into an area cleared out like a small parking lot. The admission office—really a tent—is empty. They aren't open today.

I jump up onto the tailgate of the truck to get a better view. I scan the ocean of corn, but there isn't another soul in sight.

If Scott had that kid send me on a wild goose chase...

My phone buzzes with a text from Reece. *Boone just showed. Where r u?*

Jesus. Relief washes over me and I exhale deeply. *Be there in ten.*

Maybe the game won't be a shitshow.

As I'm reversing direction, Reece sends another text. *It's bad.*

Anxiety comes roaring back to the surface.

Is Boone drunk? Did he get beat up?

My stomach pitches as I think back to the night I helped Julia.

Parker is a vindictive dick. He'll want to get even. The question is, did he?

Ten minutes later, I pull into the parking lot of the arena, jump out, and jog to the locker rooms. As I swing open the doors, guys greet me with worried faces.

They look as if the game is already lost.

I throw my things down on the bench and peer into Coach's office. He isn't there.

"Where's Coach?" I ask the room. "Where's Boone? Reece?"

One of the second line players points to the showers.

I make a break for the shower room and find a small

group of guys standing around someone under the stream of water.

Pushing guys aside, I see Coach, who's kneeling next to a naked Boone.

My breath stops. I swallow thickly.

Boone's curled in the fetal position as he rests against the corner of the shower wall. His head is dipped as shudders rack his body. I think he's crying. There's some yellow muck that looks like vomit in the drain.

Our team doctor kneels next to him, getting soaked as he works with an IV.

Hot steam hits my face, and with it the stench of vomit.

My mouth opens but I can't find words.

"Possible alcohol poisoning," our team doctor says as he looks at Coach. "He's conscious, which is good. His skin isn't pale or blue." He pauses. "Still, I'd call an ambulance. His lungs need to be checked to make sure he hasn't aspirated."

I lick my lips. "How..."

Coach glances at me, then back at Boone, the lines on his forehead deepening. "He showed up like this. Barely coherent."

"How did he get here?" I ask.

"Some pledges dropped him off. They got him out of their truck, banged on the locker room doors, then drove off," Reece mutters.

I crouch next to him, uncaring about the spray of water that gets on my face and clothes. "Boone, bro. We're here. You're safe."

He cracks a single, weary eye. His wet hair is plastered to his skull. "Hansen?"

"Yeah," I murmur. "You're in good hands. Doc is here."

He nods, swallowing. "I got this. I'm good. Need my uniform."

He starts to move around then sees the IV in his arm. His forehead creases, and he shakes his head. "No. No. Please don't. Coach, I wanna play. My parents are here—"

His chest lurches forward as he gags. Nothing comes out but dry heaves. He falls back, his cheek pressing against the tile wall. "Eric," he breathes. "Don't tell my parents, yeah? I'll be fine. Make something up. Say I have a fever or something."

Damn, he probably *does* have a fever.

I groan inwardly. His parents need to know. They'll want to be at the hospital with him.

Coach and the doctor have stepped back a few feet, and I hear them discussing getting his parents' cell numbers from the records they have in Coach's office.

Boone hears them, defeat settling on his face as his eyes water.

I want to fix this. Fix him.

He's just a kid. I mean, he's only two years younger than me, but he's like a baby compared to me. He's so damn trusting. And nice. He didn't deserve this shit.

I kneel closer, my clothes getting soaked. "What happened to you?"

He shivers violently. "They took us to the fields. Told us some creepy story about a girl with an axe. They let us loose to get through the maze, and every time we hit a dead end, we had to do a shot and remove a piece of clothing. It was pitch black and they didn't give us flashlights. I-I wasn't very good at the game. I got trashed, then couldn't think straight . . ."

My lips tighten and Reece lets out a string of curses. The guys around us grumble, anger flashing on their faces.

Boone makes a fist with his hands. "At first it was fun, but I got separated from my friends. Maybe they made it out, I don't know. I stayed there all night, freezing, and they still didn't come for me. After that, I don't know, man. I passed out."

I exhale. "We've got you now."

"I want to play. Please," he begs, his voice cracking.

Two emotions ripple over me: worry for him and rage for the Kappas.

I squeeze his shoulder. "You've got to get better. There'll be other games."

He licks his lips. "You need me, Eric."

"Nah. We're gonna kill them without you. Just get better for the next game," I say.

Coach appears behind me. "Hansen, Doc has this. Get suited up. You need to be on the ice."

Taking one last look at Boone, I head off toward my locker to change.

19

Julia

I squeeze myself over the feet of other people in the row and take my seat between Taylor and Poppy.

"Who are our guys?" Taylor asks me, squinting.

I know he's teasing.

"We're the black and gold," I say, craning my neck to spot Eric on the ice. I forgot to ask what number he was. I thought I'd be able to pick him out immediately, but these guys look the same.

Taylor takes a sip of his soda. "Okay, so what's the purpose of this game?"

Poppy nudges him. "Those guys are going to try to get the puck-thingy in that net." She points wildly. "And the other guys try to stop him from making a net, which is two points."

I chuckle. "I think you're confused with basketball."

She shrugs. "It's a distinct possibility. I'm not sporty."

None of us are. Everyone around us wears their gold and

black gear, and we're, well... not. Taylor sports bright lavender, Poppy has her pearls and a pink cardigan, and I managed to find a black hoodie, but there's no logo on it.

"Hmm, I'm wondering what makes this game so special tonight," Poppy murmurs with a side eye at me.

"No reason," I say tartly. Just thought Eric needed a morale boost since his parents never come.

They exchange a glance and blurt in unison like two schoolgirls. "Eric!"

They burst into giggles as I give them a warning look. "For the last time. We're just bonding over—"

Taylor winks. "It's okay if you no longer want to hate-fuck him anymore. Love-fucking isn't as exciting."

I scratch the side of my face with my middle finger, pointed right at him.

Okay, yes, I get major butterflies for Eric.

For a long time, they were angry butterflies, but they're different now.

Maybe me being here will mean something. If it wasn't for Eric, I'd be working tonight at the club, trying to get as many hours as I could to pay off Connor. I may not have wanted a knight in shining armor, but he is one regardless.

The players file off of the ice, and the stadium goes dark. Poppy offers me some popcorn. I take a handful as lights flash and the speakers boom with the announcer.

"Welcome to Hawthorne Arena, Lions family. Today, we bring you a match-up between the Clayton University Thunder and your own Hawthorne Lions! Welcome the Thunder!"

There's mild applause, but mostly boos as men in red and white jerseys skate out onto the ice.

"Wankers!" Taylor shouts.

"And without further ado... here are the Lions!"

The audience erupts into loud cheers. People jump to their feet, some of them wearing a jersey with the number seventeen on it. Of course. There's an emblem on Eric's backpack with that number.

I move forward on my seat, trying to spot him.

"... number twelve, Reece Morgan, at left wing..."

Reece does a loop and waves to the crowd.

"At center, Roy Donaldson, number six!"

There's less applause, more like a mumble of confusion.

I frown. Boone is supposed to be the center. He took Z's place after he left. I do know that much.

"And number seventeen, The Miracle, at right wing, Eric Hansen!"

The applause is deafening. People scream. A couple of girls shout, "I love you, Eric!"

He skates out and does a quick loop, a small wave, and returns to the bench.

"This is the kick-off," Poppy tells us.

"Face-off," I correct.

"Whatever. I know he's holding a stick."

I pat her on the shoulder. "Gold star for you."

I strain to see Eric's face, but it's impossible with the face mask and how far away our seats are.

Donaldson wins the face-off and passes to Eric. With my heart in my throat, I watch as he takes the puck across the line and shoots. The goalie deflects it.

As one of the Thunder tries to move the puck near our net, Eric slams him into the glass.

Ouch.

I smirk. That's Eric. Fierce.

My skin prickles in excitement as Eric sails down the ice

with a defender chasing him. Reece passes to Eric between two other defenders and Eric stuffs the puck in the corner of the goal.

A buzzer goes off as people jump to their feet, screaming. I join them.

Eric, by contrast, is cool, like he's scored a thousand goals before. He doesn't crack a smile, simply glides around the ice without effort while his teammates skate past him bumping gloves. Five other Hawthorne players enter the ice as Eric and his group head to the bench.

"When's halftime?" Poppy asks.

"I don't think there is halftime," I murmur, still watching Eric.

A guy behind us, obviously sick of our inane observations, leans in and says, "It's three periods, twenty minutes each."

"Right, then." Taylor springs up. "I'm getting a pretzel. I can't possibly wait that long. Want one?"

I wave him off.

The Lions' goalie is good, and so is the defense, but the offense can't get the puck out of their zone. After a tense few minutes, the ref blows a whistle.

"That's two minutes for number twenty-six, for boarding," the announcer says as one of the Lions heads into a separate bench.

Poppy's nose wrinkles. "Waterboarding?"

"No, it's . . ." I stop, unsure.

"*Boarding*," the dude behind us enunciates. He's in his thirties and wears a Lions hat and jersey. He rolls his eyes at Poppy. "He checked a defenseless opponent into the boards."

"Oh," Poppy says. "What's checking?"

The guy snorts. "How about you read a book before you come to a game?"

I glance over my shoulder at him. "We're new fans. Give us a break."

I turn back to the game just as the Thunder scores a goal.

The buzzer goes off and our fans let out a collective groan.

"Wankers," Taylor calls as he returns from the food area. He throws a fist in the air while holding the pretzel in his other hand.

Eric gets back on the ice and into the action, stealing the puck and taking it into Thunder territory.

"Go," I whisper under my breath. "Shoot it!"

He can't. Not with two men on him, blocking the goal. He skates to the left, faking to the right, then breaks free of the defensemen and skates toward the goal.

A Thunder player darts in, steals the puck, and skates down the ice. He's shockingly fast and easily shoots the puck between the goalie's legs.

The buzzer goes off.

Eric returns to the bench, spits out his mouthguard, and pulls off his helmet. His hair is soaked with sweat, his face expressionless.

"That was painful." Poppy buries her face in her hands. "I don't even know what's going on, but it's terrible. I'm stressed!"

"Welcome to the world of hockey," the guy behind us chimes in.

It only gets worse. By the end of the second period, they're down 4-1, and they don't get it back after the intermission. Eric starts making mistakes, ramming his opponent into the boards and trash-talking. When a Thunder defenseman hits him, he shoves him and they scuffle. When the ref breaks it up, he argues with the ref.

The final score is 5 to 1.

He's first off the ice and heads for the locker room without looking up at the fans that line the aisle.

"He was still brilliant," Taylor says. "You think he'd want to go out to dinner with us? Drown his sorrows in some terrible bar food?"

"I can ask," I say.

We'd planned on going to the Tipsy Moose since it's within walking distance. Poppy has already offered to buy me dinner since I bought the tickets for the game. Eric had offered me tickets, but I wanted to surprise him tonight.

We step out of the arena and into the lobby and ask one of the ushers for directions to the locker rooms. Once we get there, we wait behind a roped off area with a security guard as the players exit, showered and sullen.

My gut twists at the girls I see, several with Eric's number on their shirts.

Poppy sniffs. "This hallway smells like a perfume shop."

"Hmm," I say as one of the girls pops out her mirror and reapplies her lipstick.

It was stupid to think he needed me. Yes, he might have invited me, but that didn't mean he was desperate for a cheering squad. Win or lose, everyone loves him. He just wanted me to come because I'd never seen a game.

It's not like we're a real thing.

Doubts creep in.

Wouldn't he rather hang out with one of these girls? Or his hockey buddies?

"You know, maybe we should go . . ." I stop when Taylor nudges me.

The hall has erupted into high-pitched, girlish shrieks of excitement as Eric comes out of the locker room. Wearing slacks and a collared shirt, his hair is wet and slicked back. His cheekbones are stark under the lights, his eyes hooded.

He doesn't crack a smile.

"Eric! Marry me," comes from a random woman who has a baby on her hip. She looks to be in her late twenties. Obviously, it's not just college girls he attracts. He stops, takes the sharpie she's holding, and signs her shirt.

A television station camera crew steps in front of us and muscles their way in. "Eric! Tell us what went wrong tonight."

A microphone is shoved into his face, but he takes it in stride. "We were off. It happens. We had to make a change with O'Brien being out due to a last-minute injury. We made a lot of mental errors and lacked intensity. It's not something we mean to repeat. That's all I have to say."

He shoves past them and they scatter.

More women flock around him, and he goes through, almost mechanically, signing and nodding. It's only when the crowd thins that he looks over their heads and catches sight of me.

I wave and smile.

He freezes for a moment, then makes a beeline to me.

He stops in front of me, a blank look in his eyes.

"Sorry for the loss, Eric," Taylor says in a commiserating tone.

Distracted, Eric glances at him. "Yeah, it was awful."

He turns to me, his voice strained and tight. "What are you doing here?"

"I just thought I'd come and—"

"I looked like shit out there."

"No, you didn't. I was impressed," I say quietly.

"It doesn't take much, then," he snaps.

Walls slam up around my heart. My gaze narrows. "We were just going to the Tipsy Moose. I thought you might want to come with us." *Since your parents didn't come.*

He glances around at the crowd. "I just had the worst game of my college career. The last thing I want to do is hang out. I have things to take care of."

Oh, I see.

Well.

"Fine. Go do them. Your loss," I say. "We're going to go eat cheese fries and drink beer."

A somber looking player, I think his last name is Donaldson, comes over and tugs him away. Their conversation lasts for at least five minutes, and the longer it goes, the more I itch to ditch him.

They are pulled into a throng of girls and my course is set.

He's forgotten I was here.

I back away as my throat prickles with feelings I don't want to think about.

The pain of putting myself out there.

Not being good enough for the golden boy.

I start to sweat.

Why would he want to hang out with a stripper when he can have any girl here?

It doesn't make sense.

We don't make sense—even as friends.

20

Eric

Donaldson tells me that Boone is at the ER and doing well. His parents called Coach after the game and gave an update. I missed it when I left the locker room as fast as I could.

I need to go see him. Check in with his parents and see if they need anything.

I glance back where Julia and her gang were, but she's gone.

Shit. A long exhalation comes from my lips.

She came here for me.

And I'm burning down everything that means something to me.

I pry a girl's hand off my arm and break free.

When I'm outside, I gulp air and scrub my hands down my face. I keep running Boone's face through my head. He was sick. So sick he had to be hospitalized.

What pisses me off is someone had his phone and saw

my messages. I don't care about the game. I mean, I do, but the sooner I could have gotten to him, the quicker he could have gotten help.

I get into my truck, nerves on edge. I turn the key and it doesn't start. I take three breaths to calm down, but it doesn't help. I try the key again and get the same result. I bang both fists on the steering wheel, feeling it bend underneath each blow.

Finally it starts.

Smart truck.

After checking in on Boone and his parents at the hospital, it's almost midnight when I get home. The Kappa house is lit up. I watch as pledges struggle with a keg, trying to get it up onto their back porch and into the house.

"Nice game," someone shouts from their property. "Losers."

Wrong night. Wrong fucking thing to say.

I march over to the guys.

"What did you say?"

"Um, nothing," one of the pledges says nervously. "We're cool."

I smile darkly. "You sure? I'm right here if you want to talk hockey, hmm?"

They ease away as Parker comes out the back door. "If you don't want to eat shit, you shouldn't lose games."

I climb the stairs but a couple of scumbags block my path, trying to shoulder block me.

"You're on private property," one says. "You're not welcome here."

He tries to stop me as I grab him by his sweatshirt, whirl him around, and drag him up so he can see my face. "I didn't ask if I was welcome, and I sure as hell don't care."

I shove him and he falls down the stairs.

More brothers come onto the porch.

I've gone three periods with the Thunder. I should be spent. But right now, I itch to wipe that smug look off Parker's face.

"What happened to Boone at the maze?" I ask Parker. "Why did you leave him outside all night?"

"It's not my fault if he can't handle his liquor," he says, scorn dripping from his tone.

"Boone could've died. How stupid are you?" I point back toward the school administration building. "If they find out you were hazing—"

He laughs. "Really? You forget who my dad is? He was a Kappa. Just like yours. Just like your brother. These rituals have been around a long time, Hansen. Our alumni look back on those days fondly. They laugh about it and we laugh about it. And guess what? Real men can handle it. They rose to the challenge. O'Brien? Guess he's just a pussy like you."

Rage boils over.

Julia handcuffed to his bed.

Boone in the shower.

I lunge at him, but he ducks back into the house.

Scott steps up and shoves me. "If you want to see Parker, you'll have to go through me."

"Bring it," I say as he swings at me, too high, and I slip under it, then connect under his armpit. One, two, three, four. Body shots. Chest, leg, mouth, eye.

Gasping, he retreats backwards until he's against the wall of the house, blood pouring from him.

I pounce on him and my fists fly, connecting with his face again and again.

He stumbles backwards, clutching his nose in agony. With a roar, he comes at me, but I dance around him, lashing out with jabs until he weaves on his feet and slumps against the railing of the porch.

The other guys close in, maybe five, yelling. Some pull Scott away. Others grab my arms and tug. I get a punch in the gut, in the ribs. I windmill my arms to shove them off and it works for a minute.

One of them, a beefy guy I recall drinking with me after one of our hockey wins, lunges at me and I nail him in the chin. He drops like a bag of dog food.

Another member charges me, his fists meaty but his body open. I land a punch in his stomach and he doubles over.

Parker comes back out of the house with brass knuckles on. He grabs me from behind, but I shake him off and slam my fist into his face. Once, twice. I drive my fist into his stomach. He doubles over, and I deliver a final punch that sends him crashing to the ground.

A triumphant growl comes from my throat. This feels good. So damn good.

Someone hits my eye. A gush of air comes from me as I stumble and blink it off.

Shouts come as more brothers spill out of the house, some of them running from the front yard.

A flurry of blows connect with me from different directions.

Someone or something connects against my temple.

Shit.

My vision blurs, then I fall back. My shoulder slams against the rail of the porch and I'm sliding, the Kappa house stretching up and away from me.

I shake my head but it's filled with cobwebs.

I think I hear Reece yelling for me.

Or maybe I've been knocked around too much and I'm hearing things.

Reece. I hope you're here. I bit off a little too much.

Punches land on my body. I throw my arms up to protect my head and wrestle through them.

"Get off him, motherfuckers! Eric!" I glance up as Reece grabs me by the armpits and drags me up and away. Several players on the first line take my place, knocking fists with the guys who were on me.

I sway on my feet as the world tilts. He reaches out a hand to help.

"I can stand," I gasp out.

"The hell you can," he mutters as he leans me against a gate between the properties.

"Your nose is bloody," I tell him as I suck in air. My head throbs and I touch it gingerly.

"That's because I joined your fight," he growls. "Then I had to rescue you from getting swarmed by ten of those fuckers."

"Minor timeout," I say. "I'll go back in a sec. Just need a breather."

"No way. You look like shit. Plus, someone is bound to have called the cops."

No blue lights yet.

I squint into the fray. Donaldson and Falcon wrestle with some of the frat guys, their well-toned physiques easily overpowering the Kappas. I laugh as one of the freshman players, a wiry guy who's quiet as a mouse, does some kind of karate mojo on one of the big-ass Kappas and knocks him down.

Falcon lets out a piercing wolf whistle and motions the hockey guys to retreat. They rush over to where Reece and I are.

"What's the plan?" one of them asks me.

I look back at the Kappa house. They're regrouping and eyeing us. No sign of Parker. We're still outnumbered, but . . . "I'm ready for round two, yo."

Reece shakes his head. "Nope, Eric, nope. Everyone back to our place for beer and ice-packs."

Fine.

We take off as a group, weaving on our feet from our injuries as we yell curses to the frat guys.

Reece grumbles at me as we walk into Hockey House. "You could have warned us. We could have all gone over there together."

I hadn't really planned on fighting them—had I?

Maybe I had . . .

My nose flares. "Parker was hard on Boone because of me. He hurt Julia. He had it fucking coming."

The kitchen spills over with hockey players. Someone grabs a bottle of water and chugs it. Another player has dropped to the floor and does push-ups, like he's training to go back and fight.

I smile. I'm going to be hurting once the adrenaline has worn off, but for now . . . I'm floating.

"Kappas are pig fuckers," Donaldson says as he holds a bag of fries to his face. "What they did to Boone was shit. He hates being scared and we all know it."

We all agree, muttering.

I spit into our kitchen sink and see blood. I open the freezer and grab a two-year-old bag of broccoli and lay it on my face. "We got some payback though."

I stumble into the den and plant my ass on the couch. It feels like an elephant is sitting on my chest.

The team grabs beers from our fridge, and before long, we're all congregated in the den.

Falcon shakes his head as he plops himself in a recliner. "You look like shit, Hansen, but you took those punches like a pro."

"MMA gym," I murmur around my broccoli.

Someone clicks on the TV and hands me a beer.

"I'm proud of us," I say. "We lost the game, but we won the fight."

We do a toast for Boone and chant one of our cheers.

"I'm calling some girls," Donaldson says and a yell of excitement goes up.

I tip up my beer. "We won't be going to Kappa to celebrate hockey again. We can do it right here. Go Lions!"

21

Julia

After eating at the bar, I take a long shower then starfish on my bed.

I wonder where Eric is. I wonder what was wrong with him.

My phone notifies me of a voicemail and I start, realizing I had it on silent mode.

I push the button. "Hello, this message is for Julia Lauren. This is St. Luke's Memorial Hospital in Sparrow Lake. Nala Lauren was admitted this evening. You've been named as her responsible party..."

Not this again.

I hang up and dial the number immediately.

"Hi. I'm Julia Lauren," I say in a rush when the receptionist answers. "I received a voicemail about Nala Lauren."

"One moment please."

I wait, gnawing on my fingernails as she clicks over.

"Yes. She's here."

"What happened? Is she okay?"

The last time she was in the hospital, she had her stomach pumped. That was in the spring. I'd found her in her car, unresponsive, and called an ambulance.

"I suggest you come to the hospital as soon as possible."

I end the call, toss on a sweater and jeans, then race down the stairs.

Taylor and Poppy sit in the den watching a movie.

"I've got to get to the hospital," I say franticly as I snatch my purse off the hook in the hall. "My mom is there and they wouldn't say how bad it was..." My voice trails off.

Taylor's eyes flare. He gets up and grabs his keys. "I'm on it, love. I'll take you."

Relief hits. I can't imagine calling an Uber and waiting. "Thank you so much. I really appreciate it."

"Should I go?" Poppy asks.

"I-I don't know." I slip on my Converse.

She gives me a sympathetic look. "I'm going. We got this."

We dash outside and hustle into Taylor's white BMW 5 Series. I get in the passenger side while Poppy gets in the back.

Taylor squeezes my hand as we pull out. "We're right here with you, okay?"

I nod, my thoughts tumbling. I spoke to Mom last night. She was in a good mood. She told me she was thinking of trying for a job at the local diner. I didn't think it would happen, but I wanted to believe it.

Taylor pulls up to the roundabout with the ER sign, and I rush out of the car.

The hospital smells like disinfectant with artificial flowers underneath. Blue and white linoleum floors stretch out in every direction, illuminated by fluorescent lights. People bustle about, some sitting slumped on hard plastic chairs as they scroll distractedly through their phones; others speaking in hushed tones.

A lump rises in my throat.

"I'm here for Nala Lauren," I say to the older lady at the reception desk. "I'm her daughter and got a call. Can someone tell me what's happening?"

She runs a finger down a list, then motions to the waiting area. "Someone will be out to talk to you in a few minutes."

I pace around as Taylor and Poppy show up and rush over. I explain that we're waiting for a staff member to tell me what's going on.

"Sit, girl," Taylor says. "You're shaking. Come on."

"I can't."

Dread coils around me like a snake.

Something feels different this time.

"Ms. Lauren?"

I look up to see a short man with a receding hairline in a white coat.

"I'm Dr. Amherst." He gives me a slight smile as he glances around. "Can you come this way?"

The three of us sit down in a small office off the waiting room. It's bleak and white, and my heart lurches. Is this an out-of-the-way place for doctors to break bad news?

"Julia," he says, glancing at his tablet. "Your mother has been here several times, as you know. She's an addict."

The words are like nails down a chalkboard.

Yes, I know she's those things. It keeps me up at night.

If Taylor and Poppy are surprised by this knowledge, they don't let on, and it makes me adore them even more.

I clear my throat. "She got addicted to pills after two surgeries for her spine that didn't work."

He nods as if he's heard similar stories before. "The last time she came in, about a month ago . . ." He looks down at his chart and I sit up straighter.

I hadn't known she was here.

He continues. "We mentioned other medical issues she might have, but she refused further testing and left."

My mind scrambles to keep up. "What other issues?"

"She's been having fainting spells, headaches, blurred vision. Some could be attributed to the addiction, but we suspected hypertension . . ." He pauses. "You knew none of this?"

I shake my head. "I don't . . . where's my mother? She's not—"

"She's in ICU."

I lean closer to Taylor, who tightens his arm around me.

"When she arrived today with a severe headache, we performed an MRI. Your mother sustained a hemorrhagic stroke or an intracerebral hemorrhage. This is where one of her blood vessels ruptured, causing blood to accumulate in the area around the rupture. This puts pressure on the brain. Only half of people who sustain an ICH survive. Most are left with a significant disability." I hear the warning in his tone. She could die.

"I'm sorry . . . what does all that mean?"

"First, she's lucky she got here. We got to her quickly and she's currently in a medically induced coma. We're going to perform surgery to alleviate the swelling."

I nod rapidly. "Yes, whatever it takes."

He pulls out a picture of a human brain and points to

different areas with his pen as he talks about where the hemorrhage is and how he plans to fix it.

After he's done, I can barely breathe. "Can I see her? Please."

He rises. "Come this way."

Poppy and Taylor stay behind as I follow him behind two double doors and into an elevator. We get off on the third floor and pass a hub where several doctors and nurses are.

Her room is dark except for a light over her bed. There's a bedside table and two chairs, one a recliner. The irony isn't lost on me. This is the nicest place she's been in a while.

An IV is hooked up and machines beep with her heart rate, blood pressure, and oxygen. Her eyes are closed, but she doesn't look peaceful; she looks awful and so very frail.

I take her hand. "Mom. It's Julia. I'm here." I lean my face close to hers. "Please. Be okay . . ." My voice breaks.

A few minutes later, a nurse comes in, her smile kind. "Dear. I'm sorry. But you'll have to go now."

I whisper in her ear that I love her and kiss her cheek.

Poppy and Taylor have moved up to a waiting room on the same floor. They take one look at me and tears burst out of me.

They wrap their arms around me and ask how she is as I reply in broken sentences. I explain about the failed surgeries, how she lost her job and our home. We sit down on a couch and I tell them about Connor.

Poppy squeezes my hand. "Oh, Julia. That's terrible. I'm so sorry. I mean, we figured something was wrong, but you never wanted to talk about it."

I nod. "I was too embarrassed to tell you. And now this . . "

Taylor pets my hair. "We're here for you. We're here. That's the important part."

"The surgery's going to be in the morning." The nurse has followed and waits patiently as I ease away from my friends. "You should go home, get some rest, and come back."

"What time?" I ask.

"Six. We'll let you see her before she goes back."

Taylor smiles. "I can bring you."

We leave the hospital and get back in his car as my head spins.

I lean against the window and think about her splashing with me in the ocean.

Her giggles when she lit candles on tea cookies.

Even if she never gets clean, I still need my mom.

When we pull up at the house, Eric stands on the steps of the porch. He looks like he's been there a while. Geeze. It's nearly two in the morning.

Taylor sighs. "Want me to get rid of him?"

I push open the door. "You two go inside. I'll do it."

I approach him, then stop. Tension swirls around him as he leans against the railing as if it's holding him up. His eye is half-swollen shut, his jawline has a purple bruise, and there's a spot of blood on his temple.

"Looking kind of rough," Poppy says tartly as she passes him and goes inside.

"Oh my God," I whisper. "What happened?"

"A fight with the Kappas."

"Oh." I frown as I stare at the ground.

"I'm sorry for being a dick after the game," he says quietly. "I tend to think people are conditional when it comes to me. They only care about you when you're a winner. You aren't like that."

I meet his eyes. Take in the lost look on his face.

He lets out an exhale. "My life is fucked up. Peel back the layers, and there's nothing there but rot since my brother died. When I came to Hawthorne, I got good at pushing it back, but I'm weak this year. I'm losing control. My life is spinning in a direction that scares me. Taking things out on you? That was wrong."

I toe at a piece of gravel on the sidewalk.

"See me. Look at me."

My eyes rise and capture his golden ones as they search my face. His gaze is subdued, almost resigned, as if he's looking for something from me but doesn't know what it is.

He comes down the steps and stops in front of me. "But the last few weeks, being your friend. That was real. With you, I don't have to act. I can just be me. Because you like me for who I am. Not a single person in my life knows who I am, Julia. But I swear . . ." He rakes his hands through his hair. "You're the closest. And I don't—" A ragged sound comes from his throat. "I don't know what I would do without you. You're my best friend. I need you. You're the most important . . ."

"Shut up."

"What?" He shifts from foot to foot. "I'm trying to say I'm sorry—"

I bridge the distance between us and reach up and brush my fingers over his jawline.

I hate that he's been hurt.

He leans into the touch and dips his head. "Forgive me."

"I forgive you."

How can I not?

He's bared his heart.

He's been a friend, one I never expected to find.

He's championed me. With Connor. With Parker.

"Thank you," he says softly.

I push thoughts of my mom aside as I slide my hands up his chest and rise up on my tiptoes. "Will it hurt your face if we kiss?"

His mouth parts in surprise. "No. Maybe. I don't care. Can I? Kiss you?"

I nod and meet him halfway, his mouth taking mine with excruciating gentleness.

Time pauses.

The world rights itself as his lips brush against mine like a sacred whisper.

I feel the warmth of his breath on my skin, the hardness of his shoulders under my hands.

The scent of him, masculine and virile, makes sparks zip along my skin.

For the first time in years, we're kissing, only it isn't like it was in prep school. Those kisses were hurried and rushed, full of angst and lust. This is different. We have a history, a backstory that craves to be rewritten, and maybe this is how we do it.

This kiss is sweet. Poignant. Tender.

His lips change direction and slant against mine as his tongue dips into my mouth.

I feel light-headed as a buzz goes through me.

This. *Yes, this.*

There's true, honest emotion between us, the kind that's layered with meaning and knowledge. It's in the air, crackling and sizzling, yearning to be set free.

"Julia..." he gasps, and I melt into him.

22

Eric

I break apart from her and hold her at arm's length. "That was, um . . ." I sigh, not having the words.

A blush rises up her cheeks, illuminated by their porch light. "I-I was at the hospital. My mom is there . . ." She shakes her head. "Never mind. I need to rest or decompress or something. Come inside and let me get that blood off you."

We go inside and she motions to the staircase. "I have Band-Aids and antiseptic in my room. Have you looked at yourself in the mirror?"

"I had a shower, so yeah." I stood under a cold one for half an hour trying to get the swelling down. I pause at the shadows in her eyes. "Do you want to talk about your mom?"

She lets out a little sigh. "Soon. Right now? I just don't want to be alone."

We walk in a bedroom at the top of the stairs, and she

flicks on the light. It looks like somewhere she'd live. There's butterfly wallpaper, sketches on the walls above her iron bed, books scattered around, clothes on the floor. She's kind of a slob.

"Nice lighting," I say, gazing up at a wonky gold light fixture with sparkly rhinestones.

"Hasn't fallen yet. I like it. The house has character. Sit on the bed," she says as she disappears for a minute, then comes back with a white washcloth, antiseptic, and Band-Aids.

She soaks the cloth with the liquid, then dabs it on my temple and my jaw. Her lips compress in a tight line. "Tell me about this fight."

My nose flares. "The usual. They mouthed off and I snapped."

She pauses as she dabs at the broken skin on my knuckles. "Was this about me?"

"Some. They fucked with Boone, left him in a field all night in the cold while he was trashed." Anger digs into my gut. "You don't mess with our family."

"Is he okay?"

"They took him to the ER. He's already been released and is in a hotel with his parents."

She finishes applying a Band-Aid to a cut on my head.

I catch her arm. "Hey. Tell me about your mom."

She sits next to me. "You know about her issues." She plucks at the quilt on her bed. "She hasn't been taking care of herself, obviously, and now she has a bleed on her brain."

Shit. "I'm so sorry."

Exhaustion seems to ripple over her as she pushes at the hair in her face. "I need to wake up early and get to the hospital."

Is that my cue to leave?

Fuck. Don't make it my cue to leave. "All right, I can—"

She takes my hand. "Would you just be with me tonight?"

I study her face. "Yeah, sure, whatever you need."

"Good." She smiles as she gets up to turn off the lights. Moonlight streams in the window as she turns her back and pulls her sweater over her head. No bra, but I knew that already. She grabs a roomy shirt out of a drawer and slips it on. Her hands loosen her jeans and they fall to the ground.

Her panties are blue and demure, but my cock thickens to a steel pipe. I keep my groan inside.

She pauses in front of me and brushes her hand over my hoodie. Her words are hushed and soft. "I want to feel your skin. Is that weird? Is it okay?"

Not weird. "Um, yeah."

I slide off my joggers, then my shirt. I stand in my boxers as she takes me in, her eyes drifting over my body.

She takes in the bruise on my chest.

On my side.

On my outer thigh.

A frown forms on her forehead and her voice is strained. "Oh. Eric..."

"I'm okay. I'm tough."

She bites her lip as if she wants to argue, then pulls back the sheet and gets in.

I climb in and turn on my side towards her as I wrap her in my arms, burying my nose in her hair.

Something inside me that was hard and razor sharp, loosens.

"Kiss me again?"

"Yeah," I murmur.

She tilts her face up, and I taste her mouth with careful brushes of my lips, my hands roving down her spine in gentle motions as I keep my hands on the outside of her shirt.

Fire zings over me as I slant my mouth across her pillowy lips.

Need rushes through my veins like a waterfall.

I haven't been with someone in so damn long.

Her arms curl around my neck and tug at my hair as if she wants more.

"Julia..." I groan.

"Don't stop..."

Lips and skin collide.

Sometimes it's chaste. Sometimes hungry. Our tongues entwine and dance, exploring this new thing between us. My pulse quickens at her breathy gasps and sighs. My hands palm her scalp, massaging into her thick hair.

Throwing insecurities to the wind, I give in wholeheartedly to that kiss, reveling in the intoxication. I put my feelings in it as our tongues caress.

How beautiful she is.

How strong I think she is.

How broken I felt when I hurt her at the arena.

She's dazed as we pull back.

She nuzzles her face into my chest as we slowly wind down.

I stroke her back in lazy circles, telling her I'll take care of her and her mom, that I'll make sure everything works out.

Her arms slide around my waist, careful of my bruises. Eventually her breathing deepens and my throat prickles with emotion.

When's the last time I just... held a girl as we slept?

I can't recall.

I press my lips to her forehead and fall asleep.

I wake up when Julia's alarm goes off at half past four. We only got a few hours of sleep, but whatever we've done here is worth a thousand nights of rest.

I hold her face in my hands and kiss her hairline. "Do you want me to take you to the hospital?"

She stares at me for a few moments in wonder, then nods. "Thank you."

She stops to knock on Taylor's door and tells him that I'm taking her.

Hours pass as we sit in the waiting room. I run across the street and grab us a breakfast from Starbucks. She picks at her egg and sausage sandwich and I keep hounding her until she agrees to eat the whole thing. It's three hours later when the doctor comes out.

He comes our way. "Everything went as well as can be expected. We stopped the bleeding, drained the hematoma, and removed the pressure in her skull. Right now, she's asleep and resting. Later, we'll assess the severity and what's next." He gives Julia a slight smile. "It'll be a long recovery, but she's stable. You can visit with her now."

A long sigh of relief comes from Julia.

And I don't have to ask if she wants me with her.

She squeezes my hand and we head to her mother's room.

23

Julia

Eric isn't just a miracle.

He's vulnerable underneath, a man with kindness. He lashed out at me because he's always had to prove himself to his parents.

I realize that as I'm sitting in his truck, watching him help an older woman, maybe in her seventies, take her wheelchair-bound husband to their car. He's chatting with them, then helps him inside their car. She must ask for an autograph because she hands him a piece of paper from her car and he signs it.

I smile.

We've been at the hospital for hours, and he never left my side except to get food then stand guard as I forced it down.

My mom is resting. I sat by her bedside for the amount of time they let me, but now my body drags, and I need to take care of me so I can see her tomorrow.

"Back to your place?" Eric asks as he gets in the truck.

I need a change of scenery to take my mind off things.

"Can we go to your place?"

He looks over at me as he puts the car in reverse. "Alright."

I nod, liking that he doesn't ask questions on the why of it. I watch his strong hands as he steers us out of the parking lot. I take in the yellow and purple bruise around his eye, the cut on his forehead.

He's done nothing but protect me, and not because he wanted something.

Emotions stir in my chest as I take his hand off the gearshift and put it on my leg. He considers this, rubbing my skin slightly.

"What are you doing?"

"I want you to touch me. I need touch."

He finally gets the picture and his fingers skate up my leg then stroke back down.

It's not sexual. His hands massage as if to soothe, and my eyes lower as tingles of pleasure course through my body.

We arrive at his house and pull in. When Sugar and Z dated, I was here a couple of times but avoided it as much as I could.

We walk inside. It's messy with Chinese take-out boxes and beer cans. Hockey sticks and gear are piled up in the corner. It smells like sweat and men. I laugh. Just what I expected.

"Sorry. Um, the hockey guys had a little party last night. It was better than going back to Kappa."

I take his hand and lead him toward the stairs. I have a mission. "Where's your room?"

He points at a door.

I start to climb up the stairs then stop as I catch a pair of eyes watching from the top of the landing. "Oh, how cute!"

"Motherfucking ferret," he groans as I scoop the creature into my arms.

"Hello, little guy. I didn't know you had a pet! What's his name?"

"Lucifer," he mutters. "Don't fraternize with the enemy."

"You don't like animals? What's wrong with you?"

"Cats and dogs are cool. But the rat has a twisted fascination with me."

I let the ferret go as he opens his door. It tries to follow me in, but Eric nudges it out with his leg, slamming the door in its face. "Beat it. I want her to myself."

I like that.

I gaze around the room, taking in the navy sheets and comforter, the trophies on his dresser, the open door of his closet where clothes spill out. He's a slob.

He stands by the window, his chest rising as his eyes smolder.

An ache starts in my body. One that demands.

"Do you want me to hold you again?"

My breath hitches. "More than that."

Without saying a word, he walks over to his bed, beckoning me towards him. A jolt of electricity hits, searing me. My legs feel like jelly as I move closer to him.

Feigning confidence, I kick my Converse off, plop down on his bed, and stretch out.

He stretches out alongside me, and I laugh nervously.

He reaches out and traces a finger down my profile. "You're in my room, Julia. Is that..."

"Yes," I say as I roll into him.

"Fuck," he says in a wondering tone, then leans in to kiss me. It's not gentle like last night, but hungry and greedy.

I wrap my leg around him and run my hands down the corded muscles of his broad back, up under his shirt, feeling his sculpted chest. My pulse hammers.

With one hand threaded through my hair, he pulls his mouth away, eyes boring into mine. "Tell me you want this, too."

"Please."

"I want to see you," he says as he tugs at my shirt, slowly easing it up until he can pull it off my shoulders. His fingers trace the line of my collarbone before he moves to my bra.

His fingers brush across my skin as desire rushes in like a wave. It's been a while since I let myself be open enough to allow this to happen.

He undoes the clasp of my bra and eases it off. He pauses to take me in, and his gaze is like a physical touch—then his tongue dips to each breast, licking each pebbled peak.

I gasp as I arch up.

"So sweet, Julia..."

Our gazes cling as he unzips my jeans and shimmies them down my legs. He pushes them over my feet and tosses them over his shoulder with a grin.

I laugh, then stop when he kisses me, his lips insistent against mine. His tongue flicks against mine, tasting me. His fingers graze my neck, down the center of my chest, then between my legs.

"Eric..." I moan. "More of that."

"Trying to go slow." He maneuvers around and lifts my legs, then lowers them down on either of his shoulders until his head is at my apex.

I shudder with desire. There's something wholly erotic about a man who has you naked while he isn't.

"You're so pretty. And your pussy is soaked." His fingers rub my juices and my core flutters in greed.

He puts his mouth on me.

I cry out, then bring my hand up to silence myself, but he reaches up and grabs it. "Let it out. Please. I want to hear you scream while I fuck you with my tongue."

I whimper.

He takes his time and moves his hands to my thighs, spreading me apart. His hot, wet tongue slides slowly up the creases of my most secret parts. My head falls back and I moan as he licks from bottom to top with the flat of his tongue. He darts inside my channel, his teeth nibbling on my clit, then sucking.

He teases my nub, his breath hot against my skin.

"Eric . . ."

He wraps his arms around my thighs and kneads my ass. A fire alights inside me as sensation builds at my spine, burning and tingling.

I'm getting close, so close, almost there, then he pulls back, slowing his movements.

I cry out my displeasure.

"What do you want me to do?"

I open my eyes and there's a smirk on his face.

"Come on, don't stop . . ." I writhe in frustration.

"What do you want?" he repeats. "Say it."

I lick my lips. "You. Make me come. Eat my pussy."

"Perfect." He dips to my clit again, his tongue relentless, flicking, swirling, playing. I teeter on the edge and arch against him. My legs clamp around him as I reach for the precipice, and if he stops now, I might kill him. He pulls on my clit gently with his teeth, and I grab the edge of his comforter.

He fingers me lazily with one, then two digits, as I thrash my head from side to side. His arms tighten around my legs, pulling me against his mouth. "Eric. Oh, fuck..."

The orgasm rips through me like a cannon, and I come for what feels like minutes, my core clenching as it tugs around his fingers.

He presses a kiss to the top of my mound.

"You taste so sweet, Julia," he murmurs.

I sputter, trying to compose myself. Our first time was definitely not like this. Yes, it was good after the pain wore off, but this was a more experienced man.

I can't stop trembling.

"I think I just found my new favorite pastime," I say and he laughs.

"Anytime you want. Just sit on my face and I'll take care of you."

I reach for the waist of his joggers, loosening them. "I want you naked."

He grabs my hands. "Wait."

I blink. "What, you don't want to?"

"I do. But..."

"But what?" I chew on my lips. "We can have sex. It doesn't have to be a big deal." *I know how you operate, Eric. I have to remember that.*

He doesn't seem to like my reply, a frown appearing, but then it's gone. "Right. Okay."

He kisses me and I taste myself on him as our tongues tangle. I reach for his shirt and pull it over his head as he shoves down his joggers to his ankles. He kicks them away along with his socks and shoes.

He's exquisite naked. A muscled beast with emotional, needy eyes.

His gaze rakes down my body. "Fucking gorgeous. You don't ever have to ask if I want to fuck you. The answer will always be yes. And right now, I want this..."

He scoops a hand under my hips and twists me around with no effort, so I'm facing the wall. He runs his hands over the globes of my ass, then smacks me. I cry out.

"Perfect ass," he says with appreciation, leaning down and running his tongue over it.

My back arches for him, reveling in the feel of his hot hands.

He brings his body close to mine, his cock at the crack of my ass. He rubs it back and forth there as wetness drips down my leg. "This is what you want?"

"I didn't realize what a ginormous tease you are," I murmur as he cups my breasts.

He tweaks my nipples as he kisses my shoulder. "I'm going to get to these perfect tits soon, but first..."

I hear a packet rip, and I turn to watch him slide a condom on one-handed. I lean forward, resting my elbows on the bed. His cock is thick and long as he strokes it.

He nudges inside me just a little.

I gasp and hang my head as he pushes in inch by inch, stretching me, but not quite going all the way.

"You're so tight," he says with a groan as he plants his hands on my hips and eases more of him in my channel. The burn is exquisite, the feel of him perfect. "You good?"

"Hmm."

He slides out, leaving just the tip inside me, then plunges in deeper. He hisses as he exits, then pumps in again, still not far enough.

"You doing good?"

"Stop talking and fuck me," I say around another needy moan.

He thrusts in all the way.

A rough sound comes from his throat as he pauses and lets me adjust. His hands massage my ass. "You feel so fucking right, Julia."

He pumps back out then in, getting into a rhythm as his hands dig into my hips. He angles up, adjusting his legs to brace himself, and whatever he's hitting inside me, it's a chord that has never been struck. Another orgasm builds inside me, and I know it'll be even fiercer than the first one.

He picks up speed, making me whimper with every thrust. His fingers dig into my skin and I wonder if he'll leave bruises. I don't care. I want them. I need the intensity.

The bed frame bangs against the wall. *Thump, thump, thump.*

Desire makes me dizzy as he drives into my pussy.

Faster. Faster.

My hips thrust back against him, eager for more. Sensations ripple over me as my walls grasp at him.

Guttural sounds come from his chest. I feel the wetness between us, the evidence of how much I want him.

He fucks like a madman, and that realization amplifies the heat between us.

His rhythm increases to a frantic pace, and my climax begs to be released.

He senses it. "You ready?"

"Soon. But I want you to . . ." I protest.

"Don't worry about me." His fingers ease around and flick furiously at my clit as I shudder in pleasure. "Come," he growls, and I let go, moaning as I fall apart.

My body trembles, my muscles relaxing as tension pours out of me. I rest my cheek on his pillow and open my legs wider, spurring him to come. Groaning, he lifts me and turns me over without breaking rhythm.

He hovers above me. I can see his face with his body pressed flush against mine. His cock drills into me, not missing a beat as he sucks on my neck, his unshaven face rubbing the skin. I wrap my legs tight around him and pull his ass to me.

A sort of wonder hits me. His pupils are blown, his hair a mess as it swings around his face. He's lost in ecstasy, and I'm the one that's taking him there.

"We're rewriting the past," I say without meaning to, but there it is, out there in the universe.

"Julia . . ." he murmurs and I imagine I see a dawning in his depths.

A new beginning. Endless possibilities.

Am I crazy?

He growls as he kisses me hard. I feel his cock swell even bigger as he comes. His neck arches up and he roars it out as he pumps.

I stroke his back, running my fingers down the contours of his body.

He rolls off of me and puts his forearm over his head.

We're both covered in a light sheen of sweat.

He looks over at me and grins. "They don't call me The Miracle for nothing."

I poke him in the ribs as he tugs me next to him and we snuggle.

24

Eric

This last week has been a blur. Coach found out about the fight and threatened to suspend the ones involved, but that would be half the team so he didn't. He only said words expected of him. We avenged one of our teammates. There's no way in hell we were going to let what happened to Boone go. I'm not sure it's over. My hands itch to go back to Kappa, call Parker out, and beat the shit out of him.

Dad called twice this week about an internship he wants me to take this summer before law school starts, but I haven't called him back.

I'm content to do what I am right now.

Spending time with her.

Julia's snuggled up beside me, her breath on my chest, her body pressed against my ribcage. I'm lying on my back, twirling a lock of hair around my finger and marveling at how pretty she is with the late-day sun streaming through my blinds.

Her heart-shaped face shows no worry as she slumbers. I gently trace my finger along her jawline, the outline of her pouty lips. There's a tiny scar on her right temple under her hair and I admire it, wondering how she got it.

I lean in and kiss her softly, inhaling her citrusy scent.

She stirs slightly in her sleep as her thick lashes blink open. Soft eyes gaze up at me. Expressive. Warm.

"Hi," she murmurs. "I didn't mean to fall asleep. What time is it?"

"Around five." We had lunch together in the student center then came back to my place. She studied and I pretended to, but nothing was getting through to my head. I watched her every movement, enraptured. The way she crossed her legs, her fingers when she twirled her hair, her little puffs of frustration when her laptop died.

"Stop staring at me," she told me half an hour in.

"Nope." I rose up and started stripping. My shirt. My jeans. I kicked my shoes across the room and stalked over to her. "I need a break. I need you."

She gaped at me, laughed, then blushed deeply, her lashes shielding her gaze, reminding me of the girl in prep school. We fucked twice. The first time was fast, our gazes glued to each other. The second time we got tired of the bed squeaking and got on the floor. She bent over and clung to the end of my bed frame as I rammed into her from behind. The tall mirror I keep propped against the wall showed us, the way her tits bounced, the slide of my dick as I sank into her pussy.

She leans up and props her chin on my chest. "You look thoughtful. What were you thinking?"

"That I want to know more about you." I slide my hand down her spine. "Like, what do you want to do after you graduate?"

She smiles and curls into me, her arm around my waist. "You won't think it's silly?"

"No." I've seen her art above her bed, noticed how she loves the outdoors, the way she turns her face up to the sky. She's introverted, intuitive, creative. Pretty much the opposite of me and I'm intrigued.

"I'd love to open an Etsy shop and sell my art as cards or magnets or posters. Maybe stores. I'd need large giclee printers first, and those aren't cheap, so I'll need a day job to get started, doing web design or illustrations for businesses." Excitement colors her voice. "The good thing is, I could go anywhere in the world to do that. I'd love to live on the West Coast." She frowns. "It depends on my mom. If she's well enough to leave the rehab center. It will be good to get her out of this town."

I tighten my arms around her. Between class and her job, she visits her mom every day. She's still in intensive care. Thankfully, her doctor arranged for her to receive free medical assistance from a rehab facility once she's recovered enough to be moved there.

"What about you?" She boops me on the nose.

"I don't want to talk about me. What's your favorite color?"

She laughs, the sound light. "You're a girl underneath all that muscle."

I put her hand on my cock. "All man."

"You're hard. Again?"

With you? Yeah.

"Hmm," I murmur. "So, tell me your favorite color."

She peppers my chest with kisses. "Green, like summer grass, but blue too, like the color on a morpho butterfly."

I groan as her lips move down to my navel, and my stomach muscles flutter in anticipation. "Never heard of that butterfly," I gasp.

She kisses the tip of my shaft. "They're one of the largest butterflies in the world. Some have a wingspan of eight inches. I've never seen one in person—they're mostly in South America. There have been reports of pilots flying over and seeing thousands of them gathered at the tops of the trees like a big blue blanket."

"Hmm."

"Their color comes from tiny little scales on their wings that reflect light. When you see a butterfly, you're supposed to make a wish." Her tongue swirls around my length and my body tightens.

"Do you . . . make a wish?" I grind out, barely able to think.

She doesn't reply. Instead, she takes me into her mouth.

"Julia . . ." My cock pulses with need, throbbing.

"Hmm." Her gaze captures mine, and I'm lost to this fierce feeling building inside of me, to this magical connection that's growing each time we're together.

But part of me is frightened of this new sensation.

I've never had a girlfriend. Women come and go and we stay acquaintances. I don't share myself and neither do they.

But with her, I can be myself.

I don't have to put up a front and be a hockey star.

I don't have to be perfect.

I can be the guy that blames himself for causing Kurt's death.

She knows about that darkness.

About my dad.

Sure, I haven't told her about my mom, not really, but whatever.

Maybe she's just looking for a good time, a pair of arms to fall into at the end of the day during a trying time.

Are we just friends with benefits?

That's all I've ever been to a girl. Puck bunnies, sorority girls. A new flavor each month so I don't have to be alone with my thoughts.

"Julia," I call out, my thoughts scattering as she takes me deep into the back of her throat and swallows. Her head bobs as she sucks, her tongue fluttering. I grab a fistful of her hair and push up to meet her as she makes a humming sound, ratcheting up my desire.

"Fuck," I say, a warning to move if she doesn't want me to blow in her mouth, but she doesn't stop.

My hips arch up as I yell and orgasm, sparks skating up my skin as goosebumps follow. My scalp tingles. My body shudders, then loosens as I relax into the bed.

I tug her up to me and kiss her, tasting the salt on her lips. I suck her bottom lip into my mouth, then nibble gently as she sighs.

My hand ghosts over her hair, putting it back in place. "That was incredible. You are incredible."

She stretches out next to me with a cat-like smile.

Reece raps on my door. "Yo! Boone is back, bro. Come on down."

In other words, we all know you're having sex but Boone needs you.

"Alright," I call out as I give her a hug. "I need to go talk to him. Do you mind?"

"Of course not. I feel so bad for him. It must have been traumatizing."

She eases out of bed and sashays over to her clothes on the chair. With greedy eyes, I watch her adjust her lacy white bra then slip on a sweatshirt. Her underwear go on next, then her jeans.

She sits on the bed. "The timing is good. I want to see Mom before I go to work."

"Can't you call out? You could come over later." Spend the night.

She smiles. "I have bills due, plus I need to pay you." She grabs her purse, pulls out an envelope, and sets it on my nightstand. "There's about two hundred in there."

My stomach flops with something ugly. "Don't leave that."

Her forehead furrows. "Eric. Come on. You don't understand what it means to owe someone. I will pay you back. Just like I paid back Poppy and Taylor last week. I will be debt free from everyone."

I exhale. "What about the photography job? You said you got it?" She sent a text today during one of her classes, but we haven't talked about it.

She nods. "It doesn't start until mid-January, though. It doesn't pay much, barely more than I made at the bookstore." She toys with her hair in the mirror, avoiding my eyes. "I'm going to keep stripping part-time at least until I graduate."

"What? Why?" I frown.

She stiffens. "I just explained it."

"I don't like it."

"I don't want to dance, Eric, but what I make is enough to finally pay off my debts. I want that feeling. Plus, who knows what's going to happen with my mom. I need to save money too. I can't leave Hawthorne flat broke."

I wish she'd just let me help her more.

She walks back over and leans over and kisses me. "I'll text you later, okay?"

"Yeah."

After she's gone, I dress and head downstairs.

Boone sits on the couch, a video controller already in his hand. He's a bit gaunt, his dark hair damp as if he just got out of the shower. A Snickers bar, a Sonic cup, and a bag of cheese fries are on the coffee table. At least he's back to normal appearances.

His shoulders slump as he meets my gaze and gives me a nod.

While he recuperated, he stayed at the hotel with his parents. He missed classes on Monday but was back by Tuesday. I imagine he could have come home earlier, but he and his parents needed to decompress from campus for a bit.

"You look a hell of a lot better," I say as I plop down next to him.

He shoots me a look. "Yeah. Nice black eye."

"Meh, it's just yellow now."

"You should see the other guys," Reece yells out from the kitchen. "Scott has a cast on his arm. Parker hasn't been seen all week. There's not a Kappa on campus who will meet my eyes. Fucking cowards."

I grab a handful of cheese fries and stuff them in my mouth. "Not one peep from them."

Reece rummages around the kitchen, opening cabinets and pulling out pots. He must have seen me eating. "Yo, don't be eating junk food. It'll spoil dinner."

"Thanks, Mom," I call back.

Boone snorts. "Since I'm sickly, does this mean I don't have to clean up after dinner?"

I look over my shoulder as Reece squints at a box of pasta, ignoring us. He knows he makes a mess.

"Yeah," I add. "Last time you cooked, there was sauce on the stove, the floor, the wall, the ceiling..."

He slams a pot down.

"Don't overcook the noodles," Boone says.

"Or burn the bread," I chime in.

"Or the sauce. Smoke-flavored isn't my favorite. I want to be able to taste the tomato," Boone snarks.

Reece curses at us. "You two will love every fucking bite."

"This is true." I grab a controller and jump in the game with Boone.

There's a lull in the game, and I glance over at Boone. "So, you wanna talk?"

He picks at some lint on his jeans. "Before we left for the maze, Scott gave me a shot of vodka. Just me." He puts his elbows on his knees and dips his head, seeming to be fascinated by the carpet.

"Something was in it?"

He shrugs. "Doctors didn't find anything, but I probably tossed it up or it was too late to detect."

My fists curl, itching to go back over there.

He doesn't notice, his voice wavering. "Reece told me the other pledges dropped me off, but I don't remember."

"Will you keep on pledging?"

A bitter laugh comes from him and his own fists clench. "I'd never, but they're saying they kicked me out. One of the pledges returned my phone at the hotel and told me. My dad threatened him and he ran off. You tried to warn me and I should have listened. My parents, they're upset. Angry with Kappa. Angry with the administration that wants to sweep it under the rug. *We'll look into it* is what they said, which we both know is bullshit."

My eyebrows go sky-high. "They filed a complaint?"

He nods. "Yeah. Jesus Christ on a bike, I'm glad they didn't see me in the locker room. My mom might have packed my bags and moved me home."

I slap him on the back. "It's over now, bro. Hockey is your frat. We've got your back no matter what, yeah?"

Reece calls from the kitchen. "Alright, get your asses in here and eat."

Boone smirks as we rise up together. "Maybe it's decent."

"I can hear you," Reece mutters.

I chuckle. "The hard part is going to be finding clean dishes."

"Remember the time we used tumblers to eat spaghetti?" Boone says. "I pretty much tossed mine back and poured it down my throat."

We walk in the kitchen. Reece stands at the stove with an apron on that says *Mr. Good-looking Is Cooking*. He stirs the sauce, drains the noodles, then grabs a potholder to take the bread out of the oven.

The aroma of tomato and olive oil lingers in the air.

"We didn't have napkins last time either. Used toilet paper," I murmur then call out a victory yell when I find a package of paper plates in the cabinet.

"And he scores!" Boone shouts.

Reece rolls his eyes then pulls out a package of new napkins from a bag. "I went to the store."

"Good job, my man," I say as I swipe at the crumbs on the table and set the table.

"We're eating in the kitchen?" Boone says. "But the den and TV are right there."

I shrug. "It's up to Reece. It's his masterpiece."

"Kitchen."

Boone grumbles, then grabs a piece of garlic bread and stuffs it in his mouth. He devours it in two bites. Things feel back to normal.

Later, as we're stuffing our faces, we talk about classes, about hockey, about me and Julia—although I cut that off pretty quick. I don't want to go there. I don't want to jinx us.

25

Julia

The rehab center we move my mother into is perfect. Well, as much as a sterile facility can be. Located a few miles outside of Sparrow Lake—I can easily ride a bike—it's on a sprawling ten-acre estate with assisted living apartments, a hospital for emergency care, and the rehabilitation wing. Pretty landscaping lined the sidewalk when I wheeled her in. A nurse met us with a smile and showed us to her room.

Eric brings in the last box from the truck and sets it on the floor. There were only two, one with her clothes that I washed at my house, the other full of photos and mementos she's been hanging on to.

The room is not big, but it is private. I pull out a purple comforter I splurged on at Target and make up her bed. A small kitchenette, basically a fridge, microwave, and sink are on the right. A desk is on the left that overlooks a walking path with trees and little gardens.

I take in the tiny Christmas tree in the corner of her room.

It's so much better than the car. Tears well up in my eyes. I swallow them down.

The doctor and his staff helped me apply for a grant from a foundation for homeless people to cover what the state doesn't. He assured me this place would assist with her loss of motor coordination on her right side, the speech therapy, plus the memory issues she's experiencing. We met her speech and occupational therapist at the hospital several days ago. A psychologist also visited. She'll be receiving counseling for her addiction.

My chest tightens with hope, strange and alien. The feeling is a precarious thing, as if I'm afraid to believe in a happy ending. It's possible her stroke was the best thing that could have happened.

Mom runs her fingers down the beige curtains in the window, and when she speaks, it's slurred. "Pretty."

I open a cannister on the counter. "They have all these teas for you to try. Peach honey? Peppermint? Do you want me to make you some?"

She points to a recliner. Eric nods and wheels her over, then eases her into it by basically picking her up and sitting her down.

I make the tea using the microwave while Eric unpacks the boxes. He picks something up and holds it up. "Who's this nerd?"

I groan at a picture of me winning a medal for an art contest in fifth grade.

"Me." I snatch it out of his hands while he hovers behind me.

"Nice mullet," he murmurs.

I poke him in the side. "Our neighbor was in beauty school. Sherry. She'd come over and offer to cut my hair to practice. You think I would have learned after the mullet, but I wanted blonde highlights once and she begged to do them. My hair came out with one giant white streak. I don't know how that even happens. Mom rushed to the drugstore and got a toner. It didn't work and I looked like a skunk. Good thing it was before you met me."

I reach up and brush a kiss over his cheek. We've been spending as much time together as we can these past few weeks. Between hockey and classes and my job, it's not much, but we're making it work.

He grins and takes the tea I made for him while I set Mom's on the side table next to her, then pause as I realize the mistake. She can't drink that. Adjusting to her needs will take some time. I rummage in the cabinets and find a tumbler with a lid and straw and pour it in.

Mom stares at the photo still in his hand. "Keep."

I raise my brows. "You want me to keep it?"

She nudges her head at Eric.

"She wants me to keep it," he drawls in a triumphant tone as he tucks the photo in his wallet.

I smile and turn on the TV to PBS, where *Downton Abbey* is on, and Mom nods her approval.

After the nurse comes in to help her with dinner, Eric and I say our goodbyes and step out into a cold wind. He tightens his arm around me and ushers me to the truck.

"You okay?" he asks as he opens my door and peers down at my face.

"It's a nice place. She looks happy."

He glances at me. "But..."

"I just hate leaving her. She doesn't know anyone, and

it's all new, and she can't even walk on her own. What will she do when she needs to get up and go to the bathroom? What if she gets sick?"

"She'll get to know people. She has a buzzer if she needs help. There are nurses monitoring her."

I sigh. "Thank you for helping us. I don't know how I would have done all this, mentally, without you."

He presses his forehead to mine. "Glad to do it. How did you get this scar?" He strokes the scar on my temple that my hair usually hides.

"You noticed, huh?"

"Hey, I dig scars." He points out one on his chin, the bridge of his nose, and his jaw. "I'm a rough boy."

"Eighth grade. I was in a knife fight with this girl, dodging and jumping around. But she was good. Really good. Out of nowhere, she darts at me and slices my temple open. It bled like a geyser."

Eric whistles. "That's pretty badass."

"You know I'm kidding, right?"

"Totally, but I was a little turned on."

I laugh, feeling girlish and silly, as I toy with the ends of his hair. "Truth, I was trying to impress my eighth-grade crush by doing a handstand. I got up for a few seconds, then crashed into the dugouts on the baseball field. It did bleed a lot."

He brushes his lips over it, and I hear him breathe me in deeply.

A light-headed sensation washes over me, and I laugh nervously. Eric makes me nervous. Makes me aware of my skin. My bones.

"The crush didn't even know I was alive. Meh, I've figured out to be myself now. If people like me, they will. If they don't, then it wasn't meant to be anyway. I shouldn't have to impress anyone."

A strange expression flits over his face. "My family lives to impress. Gotta keep up the appearance that everything is fine, even when it's going to hell."

"I'm sorry."

"Don't be." He picks up my wrist and presses a hot kiss there. "Let's go home," he says and shuts my door and gets in on the other side.

When we're halfway back to my place, it starts to snow, graceful flakes of sparkle falling from the sky. Snow is nothing new in Minnesota, but it's the first one of the year.

It drifts down and settles in the grass, the trees. The air is hushed, as if the world is in a lull, waiting for something new.

"It's so pretty," I muse, craning my neck to see out the window. We pass the town square and I squeal as I show Eric the tree they've put up. All the lights are gold and glittery.

"I'm happy Mom will be able to spend Christmas in a place like that," I say.

He clears his throat. "Speaking of, what are you doing for the holidays?"

The semester ends on Friday, then we have the week of Christmas.

"Working a few days this week. We don't get a lot of business the last two weeks of December, but Eddie said I can come in and bartend. Marcia gets the dance hours since she's been there longer. I'll spend several days with my mom."

"Are you busy on the twenty-third?"

I give him a sideways glance. "Do you have something in mind?"

"Would you want to go to my parents'?"

"Really?" My stomach flip-flops.

"Sure," he murmurs, yet tension radiates off him. "Don't you want to see the house I grew up in?"

It's a dating step.

Not that we've defined what we're doing.

I nod. "Yeah, sure. I'd love to."

The second I say it, nerves tighten.

He doesn't get along with his parents, his father especially.

If he doesn't like his father, does that mean his father won't like me?

"Alright." He doesn't seem happy, though, and I get the feeling he's dreading it.

And if he hates it, I probably will, too.

"It'll be fun," I add, trying to gauge his reaction.

His jaw sets. No, in his mind, it will not be fun at all.

He pulls up in front of my house. "I've got to go home this Friday. But I'll come back and pick you up." He rubs the pad of his thumb gently over my cheek, then leans in to kiss me. He stops as his eyes flicker past me. "What the..."

I whirl in my seat to see two policemen standing at my door. Not even campus police. Real, Sparrow Lake police officers.

Jumping out, I rush up the steps. "Hello. What's this about?"

They meet me on the porch, eyes assessing. The younger one says, "I'm Officer Warren, this is Officer Thomas. We're looking for Julia Lauren."

Office Warren starts when he sees me. Pretty sure I

recognize him from the club. He's young, early twenties, with brown hair. A wholesome look about him. Nice smile. Blue eyes.

The other one, Officer Thomas, is older with a paunch, a mustache, and wire glasses.

"That's me. Is there something I can help you with?"

The older policeman holds up a piece of paper. "I have a search warrant. We received a complaint that some items were stolen and might be here."

"Stealing? I don't—" I look over at Eric, who's glaring at them.

"What was stolen?" he asks.

The older one flips through the papers in his hand. "An expensive camera and some accessories."

"Channing," I breathe. He couldn't just come and ask me for them back. He had to involve the police.

I ease past them and go to the door. "I didn't steal them. He was a friend and we had a falling out. He said it was his old camera and I could use it as long as I wanted. Time's up, huh?"

The younger officer nods, a blush stealing up his face. "We'll take that into consideration. Please open the door and stand back."

I do as they say, feeling like a criminal.

I unlock the door and usher them inside. They ask me to go get the camera, and I dart up the stairs, grab it, and hurry back down.

Eric moves to stand next to me, his eyes flashing as he mutters. "It's a hassle for anyone else to get a warrant, but not Kappa."

He's still upset that Boone reported the hazing incident to the dean and got nothing in return.

Pushing my nerves down—I've done nothing wrong—I hand over the camera bag to the nice officer, my chin tilted up. "If he wanted it back, all he had to do was ask."

Officer Thomas glances at Eric. "How do you know Miss Lauren?"

Eric crosses his arms. "We're dating. She's my girlfriend."

I start.

He flashes his eyes at me, shrugs, then grins.

Okay, then.

I ease the younger policeman away from Eric and the older man. "Do I know you?"

He sputters as his gaze darts from me to his superior. "No, ma'am."

"I work at Platinum Nights. You ever come in?"

Eric grows still, his eyes cutting to us. Clearly, he's eavesdropping.

I ignore it.

The young cop tugs at his shirt. "Hey, I'm, um, engaged to his daughter." He nudges his head at the other cop. "Can you, um, pretend like you don't know me?"

I wave my hand at the camera bag on the floor. "Make this go away and I'd be thrilled."

He nods almost immediately and heads over to the other officer. He pulls him away and they have a discussion.

Eric joins me. "What did you do?"

"Pushed my weight around."

Officer Thomas clears his throat as they finish then walks back to us. "Sorry to interrupt your day over a misunderstanding. We'll return this camera and put into the file your side of the story and that you were helpful. That should settle the issue."

"Thank you," I say with grim satisfaction. I did that. Myself.

Eric shakes their hands. "We appreciate that, officers."

Once they are gone, my smile disappears and I go inside. I've been using that camera. The first thing the newspaper editor asked me was if I had my own equipment. I'd said yes. Kind of a lie. Stupid. I should have known I'd have to return it.

I can't afford equipment like that. Another thing to add to the list.

"Was that young cop one of your clients?"

"He's been in a few times," I reply.

"Private dances?"

I roll my eyes. "You are so jealous, and no."

"Good. 'Cause I'd hate to chase after him and get arrested."

"You can't do things like that—even if we are dating." My eyes twinkle.

His big hand engulfs my cheek. "The only person I want seeing you half-naked is me."

I stand on my toes and brush my lips over his. "Thank you for caring."

I pull my shirt over my head as I take the stairs. "I'm going to bed, hockey player. Wanna come with?" I throw a look over my shoulder at him.

His gaze darkens as he follows me, tight on my ass.

I'm nearly to the top when he catches me. I shriek as he turns me and picks me up, my legs wrapping around his waist as he takes off to my room and rushes inside.

He tosses me on the bed sideways as his eyes lower to my cleavage. "I want you." His eyes burn down at me. I revel in it.

"Same," I breathe.

He tugs one bra strap off my shoulder, then the other. He eases the cups down, revealing my breasts. Air ghosts over the erect nipples as goosebumps rise. My back arches in anticipation.

He stands back and takes me in. "You deserve to be worshipped like the fucking goddess you are."

"I'm not a goddess," I say weakly. "But if you insist on calling me one..."

"I do." His fingers graze my skin, sending bolts of fire through my nerves. He rubs the pad of his thumb over one nipple, and it peaks under his callouses. Then he draws it into his mouth, sucking. Caressing the other, his tongue draws lazy circles on the rosy pebbles.

He unbuttons my jeans, sliding them to the ground, then wraps his hands around my ass, kissing the V where my thighs come together. "Lay back. You don't have to do a thing."

He scoots me up on the bed. He starts with my chin, then moves to my neck and shoulder, to my upper arms, his stubble brushing against my sensitive skin. He delivers a series of tiny, nibbling kisses down to my navel, across the curves of my hips, and down over each thigh. He spreads my legs wide, and I wait desperately to feel his mouth.

But he doesn't.

Maddeningly, he continues down, kissing my knees, my shins, right down to my toes.

I'm writhing, senseless with need.

He stands up, pulls his shirt over his head, and sheds his jeans. "Come here," he says, sitting down on the bed and hoisting me onto him so I'm straddling his lap. I'm naked on him, his cock nestled between my legs, and I want nothing more than to feel it inside me.

He opens a condom and I help slide it on. His cock is flushed red and bobs against his stomach. With one hand around his neck and one on his length, I lift so that his tip is right at my entrance. I inch him inside me, slowly, then fully seat myself. I move my hips in a slow, circular motion, then speed up. He holds my waist, helping me keep a steady rhythm.

He cups my ass with his hands as he groans. "Your show. Do what you want. Use your power."

My breath catches. He understands that I need someone to remind me that I'm strong even though my life feels out of control.

He wants me to come to the party. I'm his girlfriend.

It's not an admission of deep feelings, but with him . . .

It means something.

His erection thickens and my own body responds as juices drip between us. The air smells like him, me, us. I kiss him savagely, our lips tearing at each other.

Lust builds between us, higher and higher.

He rocks me back and forth, but I dictate the pace, the depth, the angle.

We fuck.

And fuck.

Every thrust sends ecstasy crashing over me. Eric's eyes glow as he watches me ride. There's something empowering about knowing that I have control over my own pleasure —and his.

I grind against him, rubbing myself to get the friction I need against my clit.

He leans his head back, euphoria on his face.

He's right. I *am* a fucking goddess.

My orgasm hovers, close, but I stretch it out, hold onto it by moving different ways, waiting for the right moment.

"Julia, Julia . . ." Sweat drips from his face, his voice ragged.

His thumb rubs my clit, circling it with light, then hard strokes. I'm so there.

I fall forward against his shoulder. "Come for me."

And he does, tensing, grabbing the edges of the bed for leverage and thrusting hard into me as he growls. I replace his fingers with my own, watching him come apart beautifully, and then I go with him. He buries his face between my breasts, delivering kisses to my neck.

"I know. I'm a miracle," I whisper into his skin.

26

Eric

A few days after the police incident, I open my eyes to find Julia studying my face. She boops my nose. "You're finally awake, sunshine."

I nod. "Morning."

Her fingers twirl with a piece of my hair. "You wanna go grab breakfast somewhere? I only have one final today and it isn't until this afternoon."

"Food isn't on my mind right now." I roll her off and cage her under me, my head dipping to scent the citrusy shampoo in her hair. For the rest of my life, every time I see a lemon or an orange, I'll think of her.

She laughs up at me.

"Hmm." I spread her legs with my thighs and nestle myself between them.

She sighs in contentment at our proximity while I take in her silky skin, the rise of her gorgeous tits.

I want to memorize each dip and curve.

I want to imprint her on my brain so I don't forget.

My head dips as I flick my tongue over one of her nipples. My hand caresses the other, plucking at it like a guitar. Her nipples harden as I nibble at the rosy flesh before sucking it.

Little gasps of pleasure come from her as she strains to be closer. I switch to her other breast as she opens her legs wider and her leg hooks around my hips.

I tug on each pebble, rubbing them between my fingers as I watch her face. "Julia..."

Her needy eyes.

The way she bites her lip.

Reaching over to the nightstand, I roll on a condom. Holding my cock, I tease her entrance, getting her wetness on me, then sliding out to tap against her clit.

She sighs in pleasure, then gets a serious look on her face. "I have something to ask you," she breathes.

Adding my thumb to the mix, I tease her nub, watching it swell. My eyes move to hers. "Yeah? Same. You go first."

Taking her hips, I slide all the way home and swivel my hips.

She cries out with desire. "Maybe later."

"You're a tease." I kiss her, my tongue caressing hers.

She eases away and sends me a fake glare. "You're the tease."

I stroke out, then back in. "You don't fucking know what you do to me, do you?"

"Tell me."

I thrust in deep. "Maybe later."

"Eric!"

I stop, my chest heaving. "Right now, I want to fuck you. Can I be rough?"

"Try your best, sunshine."

I'm starting to know what makes her pulse race. I pull her hair and she arches up to reach me as I suck and bite, leaving my brand on her skin.

I want marks. From me. So everyone knows she's mine.

She matches me, biting my earlobes and neck.

Our mouths meet open-mouthed and do an erotic dance as I thrust into her.

My cock throbs. Pulses.

I fuck into her.

Again and again.

Relentless strokes.

I reach underneath her and raise her ass to get deeper.

Her smell. Her hair. That sweet, delicious, hot pussy.

Over. And over.

We fuck. And fuck.

My thumb circles her bundle of nerves as I tell her to let go, that I can't wait to feel her cunt fluttering around my cock. I tell her every dirty thing I want to do. Fuck her ass. Fuck her mouth. Fuck her forever.

She shouts my name, her body tightening, then shuddering as her contractions milk me. I grab her hips, my fingers digging in, grabbing for my own release.

Sharp sensations of pleasure build in my spine, spreading up to my shoulders and arms and neck.

More, yeah, more.

It's so fucking good.

Each wet glide.

I'm lost in the lust.

She arches and writhes. Her nails dig into my ass, and I stiffen and yell my release in a guttural sound that comes straight from my chest.

I fall on top of her, heart thudding, head blissfully blank.

After several moments, I roll off of her and tug her into my arms. I kiss her lips, slow and sweet. It's dumb to tell her how fucking good our sex is, so I stay silent.

Minutes pass without us talking.

Until her phone chimes with a text and she looks up at me, brushing the hair out of my face.

"I should probably go home and study."

"Not yet." I hold my grip on her as she tries to get up.

"I'm serious!" She laughs.

"So am I, but fine."

She disentangles my limbs from her own and climbs to the edge of the bed. I feel cold at once.

Maybe it's because I know I'll be seeing my parents soon.

She throws me a mischievous smile. "Want to take a shower together before I go?"

I'm powerless to resist.

Stark naked, I open the door and peer out in the hallway. Nobody except Lucifer, who gives me a pleading look. I give him the finger and take her hand in mine.

It's early yet, and Boone and Reece are still asleep. "Coast is clear."

Rushing and trying not to laugh, we dart to the bathroom.

She leans against the door, her face flushed. "I can't believe we did that."

"Living on the edge." I grin as I open the stall shower door and start up the water.

She looks at the shower and gapes. "Wow. Can you even fit in there?"

The showerhead only goes as high as my forehead, so I usually have to bend and turn myself to get my whole body wet. "Barely." I wink. "We won't take up too much room. What did you have to ask me?"

A slow smile comes from her. "What did you have to ask me?"

Steam is wafting up from inside the shower, casting everything in a hazy mist.

I shrug. "You go first."

"No. You."

I pretend to think. "I forgot."

"I bet." She steps in and water soaks her hair then drips down her curves.

"I remember," I say, knowing I need to get it over with. "I like you naked, but you do have to wear something to my parents' house."

"Duh. I wasn't planning on going like this."

"Only thing is . . ." I step in with her, flattening myself against the wall. Even doing that, she's an inch away from me. I'm not complaining. I grab soap and start to lather up. "You don't happen to have a formal dress, do you?"

Her eyes widen.

"Dad's events are over the top." I grimace. "Don't be intimidated, though. I'll be there."

"Oh."

"If you don't want to . . ."

She winces. "I thought it'd be us and your parents. It's a party?"

"The guest list is over two hundred people. My father has it every year." I begin to lather her skin. My hands massage her, but her muscles are tight and tense. I've worried her.

I wash her back, then her front.

"So . . . dress. Do you have one?"

She doesn't meet my eyes, instead finding the wall of the shower fascinating. "I don't own fancy clothes. I mean, I have a prom dress from prep school, but I've filled out since then."

I recall her at prom. She wore a strapless white dress that sparkled. She came alone and sat with her friends.

I'd been to a pre-party with the hockey team and arrived trashed. I wanted to talk to her, but part of me, the sane side, held back. I'd taken her virginity, then dumped her. What could I say?

"At prom... you looked pretty."

Like a lost princess who didn't know how to navigate the world.

I was similarly lost. I didn't know how to manage not being Kurt.

Her gaze searches mine, then she clears her throat. "Oh. Thanks. Alright, let me think... a dress."

I open my mouth to tell her I'll buy her one but stop. She'll say no.

"Poppy's a bit of a debutante, and we're the same size, although she's shorter. She'll have something."

I watch her, trying to gauge her true feelings. "I should have told you earlier it was a party."

There it is. The anxiousness. She draws her lower lip under her teeth.

"We'll have fun," I say, but the truth is she could be a queen and my father would complain she's getting in the way of my career. Kurt had a girlfriend. Janis. Dad never liked her and tried to get between them.

That won't happen with me and Julia.

Law, hedge funds... I want her to be part of it.

"My parents can be stuck-up, but my mind about you is

already made up," I say with a grin, trying to lighten the mood.

She holds out her hand for the soap. "It is?"

I hand it over. "Yep. You're a pain in the ass."

She hip checks me out of the water to where it's freezing.

I chuckle. "Kidding."

Grinning, she pulls me back in and lathers me up, her hands moving over my body. When she reaches for my cock, she pumps me up and down, her fingers grazing over my crown.

"What did you have to say to me?"

She stops and frowns. "Oh... just that I have some ideas for a Christmas gift for you."

"I already got you something."

Her surprise is glorious, then dims. "I hope you didn't spend much."

I snake a hand around her waist and pull her to me. "You being with me is present enough."

She eyes me doubtfully.

"You don't believe it?"

"Maybe." She pauses. "I went to Parker's aunt's house once for a birthday party. Not because he wanted me to meet his parents. It was because he told me he had a fantasy of fucking me in the pool house while all of his uncles and aunts and cousins were there."

She turns to open the shower door. I can feel the unease in her, that she's comparing me to Parker.

It dawns on me. "Fuck."

She drapes a towel around her chest. "What?"

"Parker's parents. They always come to the Christmas party. My dad and him were Kappas together."

Her eyes widen.

I exhale, nodding. "Are Parker's parents a problem?"

She shakes her head. "I don't think so. We barely spoke. We didn't do anything in the pool house. We stayed for half an hour and left."

I get that. There are so many people at our Christmas party, there's usually only time for superficial talk. The whole Kappa/Julia thing probably won't come up. "My dad's crowd have a pretty short memory, especially with alcohol flowing."

Unless you fuck up.

Then, they remember it forever.

"As long as you don't try to drag me into your pool house, I think I'll survive."

"I'd be an asshole if that's what I wanted you there for."

"Then what do you want me for?"

"I wanted you before I got into bed with you. I just didn't want to admit it to myself after everything I did in prep school."

"You have me now."

"And you have me." I kiss her.

But I can't help the unease that pricks at me as we dart back to my bedroom. I watch her dress with a needle digging under my skin.

Things are good.

We're too good.

And anytime something feels this perfect, I know that the bad is coming.

27

Julia

I attach the fake eyelashes to the magnetic adhesive on my lids. Nice. Turning my head in the mirror, I take in my upswept chignon. A few tendrils hang around my face, softening the style. My lips are a glossy nude and my cheeks are contoured and highlighted.

My lips quirk. The classy stripper.

The doorbell rings and echoes in the house. Poppy and Taylor have already left for the holidays, but they'll be back before New Year's so we can celebrate together.

"One second," I call as I rush down the stairs in my bare feet.

I swing open the door with a big smile.

Eric leans against the doorjamb, looking devastatingly handsome in a black tux, obviously tailored to fit, the silky fabric snug over his shoulders and chest. His hair is tamed and swept off his face. On his feet are polished black loafers.

"You weren't kidding when you said it was formal," I say,

smiling.

"You look good enough to eat." His eyes drink me in, starting at my hair then roving down to my pale pink toenails.

"Thanks." I smooth down the lines of my cocktail dress. Made from raw black silk, it's a textured, lush fabric. The bodice has spaghetti straps and a square neckline. Reminiscent of the fifties, the skirt is flared out with a petticoat underneath. On top of the skirt is a layer of Italian lace in a rose lace design. I feel like a million bucks.

I step into strappy black heels, then reach behind the sofa and pull out a flat, wrapped package. "You said we'd exchange gifts before the party, so..."

"Whoa, this thing is huge," he says as he takes it from me and sits on the couch. He grins. "The wrapping paper is reindeers playing hockey. You did good."

I nod, anticipation rippling over me as he tears it open.

"Julia. This is awesome." His eyes track over the poster-sized hockey photo of him I had professionally framed. It's the one where he looks like a blur on the ice. He gets a bemused look on his face.

"What?" I sit next to him.

"I don't know. Just not used to getting such a great gift from a girl. It's nice."

"You're welcome."

He draws me close and kisses the top of my head. "This pic is going on my wall."

I rub my hands together, then hold them out to him. "Mine?"

"Eager, huh? Hang on." He strides out to the porch, then comes back inside holding a red box with a white bow. "This is part one."

"Part one? You're spoiling me." I tear open the lid and gasp. "Is this . . ."

"A Nikon. I read all the pros and cons and this one came out on top. It comes with a bag and all sorts of lenses."

It's clear he spent more on my gift than I did his.

"You like it?"

I nod jerkily, feeling the gulf between us but also not caring. He's wonderful.

I wrap my arms around him and hug him for all I'm worth. "I can take that job in January for sure."

He caresses my back, then pulls away to smile. "Good, good. You want the next gift?"

"Duh."

"Hmm, it's coming soon."

"Tease," I exclaim. "When do I get it?"

"Maybe you already did."

I mock scowl. "Is it you? Are you the gift?"

He kisses my lips lightly, being careful not to mess up my lipstick. "Not telling."

AN HOUR LATER, we pull into a long circular drive to a house with acres and acres of maintained landscaping. The bushes and trees are covered in twinkling white lights.

My mouth parts when I see a fountain that looks like something out of Versailles.

The house itself could be a museum. The entire thing is white. Spotless. Unspoiled.

Eric shoots a glance at me. "Impressed?"

"I'm certainly blinded by the light."

He points at the white and gray marble columns that

line the long porch. "Growing up in this house, it wasn't as great as you might think. Beautiful things can be fucked up."

Before I can reply, an actual valet opens my door and Eric comes around and puts my hand in his.

"Which reminds me," he murmurs as we walk on a red carpet that's been rolled out. "There's something I should tell you. My mother..." He winces.

"Yes?"

He shakes his head. "Nothing. I'll tell you later. Let's head to the party."

We reach an arched double doorway that's decorated with pine boughs and an explosion of red and white ribbons.

"Don't worry," Eric murmurs, sweeping me inside. "Everything's fine."

But he's mostly talking to himself.

The foyer is as big as my den. Elaborate floral displays and luxurious Country French furniture dot the area. Sculptures and art grab my attention. I see a Rembrandt. Maybe a Van Gogh. My throat tightens. This is an entirely different world from the one I grew up in.

We walk down a hall, turn a corner, and enter a huge ballroom. Everywhere I look, there's something to gasp at. A champagne fountain. A chandelier the size of a small star. A Christmas tree, one that rivals the one in Rockefeller Center. The walls are hung with greenery, sparkling lights are twined around pillars, and elaborate pine boughs and ribbons and lit candles adorn four crackling fireplaces on each wall.

A live band plays soft music to the right. Round, linen-covered tables are on the left. A herringbone parquet dance floor is in the middle. Servers dart around with platters of champagne and appetizers.

"You have a freaking ballroom in your house."

"You have something against slow dancing?"

"It doesn't bring the tips. Do they know I'm a stripper?"

He tenses. "No. It's none of their business."

My palms start to sweat.

He kisses my knuckles. "Don't be nervous. You're the most beautiful woman in the room."

"Not concerned with you running off with the competition." I push up a smile as I glance around. Most of the people are middle-aged or older.

He swans me around the perimeter, nodding and smiling at people but not pausing. "It's completely extra considering we only use this room a few days a year."

"Same, our heat only worked a few days a year."

He smirks. "Regardless of what you do or where you come from, it only matters if you let it."

"Nice speech, but were you talking to me or trying to convince yourself?" I say as I fix his bowtie, although it was already perfect. I try to put it back the way it was before I touched it.

He smiles. "Come on. I'll introduce you to my parents."

We weave our way through the crowd. People stop what they're doing to greet him as he passes. He looms over most of the men, and he's full of charm but doesn't break stride until he stops in front of a couple at the bottom of a flight of stairs. They look vaguely familiar. I'm sure they came to graduation at our prep school, but that was years ago.

Maybe in his fifties, his father is tall and fit as if he spends time in a gym maintaining his physique. His hair is completely gray but full and lustrous. He has piercing green eyes, and the intensity of them is like being stabbed with a knife.

He gives me a hooded up and down, then dismisses me as he turns to Eric.

"You're late."

"Hi to you too, Dad." Eric shakes his hand. "Yeah, traffic was a bitch. Sorry."

Mr. Hansen scoffs then takes a sip of his champagne, his gaze jumping back to me.

I give him a frozen smile. If I just keep smiling, everything will be alright.

Eric kisses his mom's cheek. Barely a touch.

Elegantly dressed in a floor-length black velvet evening gown, her hair is long and white-blonde. A perfect porcelain doll, her eyes are an icy blue, her smile barely there and vacant.

He pulls me closer. "Mom, Dad, I want you to—"

"Come this way," his father says as he cuts him off and drags him away to the center of the floor. He hands a champagne flute to Eric, then clears his throat. "Everyone! Everyone! My son has finally arrived, and I have an announcement to make."

A strained expression flits over Eric's face as the music and chatter ebb away.

"Eric has been accepted into Hawthorne Law School. He's decided against the Ivy league to follow my education path." He pats Eric on the back. "He's a future leader at Hansen Investments, where he'll take us into the next generation."

Applause and congratulatory calls come from the room and Eric smiles. They walk back to me and Mrs. Hansen—who hasn't spoken a word—even though I'm standing right here. Smiling.

Eric wraps an arm around my waist, almost clinging to me. "Alright. Now. I'd like to introduce you to Julia Lauren. My girlfriend."

They both blink as if Eric just said the world is flat. I mean, I am a girl and I am on his arm.

"Hi," I manage. "Surprise?"

Eric lets out a husky laugh.

His father's eyebrows come together. "You didn't mention you were bringing a girlfriend. What was your name again?"

"Julia Lauren. Nice to meet you."

His mother reaches a delicate, manicured hand out to me. She grazes my palm with the tips of her fingers in a limp shake. "Nice to meet you, darling."

Eric gives me a pained smile. "I guess they thought you were a random girl I escorted inside the party."

"Funny," I say, but my eyes say *Why didn't you tell them I was coming?*

"Be careful with this one," Mr. Hansen continues. "He has quite the reputation."

"I wouldn't know," I reply coolly. Lie.

"Then you haven't given him time," Mr. Hansen replies as he plucks two champagne flutes from a server and hands one to me, then to his wife. "Welcome to our home."

We clink glasses, and I take a big gulp. I might need it to make this evening pass quickly.

"Tell me about yourself," Mr. Hansen asks, eyeballing me as if I'm under a microscope.

"Um, I'm a senior at HU. I'm getting a Fine Arts degree. I know Eric from prep school."

"Last name?"

"*Lauren.* I was one of the scholarship students."

He repeats my name a few times, then shakes his head. "I don't recall you. But then it was a big class."

And I was a nobody.

A long silence stretches and tension bubbles in the air.

Mrs. Hansen breaks it by looping an arm through mine and starts tugging me away. "Sorry, guys, she's mine now."

Eric's hand tightens on mine. "Mother. Where are you—"

"I'm taking her on a tour of the house. Of course."

"Of course," I whisper back as his eyes meet mine for a beat.

She sweeps me out of the giant ballroom, waving to people on the way as she bends her head to mine and tells me who the various people are. I barely remember any of their names.

She leads me to a beautiful, paneled library, then an elegant parlor where she receives her appointments. Apparently, she works for three separate charities.

At the base of a giant double staircase, her eyes glint. "Let's take a peek upstairs. I bet you'd like to see his bedroom, wouldn't you, Janis?"

"Julia and, uh, sure."

"Great." She doesn't acknowledge the name correction but lifts the hem of her gown and goes up the stairs. I follow.

We reach an arched hallway that leads to several doors. She opens the first one. "This is my son's room."

I peer inside.

Odd.

First, it looks frozen in time, yet super clean. Second, this can't be Eric's room.

My childhood bedroom had trinkets and posters on the

walls. I expected Eric's to be filled with sporty stuff. Hockey sticks. Trophies. Photos of him.

His king-sized bed has a crimson and black comforter and the walls are navy. Over the bed is a red flag with Latin on it like a college flag. It's not Hawthorne's.

"This was his bedroom?"

She smiles, her expression as blank as a piece of paper. "He loved to read in front of that window, the one that overlooks the gardens."

Read? I mean, sure, he's a smart guy, but he isn't the type to sit and read. He'd be out playing basketball or skating on the lake. "He must have been happy here," I murmur.

"Very neat, yes? That's our Kurt. You get one bit of lint on the floor and he'll notice. He likes everything organized and clean. I'm so proud he got into law school."

Was Harvard Law the collegiate flag over the bed?

I'm so confused.

"You mean Eric?"

She shakes her head adamantly. "I mean Kurt. He's your boyfriend. Keep up, darling."

My bones chill.

She thinks Eric is Kurt? Or pretends?

Eric mentioned she stayed in a psych ward while he was in high school.

We all have ways of coping with loss. I get that. But this is . . .

I put it aside as we walk down the hallway. I catch family photos on the wall. Mom. Dad. A young Eric, smiling like he has a secret. He looks different with his buzz-cut and baby fat. I want to pinch his chubby cheeks.

I see the other boy, Kurt. He resembles Eric, but his eyes are blue, and his hair is blond. He looks like his mother.

"Are you moving to Boston after you graduate?"

"No," I say gently. "My mom is in a rehabilitation center after a stroke incident. I'm not sure where I'll end up."

"Oh no, that's terrible. It must be hard with Kurt at school and you in Sparrow Lake."

I'm not sure what to say. Tell the truth? Play along?

"Eric is also in Sparrow Lake."

"Tell me, how serious are you and Kurt?"

I give in.

"Um, we're dating. It's kind of new."

She hooks her arm through mine and we leave. When we get back to the ballroom, she drifts off to talk to some guests while I search for Eric.

I wave at him across the room, and he downs his champagne and breaks away from his father. He takes my hand and leads me through the crowd and outside to a covered patio with twinkling lights everywhere. Gas heaters line the perimeter. A few people mill around, but it's mostly empty. In the distance, I can make out a lake covered in a white swath of snow.

He squeezes my hand. "What did Mom say?"

I wince, straining for tactful, but . . . "She called me Janis and referred to you as your brother. She showed me his room."

He shuts his eyes and goes to the railing and gazes off into the distance. His hands clench the ornamental iron. "I'm sorry. She isn't always like that. It's the time of year. He died in December and she's delicate."

He pauses a moment, then continues.

"She wishes it were true, you know," he murmurs. "She loved him more than me."

I keep my face impassive even as his words make me want to gasp.

He sighs. "He dated this girl named Janis. And then your name is similar. She calls me on the phone sometimes and pretends I'm Kurt. I just go along."

"I did the same. I didn't know what else to do."

He scrubs his face. "Kurt ticked all the boxes for them. Even in death, I can't compete."

"You're pretty awesome too."

He glances up at the stars. "Maybe."

"No, you are," I insist. "Do you want to be him? Is that what law school is about?"

Tormented topaz eyes catch mine. "I'm trying to be what my parents want."

I shake my head, trying to make sense of it. "Because you feel guilty that you were there when your brother died?"

"I'm the one who walked in that trailer. If I hadn't, he'd still be here."

"Oh, Eric. It's not your fault and your brother wouldn't want you to think that."

"Let's drop it, yeah?"

"No," I insist, wanting to help. "You can't live up to a ghost that your parents have on a pedestal." He was doing drugs, so he wasn't *that* perfect. I hold my tongue on that point. "You have to think about who you are and what *you* need."

"I said I don't want to talk about it," he says in an abrupt tone.

I flinch.

He groans. "Sorry, Julia. It's just ... being here is hard for me. It brings back some weird feelings."

Oh, I can see why.

28

Eric

I throw an arm around her, itching to push the issue of Kurt behind us. "You're starting to get cold. Want to go in?"

She nods. "They're probably looking for you."

We walk inside and grab more champagne from the bar. The room has thickened with people, the din of noise louder.

"Eric?" a voice says behind me.

I turn to find one of my father's clients. "Michael McClure," he says, shaking my hand. "I just wanted to say congrats on the acceptance to Hawthorne Law."

I introduce Julia, and we exchange stilted small talk.

I'm talking about my last hockey game—it's the only thing I know well—when I see Dr. and Mrs. Cavendish stroll into the entrance of the ballroom, dripping with arrogance as they hold their noses in the air. They speak to my parents, acknowledging them with a haughtiness that screams *I'm richer than you.*

I cringe as my dad fawns over them, getting them drinks and laughing loudly at their conversation.

I nearly spit out my champagne when Parker walks in behind them.

He's never come to one of these parties, and he sure as hell isn't welcome.

Wearing a smug expression, he throws back a glass of whiskey as he scans the area. He glares at me, then Julia. A livid expression flashes on his face. His throat moves.

Dude has it bad for her in a fucked up way.

He turns and says something to his father. They both glance at me. Then Julia.

She stiffens. "What is he doing here?"

I clasp her hand. "I can deal with him. This is my house. Don't worry."

"I haven't seen him since the incident at the Kappa house." Her brow furrows as she sucks in her lower lip. She's a little scared of him and I hate it.

"Stay here." I make my way toward Parker and he does the same, meeting me near the bar.

"What are you doing here?" I say quietly, but there's no doubt of the menace in my tone.

"Parties are my thing. There are so many people. Important people. Do they know your little secrets, I wonder?"

"I don't have any secrets," I mutter.

I feel Julia sliding up next to me. She clings to my arm as her chest rises rapidly.

"Hey, Ju-Ju," he croons. "Nice dress. You look fuckable."

My hands clench. If we weren't surrounded by my

father's colleagues, I'd take him by his collar and drag him to the door. "Don't even look at her."

"Don't make a scene, Parker," Julia says in a hushed voice.

"Never, Ju-Ju. I'll be as quiet as a mouse." He smirks at me. "I've done a lot more than look at her, Hansen. I've fucked her. And she's not even that good. For a whore."

Blood boils in my veins and I grit out my words. "Get out."

"Calm down." He motions to a passing waiter and takes a glass of champagne, his sip slow and easy. "I came here to deliver a message."

I glare. "Then deliver it."

"Not to you." He rolls his eyes. "Where's your father?"

My gaze thins. "What do you want with him?"

He rocks from his heels to his toes, his voice rising. "I heard the news that you got into law school. Congratulations." He glances around as if to see if anyone is listening. "Damn, I love an audience."

"If it wasn't for them, I'd knock your teeth out," I say.

He makes a tutting noise. "You're getting red in the face, Hansen. People are starting to stare."

They are. Eyes flit to us then bounce away.

"I had someone look up your application," he calls loudly. "I can do that, you know. There are plenty of Kappas on the board of admissions at Hawthorne Law. Your application wasn't very impressive. Dude, you're stupid."

Anger burns brighter. On my skin. In my bones.

He smirks. "Of course, the admissions committee was shocked to learn of your violent streak. Five Kappas have come forward and filed complaints against you for assault at our house. We caught it on tape. It shows you storming onto our property with fists flying, and when a few good Samaritans tried to break it up, you assaulted them as well."

"Guess it didn't show the part where it was ten of you on top of me, did it?"

He gives me a dark smile. "Your admission has been put on hold until it can be investigated. It's possible it will be rescinded, and good luck getting another law school to even look your way. You're going to be blackballed from every serious school in the US."

My mom and dad break through the crowd and join us. "Eric? Parker? What's going on? What's this about a fight?"

Parker's eyes never leave mine. "Sorry, Mr. Hansen, I assumed the family knew."

My father's lips compress as he looks from me to Parker. "I'm sure this is just some disagreement between fraternity brothers. There's no need to file complaints."

Parker laughs. "Mr. Hansen, I was shocked to hear from my father that you think Eric is a Kappa. He was kicked out years ago—for hitting me actually. I let that one go as, like you said, a disagreement between frat brothers, but clearly that was a mistake. He hasn't learned his lesson."

My father's eyes drill into me like flints of rock. "Is this true?"

"I was defending Boone, Dad. He's my friend—not that you'd know this. They nearly killed him during pledging. They left him in the cornfields overnight without clothes, and drunk."

My father frowns, confusion on his face. "But wait, you're not a Kappa?"

"No," I admit with a resigned sigh.

Parker nudges his head at Julia. "His girlfriend is a stripper with a druggie mom. I mean, I'm just sharing this because I thought you'd want to know, Mr. Hansen. Eric is making bad choices."

My mom gasps and darts her eyes to Julia, her brow wrinkling. "Oh. And I showed her around the house."

Julia's breath hitches.

"Merry Christmas," Parker says, then turns and saunters away from us.

I blink to push the tide of emotion away. There's so much boiling inside of me that I don't know how to react.

Julia trembles, her face reddening as she looks up at me. Shit.

It's not just me that got humiliated.

"Don't let him get to you, okay?" I say softly.

"Everyone heard him," she whispers, then glances at my parents. She undoes her hand from mine and pulls away. "I-I need to leave. Are you ready to go?" Her eyes plead with me.

"Yeah." I move to follow her but my father grabs my shoulder.

"Eric," he mutters. "My office. We need to discuss the charges against you—and a new law school."

"I can't. I have to—"

"Now," he says, then puts on a smile and claps the nearest man on the back and says, "Scene's over, everyone. We'll sort this out. Please, enjoy the party."

I shift my gaze to find Julia, but she's already disappeared.

I should go find her, but I just need a minute to talk to my dad.

We walk into his office. It has a desk with five monitors on it. Mounted to the wall are his Hawthorne diplomas and the Kappa picture when he was president.

He closes the heavy oak door. "What the fuck was that about?"

"Parker is a dick. He's pissed that I beat the shit out of him." And that I'm with Julia.

"I don't even know where to start." He runs a hand through his hair as he sits at his desk. "I can probably get the charges dropped with a few phone calls, but Cavendish has more pull than me over Hawthorne. What were you thinking? How long have you lied to us?"

I huff out a bitter laugh. "I didn't want to tell you I wasn't in Kappa because I knew how much you wanted it."

"I had nothing when I started at Hawthorne, a scholarship kid from the middle of nowhere Minnesota. I studied, I networked, and met the right people. That's how I gave you all of this. All I ever wanted was for you to continue what I started." He exhales. "You know how much this means to your mother. You know—"

"She doesn't even know who I am," I snap.

He slams his fist on the desk and the sound reverberates off the wood paneling.

"If she finds out you aren't going to go to law school, she'll be hurt. You can't disappoint her."

My jaw tics. "This has nothing to do with her. It's your dream, not hers."

He rises up and charges toward me and puts his nose inches from mine, and points to a chair. "Sit down."

My hands twitch to hit something.

I don't back down from anyone on the ice or off.

But in his castle, with him staring me down, I feel like the kid I was after Kurt died. Guilty. The person responsible for screwing up our family.

With a heavy exhale, I sit down. Texts come in from Julia and I barely read them.

He goes back behind his desk. "This is what we're going to do. You're going to move off-campus and live with us."

He means prison.

"What? No. I need to be closer to school for hockey."

"Fuck hockey, boy! Don't you care about your future?"

I look down at the floor. "Of course, I do."

"I have a friend on the board at a law school in Vermont. It's small but good. She can get you in there."

"Vermont... but—"

"Lots of old money there. You can spread our influence into the Northeast."

My eyes bulge. Thousands of miles away. For the next three years. "But I can't—"

He taps on his computer. "I'll send an email and see if we can't get you an interview for the winter break. I'll ask her what size donation will help expedite the process of finding you a spot."

"But..."

Everything tilts on edge.

He wants to get rid of me. To a place where there will be no Julia.

He barely looks up from his laptop. "And Eric? That girl? The stripper you called your girlfriend?"

This is the final nail in the coffin.

He doesn't even have to pound it in.

I already know what's coming. "She's not what you think—"

"I don't care. Lose her. Whatever she is, whatever she's done, she isn't on our level."

I slump into the seat, my head spinning.

He can't do this.
I'm in control of my life, not him.
I watch as he types away.
But...
I can't disappoint him. I owe it to Kurt.

29

Julia

I rush out of the mansion and stop at the bottom as I inhale a deep breath of cold air. My hands shake as I press them to my face. Jesus. How humiliating. The disgust in Mr. Hansen's eyes. His mother's gasp of disbelief. The people around us who gave me scathing looks.

Mrs. Hansen opens the door and stands on the top step. "Darling, are you okay?"

I drop my hands and glance up. "Um, well, no."

She comes down to where I am. "I apologize for Parker, even though he should himself. He's always been jealous of . . . Eric."

I rub my arms in the cold. "Eric mentioned it."

She hands over a pretty black shawl she must have grabbed on the way out. "I'm sorry for saying what I did. It was a knee-jerk reaction, darling, and nothing more. Just the shock of the scene, I suppose. We want Eric to go to law school, and hearing that he's been fighting and his admission might be rescinded is a big deal."

"Right." My teeth chatter.

"Eric brought you here, so I'm sure he likes you."

Does he? Then why didn't he come outside with me?

"He does need to talk to his father, though," she adds. "There's no denying that. You're welcome to come inside and wait? I can find a quiet room for you if you want?"

She's truly trying to be helpful, but walking back inside that pristine house isn't going to happen.

"I'm fine where I am."

She sighs, a sad look on her face. "You have pride. I understand. I'll let Eric know where you are, yes?"

I nod and she disappears back inside the house.

I chew on my lip as I send a text to Eric.

I'm outside and want 2 go home.

No reply but it shows as read.

I stare at the beautiful fountain in the circle drive, my thoughts dark and thorny. Money can ruin people. Parker. Mr. Hansen. Eric?

My heart thumps as I linger at the entrance, expecting the door behind me to open, that he'll finish with his dad and come out.

I wait.

Five more minutes. Ten.

I wait longer.

Fifteen. Twenty. Thirty.

I shiver as the wind blows. The shawl isn't going to keep me warm.

I pace around the entrance, then linger out to the driveway and gaze up at the stars.

My fists tighten as I remind myself of Taylor's words.

I am my own universe. I'm made up of black holes and glittering galaxies.

I'm vast. Limitless. I can't be contained. I. Am. Beautiful.

So why am I waiting on him like a silly schoolgirl, like the one I was all those years ago?

I push back tears as thoughts flit through my mind.

Is it possible I'm just a novelty to him? Someone to pass the time until he goes to law school?

I hate the doubt that creeps in, I do, because he's done so much for me, but tonight has eviscerated me.

He was also humiliated, though. He's probably not going to get into Hawthorne Law.

My lashes flutter. But it's been over half an hour. Why hasn't he texted me?

People let me down. He has before.

I am my own universe. I am. *I am.*

"Can I help you, miss?" A valet says as he approaches. "You're going to freeze." He's young, maybe twenty. His co-workers are behind him, working on someone's flat tire.

"I'm fine," I push out. "Hey. Do you think one of you could give me a ride to Sparrow Lake?"

"You lost your ride?"

"I think so."

"I would take you in my car, but I'm on the clock until the guests are gone. We're expecting the party to be over by midnight or so."

It's only ten and the party is in full swing.

"No problem. I'll figure it out." I pull my phone out of my clutch and check for Uber and Lyft. No drivers out.

Merry Christmas.

Forty-five minutes now.

I sigh and shiver some more, then survey my surroundings. I went to school in this town, but I have no idea where this neighborhood even is. I can't walk home anyway. It's too far.

Frustration builds, mixing with the anger and mortification. Tears cloud my eyes and I swipe at them.

I shake my head as it dawns on me, as I recognize the feeling that's been building in my chest for weeks. Funny how it takes a momentous event to see your feelings clearly.

I love Eric. Wholeheartedly. Completely. Unconditionally.

I love his spontaneity. The layers of darkness inside him. The way he holds me. The shape of his lips. The warmth of his hand in mine.

But family is the backbone of everything he's ever known.

He's eaten up with guilt and shame.

He wears the mantle like a robe.

Hedge fund manager. Billionaire. He's going to live the life his family wants.

And I have to live mine.

Sniffing, I walk to the valet station and smile as I lie through my teeth. "You know what? I just got a text from Eric. He told me to take his truck back and he'll catch a ride with someone else."

Relief hits him. Obviously, he was worried about me. "Great. I'll pull it around for you." He grabs a set of keys from the board.

The moment he disappears, the headlights of another car pull up into the circle, a sleek black Mercedes AMG GT. The vehicle stops in front of me, the passenger-side window powering down.

"Need a ride, Ju-Ju?" Parker asks.

I rear back. "I have one."

He puts the car in park and leans over the window. "Ah, did Eric leave you out here all alone?"

"Fuck off."

He checks his rearview mirror and calls to the valet, "Hey, if you want a tip, ask for the blow job. She's shit with everything else."

My blood boils as rage awakens and begs to be let out to play.

Maybe it's because I never got vindication after he cuffed me to his bed. Maybe it's because he came here tonight to ruin Eric and embarrass me. Maybe it's because I love Eric and I'm terrified of the pain that's going to come with it.

The valet left the tire iron on the ground from earlier. I snatch it and wield it like a weapon.

Parker laughs. "Ju-Ju. You can barely hold that thing. Put it down."

He's never going to learn. He'll keep hurting people as long as he breathes.

Why didn't I report him? Even if it would have brought awful scrutiny into my life.

Adrenaline pumps through my veins. Once, I loved him. The mere idea seems preposterous.

I pull the tire iron back and slam it against his passenger-side mirror.

A loud popping noise reverberates as my hands tingle from the impact. The mirror jiggles for a moment, then drops and hangs by a single wire.

His eyes flare. "What the fuck!"

I slam it down again, hitting the glass of the windshield. It emits a sickening crunch and spider webs.

"Stop it, you crazy whore!"

Not that word. Not ever.

"Whoa," the valets calls, giving himself plenty of space as he approaches us. "Let's bring this down a notch."

My chest rises rapidly, the metal stick heavy in my hands. I swallow thickly, but don't want to let the anger go.

The other valet returns with Eric's truck and the headlights flash in my face.

Parker throws open the door and stalks over to me, hands raised. "You stupid—"

I raise the weapon back up. "My next shot will be your balls."

He freezes, gauging the situation. "Why?"

Why?

"Leave. Eric. Alone."

"Yeah, all right! Fine!" he snaps, then without warning, he reaches and tries to grab it from me. I swipe it down, connecting with his knuckles.

"What the—what the fuck?" He grabs his hand. "We've got a bowl game, you—"

I take the tire iron in both hands and press it up against his chest and shove.

He stumbles to the ground and our eyes connect.

I laugh, the sound a little off.

"How does it feel? To be scared?" I ask. "That's how I felt when you tackled me and took me to your room."

With one last glare at him, I drop the tire iron and walk to Eric's truck. Half of my hair is out of the up-do, so I remove the clip and shake it out, letting it fall to my shoulders. My heart beats rapidly. My skin feels singed by fire. I feel . . .

Alive.

By the time I pull out, Parker has jetted away like a scalded cat.

I crank up the music as I pull out of the drive. I hit a couple of dead-ends as I try different roads to get out of the subdivision. Soon, the mansions give way to smaller row homes, and in the blink of an eye, I'm in Sparrow Lake.

My hands ache as I clench the steering wheel.

I am my own universe. I'm made of black holes and glittering galaxies.

It doesn't matter that I take my clothes off for money.

I matter.

I fucking matter.

The truck pulls into the police station. I get out of the truck, walk in, and approach the lady at the front desk. She's wearing a uniform. Her name tag says Officer Carden.

She gives me a careful look, taking in the dress. Probably my wild hair. "What can I do for you?"

"I need to report something. I'm not sure what to call it when a man throws you over his shoulder, unwillingly, then handcuffs you to a bed without your consent. He kissed me. He grabbed my breast."

She stands. Looks me over. "Come back and have a seat. Did this happen tonight?"

I fidget as I sit, crossing my legs. "A few weeks ago. I saw him tonight, though." I stare down at my hands. "I beat his car with a tire iron and threatened him. He'll probably report it. His name is Parker Cavendish."

She blinks. "I understand. Let me get a detective."

30

Julia

I'm in bed at two in the afternoon when my bedroom door bursts open and Taylor waltzes in and plops down. "Rise and shine, love. I'm back from Christmas and wanna hear everything about your party at Eric's."

Like a splash of happy, he's wearing green pants and a bright yellow sweater.

I'm so happy to see him that I squeal and throw my arms around him.

"You have no idea what's been going on," I say as I sit up in bed and pull my knees up to my chest. My mirror against the wall tells the story. Tangled hair, red eyes, and there's even a spot of red pizza sauce on my chin.

In the five days since the party, I've barely noticed life. I spent Christmas Eve and Christmas Day with my mom and put on a happy face, but when I came home—alone—I ate whatever I could find and watched a long line of Christmas movies. Last night I worked at the club bartending and was glad to be around people.

I've been to the police station once more since that first night when I sat in a small room and wrote my witness statement. At the last visit, I was interviewed by a special investigator. I recounted my relationship with Parker, his phone texts, his brothers who wouldn't let me leave the Kappa house that night.

After I left the station, I felt more in control of my life than I had in a year. I drove to Eric's house in town, left his keys in the ignition, and walked home.

"Spill all the tea. Was it a big house? Did you have a blast? Also, what are we doing for New Year's Eve?" He smiles, then sobers as he gets a look at my face. He sweeps the hair out of my face. "Julia?"

I pour the entire story out in a rush, from the party to Parker showing up, to the police station.

"That was very brave," he says softly. "Reporting him is a way to bring light to sexual assault on campus. Or anywhere."

I nod. "He'll just keep doing it to other girls. I don't want that."

"And Eric? Have you heard from him since that night?"

I worry my lip between my teeth. "He finally texted the night of the party." But only because the valet had gone inside to tell them what happened between me and Parker.

"And?"

"I told him I needed space." I pluck at the quilt on my bed as I recall our brief texts. He wanted to call me, but I didn't want to talk. It felt too fresh. And I was still reeling with the police stuff—which I didn't mention. "I mean, obviously, he needs time. He ditched me for his dad." My throat prickles.

"Sweetheart..."

"I don't mean to sound petty. It's not *just* about him not rushing after me at the party. I get that his father has a hold on him. I get that he wants to make his parents happy. The thing is, he never even told them I was coming. I need to forget about him and focus on my mom and me." My voice hitches.

Maybe I should have waited inside for him. I don't know.
Maybe he should have chased after me. I don't know.
What is true, is that we need a breather.
He pats my hand. "You love him?"
"Unfortunately."
"Bollocks," Taylor says as he hugs me.
He urges me up and we go downstairs.
I smile wanly. "When is Poppy coming in?"
"Sometime today."

I fix him a hot tea, hand it to him, then make mine. I sit at the table and swish in the creamer.

The doorbell rings. "Julia?" Eric calls from the porch.

I sit up straighter. "I don't want to see him." Because if I do, I might change my mind.

"Got it." Taylor grabs a fork off the table, waggles his eyebrows, then marches into the den and opens the door.

I follow and listen from the hallway.

"Hello. Sorry, but Julia is indisposed," Taylor says.

My heart clenches, and before I know it, I'm coming around the corner and stand next to Taylor.

"It's fine. I've got this, Tay."

"Sure?"

I nod.

"I'll be in the kitchen," he says as he points the fork at Eric, then sashays away.

I take him in. He's wearing jeans that cling to his thighs and a pale blue cable-knit sweater. Boots are on his feet. He drags a hand through his hair. "Hey. How are you?"

"Fine."

He licks his lips. "I, um, wanted to say that I'm sorry for not checking on you at the party. I thought you'd wait for me." He clears his throat. "You alright?"

"You already asked that." I stare at my hands and push the words out. "I went to the police and reported Parker for the incident at the Kappa house." My gaze darts to him. "I-I listed you as a witness. They'll be contacting you. Sorry."

He looks shocked, then recovers. "Sure, yeah, anything I can do. Don't be sorry. He deserves it. I'll back you a thousand percent." A huff comes from him. "Dad already has the charges against me dropped."

A long sigh comes from me. "I-I wish you'd tried to see me earlier since the party." I may have said I needed space, but I really needed him to make the first move and try to see me.

"I just needed to think." He pauses, and I feel him studying my face. "Julia. I need you to understand. There are expectations on me."

"No, I understand. The expectation is you won't bring me home to the parents."

"That's not it. My life, it's important to them. My father—"

"Wants you to go to law school. Tell him no. Tell him you make your own decisions."

"You're important to me, Julia. They know that. I've told them. You and I are together."

My eyes capture his. "We aren't."

His nose flares. "What I'm trying to say is that it wasn't you. You didn't even matter that night."

The words knife straight into my heart. So that's why he didn't follow me. I don't rate. "Which is it? Am I important, or do I *not* matter?"

He sighs. "Stop. That's not what I meant. Look, there's more—"

Be strong.

Be fierce.

I interrupt him with a hand. "Eric. Stop. You do your thing and I'll do mine. Yeah?"

Tell me no, Eric. Tell me you want me and to hell with them.

His jaw clenches as he studies my face. Then he looks away from me and into the distance for several moments. When he turns back, he's got a faraway look in his eyes.

"Maybe you're right. I don't need any distractions, I guess. I'm quitting hockey. May as well rip everything away."

My chest sears with a white-hot pain. "Okay."

"Okay."

We stare into each other's eyes—until I can't take it anymore.

I shut the door quietly, then lean against the wall to listen to him leave. Five minutes pass before he walks down the steps.

When I go back into the kitchen, Taylor takes one look at my face and opens his arms.

I fall into them and cry silently.

31

Eric

I back out of the parking lot on campus to head home.

Go to class. Go to my parents'. Study. Eat. Sleep. Wake up.

That's what I've been doing for the past two weeks since school started.

Today I have another stop to make. I need to finish getting some things at Hockey House.

As I'm driving down College Avenue, though, I see her, and my heart double-times, a familiar anguish hitting me like a ton of bricks.

I see her dark hair, tinged with gold. It must be . . .

Nope, not her.

I've heard about her, though. All of campus has. She started a snowball rolling downhill involving an investigation concerning misconduct at Kappa. At first her story was turned into a joke, as college hijinks and boys being boys.

When other girls came forward, the jokes stopped.

My father is furious about the entire situation. *Nothing like that would have happened back in my day,* he said. I don't know if that's true.

I park at the house and grab the boxes from the back.

Reece's hand falls on my shoulder when I walk inside. "Well, look who's back from the dead."

"Hey. Sorry I haven't been around." Or texted him much.

He gives me a disappointed look. "You drop off the face of the Earth. Then Coach tells me you've left the team and I'm captain now. I think I deserve a little more than a 'hey'."

He deserves a hell of a lot more than that. All the guys do.

They lost their last game without me.

My body feels leaden. "You're right. I'm just trying to figure out life, yeah? Let me just pack my stuff up."

"Fine. I need to clean up for the new roommate anyway."

"New? That didn't take long."

"Yeah. Bowers."

I exhale. Bowers is a good guy. A good player.

"Come in the den. I want you to take a look at something."

Okay, weird.

"Sure."

We walk into the den and a blur grabs me by the collar of my coat, spins me around, and envelopes me in a bearhug. "What the—"

I take in the broad-shouldered guy with curly long blond hair. He's a big dude. He must have been standing in the back, waiting on me to walk into the den.

"Z?" I exclaim in amazement. "Fuck me. Shouldn't you be in Nashville?"

His grin takes up his whole face. "Yeah, it's me, asshole. I took a personal day to fly here and talk to you."

I sputter. "Dude. I'm flattered."

He pats me, then shoves me in the recliner. "Good. Now that the niceties are done, it's time to talk."

Oh.

Boone has entered the den, and he and Reece sit on the couch. Serious expressions are on both their faces.

Z drags a chair from the kitchen and plops it down beside me.

"Uh, is this an intervention?" I ask, bemused that Z is here, but uneasy about having to explain my reasons for quitting the team. It's terrible to admit when you've given up.

Boone nods. "I've never seen anyone who needed more intervening than you. Wait. Maybe me when I rushed Kappa."

I chuckle uncertainly.

"Here. You might need this." Z hands me a water and I take a long drag, then wipe my face.

He looks me over, his eyes grave. "It's not really an intervention. Let's just call it a chat to get a certain player's head out of his ass."

I wince. "You didn't need to come all this way. I'm straight. I'm fine." I'm not.

I fucking miss hockey.

Reece grimaces. "Eric. Look at yourself. You've lost weight. Your eyes are dead. Just explain why you quit and we'll listen."

I dip my head and clench my fists to find an anchor. It used to be Julia. She made everything brighter. But without her, things have only spiraled. "My life is about following my dad's footsteps. Hockey was interfering in achieving that."

Reece snorts. "Interfering? Fuck me. Hockey is your life."

Z shushes him. "We need to listen to him. Look, Eric, I understand that these ideas come from your dad, but I know you. You love being on that ice."

A lump rises in my throat. "Okay, sure. The best part of my life has been on the ice, but that's coming to an end after this season. This is as far as I was going to go. Pro is a dream I didn't achieve."

Z smirks. "I always thought you were the best winger I ever played with."

"Hey! Standing right here," grouses Reece. "And, hello, I'm your brother."

"Sorry, bro," Z continues without taking his eyes off me. "I've always been confused why you never got a sniff from the league. So, when Reece called and told me what was going on, I asked our head of scouting. He said he had you rated high on their board a couple of years ago but was told by the Preds owner to put you on the do-not-draft-for-off-ice-reasons list."

"What?" I ask as I rear back in shock. "But how?"

Z nods. "Yeah, crazy, right? So I called our owner and asked him. He told me he had a conversation with your dad at some fundraiser a few years back. Your dad said you would never play pro hockey and to not waste their time on you. Apparently, it got around, and now every team in the league has you on their do-not-draft list."

I stand up and pace around the den. "This is bullshit. My dad wouldn't block me from going pro."

Reece glowers. "Wouldn't he? He talked you into quitting the team."

Z's eyes search mine. "If you could be a free agent at the end of the college season and sign with any team, what would *you* want to do with your life?"

I shake my head. "What's the point? I'm already off the team."

Boone points at me. "Officially you're taking time off for a mental health break. That's what I'm telling people." He grins. "Come on, you know Coach would have you back."

Reece jumps in. "If we win every game for the rest of the season, we'll have a good chance at making the playoffs." He pauses. "Or maybe you come back and we don't make the playoffs. Maybe you don't get signed by a pro team. Even if all of that happens, you'd be happier than sitting in a law school planning how you are going to squeeze an extra two percent out of some stock trade."

I scrub my face.

Z squeezes my arm. "Dude. You only make sacrifices for the things that matter. You care about hockey. Let's go to the arena and scrimmage, just a few of us. Boone has already called some of the defensive guys to meet us there. If you want to give it up after that, fine, I'll shut the fuck up. I came all this way to see your face and tell you what I think, and I have to fly out tonight. Let's do this, yeah?" Full of energy, he picks up the hockey puck someone left on the coffee table, the one with *The Best Puck* written on it.

Looking at it brings back memories. Good ones.

Like a small burst of light, I feel a tingle of hope.

And Z is here. I get to play on the ice with him.

I don't even think about my reply. "Fine."

Thirty minutes later, I suit up inside the arena.

It feels strange, taping my stick, lacing up my skates.

"Ready?" Z asks.

I smirk. "You're with the defense, so I'm sorry if my goals are gonna hurt your fragile confidence."

"Bring it," he says and skates out onto the ice.

I follow him, and as soon as my skates glide over the surface, home—and family— settles deep into my chest.

32

Eric

"Hansen! Hansen! Hansen!"

The cheer is deafening as the game ends. Another win for the Lions.

We were pure magic tonight, my first game back since I saw Z.

I do another victory lap, give the crowd one last wave, then head for the locker room.

When I get there, Coach throws an arm around my shoulder. "Another beauty," he says as I pull off my helmet and wipe the sweat from my brow. "Get a shower and come to my office when you're done. There's someone I want you to meet."

"Who?"

"You'll find out," he says with a wink, shoving me off.

I peel off my jersey as I peek through the window blinds to his office. Sure enough, there's a guy in a suit there.

"What's that all about?" Boone says, coming up behind me.

"I don't know," I say, trying to gather clues from the guy's appearance. But there isn't much. He looks like a salesman.

Reece balls up his jersey and throws it in a laundry bin. "I'll tell you what it is. Our man, here, is going to the show, yo!" He struts over to me and grins. "That guy's a scout."

Or someone who could save me on my auto insurance.

Boone shoves me forward. "Only one way to find out. Get your pretty ass in the shower and don't keep us in suspense."

Ten minutes later, hair still wet, I knock on the door to Coach's office. He motions me in.

The man in the suit stands up. "Eric Hansen!" he says in a game-show announcer voice as he extends his hand. When I put mine in his, he pumps it hard. "It's great to finally meet you."

"Good to meet you, too," I reply.

Coach nods. "This is Tip Wallace. He's a scout for the Washington Capitals."

Holy fucking hell.

Tip nods. "Nice game tonight. You played the wall great. Good stick-handling and speed. You're in with your line—that's impressive. It's like you're reading each other's minds."

"They make me look good. Why are you here?"

Tip nods. "We overlooked you because we were told you weren't interested."

"Who told you that?" I ask.

He shrugs. "Just heard it from another scout. I'm not sure where it started."

My fists twitch as I think of my dad. Once I told him I

was going back to hockey and to live with my friends, he's refused my calls.

Tip continues. "Zack Morgan called my boss and told him we should look again. It's funny, our general manager doesn't usually get calls from other teams' players, but here we are." He grins.

I plop down in a seat as he talks about my career in hockey.

The same thought keeps circling.

They want me.

For what I'm good at.

"Eric?" Coach asks, and I realize there's been a lull. "Tip just said he'd love to have you on the team."

My chest rises rapidly. The chances of a hockey player going pro are one in four thousand—and I'm being given a chance. I lick my lips. I don't want him to think I'm easy, but I am so damn easy. "I can't commit to anything until the season is over, but well, the Capitals are a kickass team and I'd love to be part of it."

Tip smiles as he presses his business card in my hands. "Of course, we just wanted to be the first to talk to you. We are, right?"

"First? Uh, yeah."

I stand to shake hands with both men. As I do, I manage to glance out the office window and see Boone, Reece, and most of the team watching us.

I leave the office and grin as I flash them the business card.

They hoot and yell. Reece picks me up and tries to swing me around, but I shove him off, laughing.

This is it. My dream, come true.

Except...

Boone throws an arm around me. "We should go celebrate, bro."

I grab my duffle. "Not tonight, but soon. I've been putting off seeing my dad, but I have to have my say."

When I pull up to their house, I cut the engine and take a deep breath before I go inside. His office door is open as he types away at his computer.

"Dad."

He doesn't look up.

"Dad," I say, louder.

"In a minute," he mutters as he holds up a finger and keeps typing.

He doesn't stop until I take the business card and slide it over to him. Even then, he only glances at it. "What's that?"

"Look at it."

He takes his hands off the keyboard and picks up the card and studies it. "And—"

"A scout came to the locker room tonight. They want me to play for the Capitals."

He pushes the card away and picks up his pen and leans back in his chair. *Tap, tap, tap.*

"I don't agree with you playing hockey—"

I slam my fists down on the desk. "It's what *I* want. Did you tell NHL owners that I didn't want to play pro?"

He pulls off his glasses and laces his fingers. He opens his mouth to speak, but I steamroll over his words.

"You did. Kurt's dream was working for you. But hockey is my life. You don't even know how good I am." An exhale comes from my lips. "I miss Kurt every day. But I'm not him. I'll never be him. I don't want to be him!"

"If you play hockey, I'm writing you out of my will."

"I don't care about your money."

"Eric?" Mom says.

I start at the sound of my name on her lips. I turn. "Mom?"

She walks into the office wearing a blue skirt and white blouse. Her hair is done up in a fancy style. She looks lucid. A little tired. "You moved out. I've missed you at breakfast. How are you?"

"Fine. A scout came to see me today. He wants me to play for them." I thrust my hand at Dad. "He's still on me about law school."

"Oh." She takes the card I hand her and studies it. "Wow, this is wonderful."

My dad scoffs. "Hockey is ridiculous."

Mom's head comes up sharply as she focuses on Dad. "Eric isn't Kurt. I heard him say it. He doesn't want to be a lawyer or work with you." She smiles tremulously as if something has loosened from her and fallen away. "He needs to get on with *his* life. I know Kurt is gone. Sometimes I just get confused. I gave Julia a tour and got a little lost in my head. Will you tell her I'm sorry, Eric?"

I nod slowly. "Of course."

She toys with a paperweight on the desk. "I'd like to meet her again, you know. She's very pretty. She told me about her mom's health struggles."

"She's had a tough life, but she's a good girl," I murmur, daring my dad to say otherwise as I flash a look at him.

She nods. "If you care for her, then I will too."

I watch as she picks up a family photo of us. Her fingers trace over our faces. "Kurt had his demons. Maybe demons your father and I created with so much expectation." Her voice hitches. "I mean, we'll never know why he started using drugs, but one thing is true . . ." She turns to my dad.

"We can't do the same thing to Eric. It's not fair. He wants another life. He wants to be happy."

My voice quakes. "Mom?"

Dad comes around his desk and stands in front of her. "Marilyn..."

She cups his cheek. "Let him be himself, darling. Let go of this legacy thing. You let yourself get all worked up over it, but it has to stop. Eric has been miserable here with us. Even I can see that."

I walk over and hug my mother tight as a shudder of relief ripples over me. I don't know what happened to wake her up. Maybe it was the incident at the party. Maybe it was hearing me say that I don't want this life.

"Thank you," I say as I kiss the top of her head.

Her lips tremble as she looks up at me. "You're a beautiful person, Eric. You've endured so much, and none of it was your fault. I want you to know that. I'm sure I said it before, and if I didn't, I should have. Now, go call Julia and let us know when you guys want to visit us again."

I glance at my dad, who's plopped back in his chair, a confused look on his face.

I'm too angry at him to care. I kiss Mom's cheek and walk out of the house.

33

Julia

The sun shines. Bees buzz. Birds chirp. And daffodils are trying to bloom.

I'm on the campus green, taking photographs of anything and everything. Even though it's late February, the temperature is in the sixties—a fluke—and everyone soaks up the pretty weather. I've traded my fleece jacket for a sundress. Poppy has a blanket out, and like the little nurturer she is, she brought a picnic basket with peanut butter sandwiches, cookies, and lemonade. I feel like I'm in a Hallmark movie.

Nearby a group of people play ultimate frisbee and their laughter floats across the park. Girls have brought towels, and a few crazy ones are in bikinis. An elderly couple walks hand in hand on the tree-lined path around the park.

I snap photo after photo. That's what my boss at the *Sparrow Lake News* wants—human interest photos. They give me a topic each week, and I dash out and take hundreds of photos, then send them to the editor, who meets with his staff to choose the pic to write about.

I make less money at the paper than I did stripping, but I'm managing thanks to another job I picked up. Hello. Meet the best server at The Noodle Bar, a ramen restaurant off campus that opened last month. It's quite the hit, and while the tips aren't up to Platinum Nights standards, it's enough. I laugh. It's ironic that I spent years eating ramen because it's cheap and now I'm serving them to college students for tips.

My mom is still recovering at the rehab facility but will be released soon. She has speech difficulties but has relearned to walk, and that's huge. She's moving in with us in another month. Taylor and Poppy and I worked on one of the empty rooms downstairs, formerly a parlor of some sort, and turned it into a space for her to have a bed and whatever else I can find at secondhand stores.

"This isn't exactly hard-hitting news," Poppy observes as I snap a photo of the old couple. They are so adorable that I sigh wistfully.

"It doesn't have to be."

I've been the subject of enough news. A couple of weeks after I reported Parker, *Sparrow Lake News* picked up the story, a vague piece about a sexual assault on campus. All the Kappas knew what it was about and soon word got around to everyone that it was me. I was scared of retaliation from them, but it never came.

The story grew when five more women filed reports. Most of the fingers pointed to Parker and Scott, and this time there was no sweeping it under the rug. I'll likely have to go to trial, or perhaps Parker will take a plea deal. I don't know yet.

To add more fuel to the fire, the Kappa chapter was hit

with a hazing scandal. When the administration didn't investigate Boone's claims, his parents sent what happened to Boone to a newspaper in St. Paul. They ran his account and Twitter went bonkers. Everyone wanted to know why our administration was ignoring hazing. Well. They aren't anymore.

The Kappa charter was revoked at Hawthorne.

Poppy slides Ray Bans up her nose. "I drove by Kappa earlier this week. It's dead empty." She smirks. "I wonder if they'll sell it. My dad might be interested in a new house to renovate."

I hold my face up to the sun. "I walked by yesterday and someone had spray painted *Pig Fuckers* in huge red letters." I smile. Good riddance, Kappa.

Poppy drops her sandwich. "Wait! I forgot to ask you about the criminal property allegation. What happened?"

I tell her the gist of it. Parker reported my damage to his car. Of course. And the valets were witnesses to the debacle—but they supported *me*. Their accounts detailed his antagonism and misogynistic remarks. I'm sure he didn't expect their defense of me because he assumes all men are like him. Sure, it's no excuse for beating the shit out of his car, but a victims advocate lawyer took my case and the judge dismissed it. I'm required to pay for the damages to his car.

"My lawyer took care of my fine," I tell her. "It was two grand. She's letting me pay her back."

"You still sending Eric money?"

I nod. "Sent him a check this morning. Slow and steady is the game. I'll get it paid off eventually."

He's sent me several texts this week asking if he can talk to me. I haven't replied.

I'm trying to take photos of a man with his dog when a long shadow appears in my light.

Poppy squeaks and I lower my camera.

It's as if my thoughts conjured him.

Eric's frame looms over us, and I hold my hand up to shield my face from the sun to see.

He's still gorgeous. Chiseled cheekbones, perfect lips, thick lashes.

I've avoided all the places I thought he might be these past weeks. The student center. The food trucks. His house.

He's wearing athletic shorts and a black mesh tank top that shows off his muscled chest. There's a frisbee in his hands, and one look past him shows that Reece and Boone and several other guys have joined the ultimate frisbee game.

His hair is under a ballcap, the strands curling around the edges. His eyes fight to hold mine, but I can't gaze into those depths.

I know what I'll see.

Regret.

Sadness.

Maybe loneliness.

"Hey," he says quietly.

"Hey."

He nods at Poppy. "Good to see you."

Her eyes are huge as saucers. "Um, Eric, long time no see." She stuffs a cookie in her mouth.

He turns back to me. "Nice dress."

"Oh." I glance down at the blue morpho butterfly pattern on my sundress. "It's a little early for spring clothes, but . . ." I trail off. Lame. So lame.

He fidgets and rubs the back of his neck. "I, uh, saw you over here and wanted to come and say hi."

"You did that," I murmur.

"I did, didn't I?"

"Hmm."

Someone calls his name, one of the players, but he doesn't budge. "Ah, the thing is, I still have your other Christmas present. You got my texts?"

I nod. "Ah, don't worry about the gift."

His hand goes to his hip. "I *want* to give it to you. It's not like I can give it to anyone else, right?"

"You can do what you want, Eric."

"And I want to give it to you," he insists.

"Why?"

"Because I bought it with you in mind."

"I see." I pluck at a blade of grass. "You can always return it."

"I don't want to, Julia." His voice is firm.

Poppy sighs. "Good Lord, just take the gift and be done with it."

"I don't have it with me," he says, then pauses. "We have a game tomorrow. I'll leave you tickets at the door. For you and Poppy and Taylor. Come and I'll give it to you then."

That's not a good idea at all.

"Fine," I hear myself saying as I swallow the lump in my throat.

His eyes linger on my face. "Good."

The moments tick by.

Five, six, seven, eight, nine, ten, eleven, twelve—

"Eric! Get over here and throw the damn frisbee," calls one of the guys.

"Later," he says with a start, then takes off running across the green.

I watch him the entire way, my heart jumping.

Poppy tosses a sandwich in my lap. "Eat this. You look pale. So, did you say 'fine' just to make him go away, or are we going to a hockey game?"

I replay the interaction over and over, trying to suss it out.

Why does he insist on giving me a gift?

I chew my lips. "I have no idea if I even want a gift from him. It might make me sad."

"You should go. Closure, plus a parting gift. Maybe it's what you need to move on."

I've told myself that I'm fine, that I'm slowly getting over him, but I'm lying to myself.

Love doesn't vanish.

Even when you wish it would.

"Are you sure you don't want anything?" Taylor asks as he orders beer and a hot dog from the concession stand.

I shake my head, looking around the crowded concourse. Two giggling girls in number seventeen jerseys walk by, and I wonder if Eric is in the locker room right now, feeling as queasy as I am, but for entirely different reasons.

Taylor and Poppy take their food and we go into the packed arena. We climb down the steps and stop at row A, almost directly behind the bench.

"Good seats," Taylor murmurs.

He isn't wrong. I can almost reach out and touch the players if the glass wasn't in the way.

By the time the music starts to blast and the spotlights swirl on the ice, I'm a ball of nerves.

Just be happy for him.

You've come to wish him well.

And closure, whatever that means.

Everyone around us erupts into cheers as our team skates out.

I scan the ice just as Poppy finds him and jiggles my arm. "There he is! Boooo!"

I scoff. "Stop that. He's on our team."

She rolls her eyes. "I thought we were hating on him."

Taylor smirks. "Cheer the team now; hate on him later."

The next time Eric loops around, my palms sweat.

He doesn't raise his head to the audience, so I don't have to think about him noticing me. He's focused on the game.

Not nervous, like me.

Boone saw me on campus recently and mentioned that Eric had quit for one game. I'm glad he's back where he belongs. Something swells inside me. Pride. Even if he doesn't care about me in the same way, I'm happy for him.

I lean forward as Eric skates down the ice with the puck. He dodges a hit, spins around behind the goal, then slams the puck to Reece who scores. Instantly, we're on our feet and jumping up and down as the siren blares.

At the last intermission, the game is tied as the players file off the ice.

Eric still doesn't come close to looking at me.

After the Zamboni does its magic and the players filter back onto the ice, I stand up and rattle the glass. "Go Lions!"

But as time ticks down to the two minute-warning, there's still no goal on either side. My eyes alternate between checking the seconds ticking down on the overhead clock and the game.

Finally, Eric skates out for his last shift in regulation. I lean forward as he and another player hit the boards, hard, not two yards from me. They grapple, sticks click-clacking together, trying to free the puck.

In the middle of the tussle, his eyes suddenly shift up ... higher, higher ... and meet mine.

He pushes off the opposing player, and maybe I imagine it, but I swear he smiles at me.

And then he's off, puck glued to his stick, heading for the opposing team's goal before his opponent even realizes he's gone.

I know the buzzer is coming. Just as the final seconds hit, Eric pulls his stick back and fires a shot that cracks through the arena like a whip. *Pow.*

The goalie dives and misses.

Goal!

The crowd roars louder than ever and I yell with them. Taylor and Poppy and I hug, then hug the strangers behind us.

On the ice, the players are hugging.

I'm sure Eric's at the center of it, getting adoration he deserves.

"Hey."

I turn around and there he is, pressed against the glass right in front of me. My heart skitters in my chest as I take him in, still breathless and sweaty.

He left the team for me.

"I'm glad you're here," he calls.

I can't help smiling. "Wanted that present."

He points his glove. "Meet me over there. In front of the locker rooms."

He skates away as the crowd cheers and the Lions shake hands with the opposing team.

"You need us?" Taylor asks as we exit our row. He gives me an arm squeeze.

"No, I can handle this."

They leave, smiling at me.

I get to the hall to the locker room but can't go any further because of the security guard. Eric taps him on the shoulder and points at me.

"That's Julia Lauren." His eyes capture mine. "She's with me. Always let her pass."

The guard nods and steps aside and I walk down the hall toward him.

I stop a few feet away, my hands tight against the strap of my purse. I drink him in. The fire in his eyes. The exhilaration from his win.

"Julia..." He pauses and exhales.

"Yes?"

He tosses off his gloves and takes my hand. "Will you give me half an hour to get changed? Just wait here for me?"

How can I say no?

I nod jerkily.

He lifts one of his hip pads and pulls out a Ziplock. Unzipping it, he tugs out a piece of paper. "This isn't your gift. It's, um, something I wrote, sort of as a way to explain." He leans against the wall as he toys with the paper. "Will you read it? While I'm showering?"

"Why?"

"I don't think I can handle it if you read it in front of me."

"Oh. Sure."

Hansen, Hansen, Hansen comes from the locker room.

A small smile crosses my face. "Your team is calling. You need to go."

He presses it in my hands, his grasp warm. "I'll be back soon."

I unfold the paper.

I'm not a poet,
That's the first thing you should know.
But sometimes it's only in the lines of words
That I can hear myself think.
The first time I saw you,
You were a lamb
With dreams in your eyes.
You reminded me of the me I wanted to be,
Innocent and sweet.
I wanted to taste that part of you, did you know that?
But I also wanted you because I'm a selfish prick.
I took your kisses,
Without care or conscience.
I'm sorry.
I can't change the person I was
Before.
But now ...
My favorite moments of us are
Your Converse on my floor,
Your hoodies on my bed,
The butterflies over your bed,
The way you fit in my arms.
When I see your eyes now,
I see a wolf.

Strong.
Fierce.
Beautiful.
Worthy.
And you know it because you tossed me aside.
I'm a dumb fuck.
I got lost.
I lost my journey.
I lost the path to hockey.
I lost you.
And happiness.
I can blame it on my parents.
On Kurt.
On guilt and blame and responsibility.
On the pressure cooker in my head.
But I was scared too.
Of trying to be someone good enough for you.
Of accepting that you cared.
Since I was a kid,
People have only loved me conditionally.
If I'm smart.
Or rich.
Or funny.
Or a star.
It's ironic
That people assume I'm carefree,
That I'm the easy one,
When I'm the one with the hole inside.
I'm not sure I've ever been loved
By a girl that didn't want a piece
Of my celebrity.
I'm learning to love my mom again.

I'm learning to love myself,
In bits and pieces.
I'm not perfect.
Never will be.
But I care about you.
I fucking love you.

My breath hitches as emotion claws at my chest. Reading his poem was like falling into the sun. I'm surrounded by warmth and light and beauty.

I'm sitting in a chair gathering my thoughts when he exits the locker room in jeans and a black knit sweater. His eyes are glued to my face.

I stand up. "Eric..."

He stops in front of me, tossing his duffle to the ground. "Wait. Before you say anything, let me get this all out. I don't blame you for breaking it off. I deserved it. You helped me."

I lick my lips. "I did?"

"I hit rock bottom, Julia. I fucking missed you. It's no excuse, but my head hasn't been in the right place all year. Everything from the past came to a head the night of the party. My whole life imploded. I tried to be like Kurt, to make them happy, but I'm just me."

Tears well in my eyes and I will them away. "You're pretty awesome."

He laces his hand with mine. "I'm not going to law school. I'm going to play hockey, most likely with the Washington Capitals. Can you believe it?"

Boone already told me about the Capitals, but I don't say so. I want Eric to feel the experience of telling me. "Congratulations. It's wonderful news. I'm so happy for you."

Moments drift by as we gaze at each other, then he exhales and drops my hand. "Right. I have this for you."

He opens his duffle and pulls out a ring box.

I open it and inhale sharply as I touch my mother's ring. "When did you get this?"

"As soon as it went up for sale at the pawn shop. I was going to give it to you after the party, then after everything that happened, it didn't feel right. It's rightfully yours, so we shouldn't even call this a present. I'm just returning something you lost. Regardless of how you feel about me, take it, keep it."

My hands clench around the box. "I can't say no to that. Thank you."

He runs a hand through his hair. "Can we go somewhere and talk?"

34

Julia

We get inside his truck. He cranks the vehicle and turns on the heat to let the cab warm up. It may have been warm these past few days, but the nights are still cold.

I feel him staring at me as the engine idles. I fidget in my seat. "Congrats on the win. You played great."

He taps his fingers on the steering wheel. "I could barely focus when I showered. I kept thinking about you reading my poem."

"I love it," I murmur.

Then we say nothing. For what seems like five whole minutes.

"I'm not as strong as you think," I say finally.

"Why do you say that?"

"Because I missed you so much." My voice cracks and I pull it back as I shake my head and look out the passenger side window.

"Hey, look at me."

I do, my heart pounding with the need to hear those words from his lips.

His topaz eyes glint with a deep well of emotion. His face softens, his lips curling up in a small smile as he trails his hand down my cheek. "I let my parents get between us, but I know my future. I'm a hardcore hockey player with little to offer you. My dad will probably disinherit me. I'm cool with that. I'm going to be starting over. A career on the ice. A new city." He studies my face, tenderness in his eyes. "I can't take Kurt's place as atonement for how he died. I need to be myself. And there's only one thing I want."

"Hockey."

"It's you. I want you."

Tears appear from out of nowhere and drift down my cheeks. He wipes one away.

"I love you, Julia. I meant those words in the poem. My world kind of begins and ends with you. You see me for who I am, the ugly parts, the good parts."

My throat tightens as a sense of wonder washes over me. "Oh, Eric, I love you too."

He smiles and laughs. "Jesus. Thank God. Thank you, thank you, thank you."

Happiness fills me up as he brushes his lips over mine, tentatively, as if it's our first kiss. I melt in his arms as his mouth touches my eyelids, my nose, my forehead, my cheeks. I quake under each gentle touch, tingles dancing over my skin.

His big hands cup my cheek. "I'd do anything for you, Julia."

"When did you know, you know, that you loved me?" I

mock-glare at him when he smirks. "What? Girls like this stuff. We're gooey inside."

He thinks for a moment. "I knew it was real the night I held you in my arms after your mom's stroke. Then there was this morning after we had sex. The sun was shining on your face. I don't know, it's dumb—but my heart was just happy."

"If only Boone and Reece could hear you say those sappy words."

He mock-glares at me. "What about you?"

My hand touches his face. "Prep school was the beginning, but it didn't dawn on me until the night of the party at your parents'. The loss I felt when you didn't come outside, it was as if part of me was destroyed..."

His eyes shut. "I'm sorry."

I press a kiss to his lips. "No, we need battles to win the war. We'll make mistakes, then work it out. No more space between us, though. I can't do that." I gaze down at the ring I slipped on my finger. "Thank you for this. It's exactly the kind of thing you'd do."

"To everyone else, I'm a stone-cold badass with no feelings, yeah?"

My hand trails down to the strong column of his throat. I lean on his chest and inhale the spicy aftershave. I soak in his strength. "Take me to your place."

"Can't. There's a hockey party." His eyes twinkle. "Yours? But I need to hit a drive-through first."

"Hungry?"

He waggles his brows. "Yes, my love."

"Oh, is that going to be a thing now, 'my love'? What would the hockey players think?"

He gives me a wry grin as we pull out of the parking lot. "I really don't care. I'm The Miracle."

35

Eric

Later, we sit on the couch in the living room and stare at each other. My chest tightens at the emotion that arcs between us. I'm thankful she's giving me another shot.

"I want you with me after graduation," I say. "You're my family. You'll come with me to Washington?"

She winces. "My mother..."

"She can come. I still have my trust, and my signing bonus will be enough for us to get started, maybe find an apartment, plus get that printer you wanted to start your business."

"Are you sure?"

"Yeah."

"Okay!" She throws her head back and laughs, the sound full of happiness. "This is so exciting."

Relief washes over me. I didn't realize how terrified I was

she'd say no. That she would say she had other plans for herself that didn't include me.

After a soft kiss, I pull her to her feet and sweep her up in my arms.

She giggles as I carry her up the stairs to her room.

I set her down and close the door. There hasn't been anyone for me since the night I saved her from Connor.

I walk backwards to the bed and tug her into my lap, my nose trailing up her neck, dragging in her scent, again and again.

I tease the soft skin of her throat with my lips and teeth as she curls her limbs around me.

Her ass is in my hands, her breathing fast.

She massages my shoulders and I groan.

I've spent the last three periods getting beaten, but she heals every bruise with her touch.

I want to sink into her.

Devour her.

Emotions inside of me demand to be released.

Love.

Passion.

I slant my lips against hers once. Twice. Over and over.

"I love you," she says, her voice quiet as she tries out the words again.

"I love you, too," I say as I nudge her coat off her shoulders. I set her on the bed and trail my hands down her body. Her gorgeous breasts. The small waist. Her curvy hips.

I'm fucking lucky to have a girl like her. Authentic. Strong.

I lean over to kiss her, teasingly. Little nips.

I want to make love to her mouth.

She sits up and raises her arms. I tug her top over her arms, then her bra, grazing my fingers over her pert nipples.

We don't break eye contact as I shimmy down her jeans, then her white lace thong. I grab a fistful of my shirt and pull it over my head, then strip down to nothing.

My cock bobs against my stomach.

I lean over, careful not to crush her, as my tongue sucks on a nipple. I nibble and tweak and swirl until it's hard as a rock and rosy red.

"I'm gonna take this slow," I say just to torment her as I start with the other one, giving it the same long attention, my tongue flicking and playing.

"Hmm," she says as I trail down the center of her chest, one hand on each breast, massaging and caressing, as my mouth licks her pussy. Soft. Gentle. Then insistent licks that make her moan.

"Beautiful little pussy, my love..."

She giggles a little at that and I double my efforts as I smile against her skin. I suck her clit into my mouth while my fingers tug on her nipples, stretching them out, then letting them go to stroke her breasts. I start a rhythm, getting in sync with my fingers and my mouth, sucking at her, touching her.

"Eric..."

"Yeah?"

"Fuck..." Her body tightens as she comes, her walls clutching and fluttering for my cock.

I tug a condom from my jeans and slide it over my dick. I pull her legs around my waist and slide into her.

I groan at the feel of her warm heaven.

Ah, it's almost too much to take.

It's sublime, like discovering a new, better part of myself.

"Fucking after saying 'I love you' is the best," I say on a growl.

She laughs again and I like that. That she and I are open and free—even during sex.

I guide her hands above her head, lace my fingers through hers, and plunge back inside her.

"Wherever you are, I'll be," I tell her as we fuck.

She puts her hand on my heartbeat. As if it grounds her. Then she pulls herself up so we can press our foreheads together.

My skin is covered in sweat, and I want to make this perfect.

I want to make this everything for her because she's everything to me.

"Fuck, Julia, tell me this is forever."

"I promise." She gazes up at me, glistening and flushed, her muscles straining as she meets my thrusts.

"I love you," I rasp because I need to make sure she understands. I've gone so long without love that I need to know it's still there.

I lift her ass off the bed and drive into her. Every time I pull out, even just a little, my world ends.

I need faster. More.

My hands go to her waist, lifting and lowering her, muscles straining as I try to wait for her to come again.

When she comes, I can't take my eyes off her. I'm awed that I can feel this close to another person. Awed that she wants to be mine. I spent so much time in the dark, and now that she's here, everything about our future's so fucking bright.

I toss my head back and roar my release, pumping into her until there's nothing left of me.

Bliss.

She curls into my arms, and I drift my hand over her hair.

She loves me without judgment.

She accepts the challenges of my issues with Kurt. With my family.

She is what motivates me to face the world.

And no matter what challenges we face, she's here.

Unconditionally.

EPILOGUE

Some years later...

Eric

"Eric, you aren't taking our five-year-olds axe throwing at some bar," Julia calls out as she helps Kurt, one of our triplets, out of the creek. He's totally me at his age. Carefree, wily, and always ready to play tricks on his siblings, Kara and Kelli.

He and his two sisters, plus Z and Sugar's two boys, Evander and Nash, age six and four respectively, have been climbing up a flat rock and jumping into the basin of a small waterfall. It's not even a foot drop into the water but you'd think they were on the Olympic team for diving. They call it "cliff jumping." My lips twitch.

Kurt has his typical mischievous (maniacal) grin on his face as he sticks his cold hands on Julia's stomach. The water *is* freezing, a stream that trickles down the Blue Ridge Mountains in Ellijay, Georgia.

Julia smirks as she bends down and gives him a quick kiss on the cheek. "I'm so hot your cold hands don't bother me, munchkin." She boops him on the nose. "Axe throwing is dangerous, and don't you ever do it."

"Swing me, mama, swing me," he sings and she does, holding him under his arms as she twirls him around. She puts him back down on the pebbled rocks of the shore and he squeals in delight as he wraps his arms around her legs for a hug. Warmth spears me as I gaze at them, an almost tangible bond emanating from me to them. "Strings of love" is what Julia calls that feeling. Yeah, she's more eloquent than me.

We hadn't planned on having three kids at once. Hell, we hadn't planned on getting pregnant a year after we got married, but hello, surprise baby. We went to the first ultrasound and saw that it wasn't just one baby but three. We walked out of the doctor's office in a daze. I don't think we said a single word the entire drive back to our house. It didn't really sink in until we started getting the nursery ready. Three cribs, three changing tables, pacifiers, toys, bouncy chairs, and so many fucking diapers. We had a walk-in closet entirely dedicated to Pampers. And when they were born, I was right there holding her hand, praying to God to let Julia and my babies be okay.

It wasn't easy being a second-year rookie in the NHL and a father of three. Yet, unexpected things in life can be the blessing you never knew you wanted. We wouldn't change anything about how our life fell into place.

Kurt lets her go and races back to the rock where the others are waiting for him. He's wearing flamingo swim trunks that come down past his knees and a long sleeve white swim shirt. His longish hair sticks out everywhere under a floppy Capitals hat.

Kara is poised to jump in, but he hip checks her out of the way and dashes off the rock in front of her. He lives for thrills. He may act like me, but he looks like Julia with his sweet brown eyes and dark hair. But Kara and Kelli? Those two have my signature hair. Kara is the "mom" of the triplets —she was born first—while Kelli is the quiet genius behind their plots to overthrow the parentals.

Kara shakes her fist at Kurt when he pops up from the water. I can't hear what she's saying but I'm sure it's all about rules and "know your place" and "I was born first so I'm the oldest" kind of thing. I'm still chuckling as Julia turns to me and puts her hands on her hips.

"Are you listening to me?" she asks.

"Hmm," I say I take her in. She's wearing a red bikini, huge sunglasses, and a big floppy hat. She looks like a movie star hiding out at an exclusive beach resort. Damn, I love her. She's talented; she's caring; she's hot as fuck. I'm living the dream with her and my Triplets of Terror.

"Have I told you you're beautiful today, my love?"

She rolls her eyes. "Not since this morning and don't use "my love" on me. You're trying to soften me up."

"Never," I say. "Is it working?"

She tosses an empty water bottle at me, and I laugh as I dodge it.

We're at a cabin that Z and Sugar own. We flew into Nashville a week ago, hung out at their house for a few days, then caravanned the few hours to get to Ellijay, a quaint town nestled in the mountains. Bordered by a creek on three sides, their house is big enough for us to vacation with them plus toss in a few more people. We've been coming here for three years, and it's perfect for a late summer getaway before the preseason starts.

"Eric? I'm serious. No axes."

I grin. "Come on now. They have cages between each throwing lane and even a special section just for kids. The Terrors are always throwing stuff in our house. At us, at each other." I waggle my eyebrows. "They'll love it. Tell her Z."

Z pauses as he pulls his oldest, Evander, out of the water. He gives me a look like he was hoping I didn't need his help. The plan was to bring this up when Julia and I were alone, then get her to talk to Sugar, but this morning she kept asking what we should do tomorrow when it might rain, and I decided to go for it.

Z turns to us with an expression of serious contemplation. "We talked to the manager yesterday. He said they have a league for kids as young as seven. The axes are smaller. I think it will be cool."

Sugar scoots up in her lounge chair and tilts her head forward to look at Z over her sunglasses. "Evander won't be seven until October and Nash is only four. None of the kids are old enough. I don't think you two were thinking at all." She blows him a kiss.

He grins. "Well, what I meant was, seven is just the league age. The manager said if we sign a waiver, any age can throw."

"See. All taken care of." I smile at our wives like that should settle the matter.

"Ha," Sugar says. "They'll let you sign a waiver, which absolves them of liability. It doesn't mean it's safe. It means the owners aren't morons."

"Come on, babe, don't go all lawyer on us. It'll be fun," Z says as he bends down to give her a little kiss.

She nudges him away with a laugh. "You're as bad as Eric. Stop trying to sweet talk me."

He brushes his hand over her shoulder in a caress. "Would I do that?"

She smiles slyly. "Maybe."

"Later, I'll tell you all the words I know and they won't be sweet," he says in a low voice as he plops down next to her and they hold hands in between their chairs.

Julia smiles. We're used to their PDA and I guess they're used to ours.

The kids swim over to the edge of the creek and haul themselves out, tossing off life jackets and goggles. They dash in our direction.

I hand Kara her Thor towel, Kelli her Wonder Woman, and Kurt his Star Wars one. Z hands out towels for Evander and Nash.

Kara and Evander pace around the shore and argue over where to sit. He wants to be back on the rock, but she wants to be in the shade near us. She wins and they follow her to a willow tree.

"Ready for our snack," Kara says to us.

Julia shakes her head, her voice low so the kids don't hear. "She's always in charge."

Sugar smirks. "Her and Evander butt heads over everything."

Julia sighs as she watches them spread out their towels. "They're so cute. Looking at them now, you'd never know how hard it was getting them to agree to a movie last night. Kara wanted *SpongeBob*, but Evander insisted on *Toy Story*. Evander won with a majority vote."

"Buzz Lightyear!" Nash calls out, ears perking up at the mention of the movie.

I hand out water, sliced grapes, and cheese sticks. Bending down next to Kelli, I pat her head. "This girl could pass for a seven-year-old. Plus, she's one of the best skaters on the hockey team."

Kurt grunts. "I'm the best!"

Kara rolls her eyes. "We're all good, dummy."

I raise an eyebrow at her. "No name calling, Kara."

"Sorry," she says to her brother.

Kelli looks over at Julia who's now digging through her bag for more sunscreen. "Mama, I wanna throw an axe."

"Me too," comes from the others at varying levels of excitement, except for Nash. He's more interested in the ants trying to get on his towel.

Kurt nudges Evander. "Hey. I can putta apple on my head then you can throw the axe and knock it wayyyyyy off."

Evander breaks into a wide grin. "Yeah!"

I start. "Wait, no, uh—"

"I wanna apple on my head!" Kara calls out then picks up a grape. "Or a grape!"

Z chimes in. "No apples or grapes, guys. The game is throwing the axe at a target and trying to get a bullseye. Doesn't that sound fun?"

Kurt frowns. "We throw axes at bulls? Is that a cow?"

Evander gives him a superior look. "Of course."

Kelli tears off a piece of her cheese stick and chews it. "Is the cow in the bar?" Obviously, she'd been listening to our conversation on the shore. My little genius.

"Of course it's in the bar," Evander says. "They have to eat."

Kelli cocks her head. "They eat grass. Why do people let it inside?"

Kara snorts. "They don't. A cow is outside and we chase it with our axes till we get it. We pluck out its eyeballs."

Kelli blinks. "I like cows! I don't wanna throw axes anymore!"

"No one is chasing a bull or a cow outside. It's not an animal. It's a thing. A *bullseye* is the center of a round target that you throw at," I say.

Nash forgets the ants on his towel and pouts, a serious look in his eyes. "Bad people hurt cows."

Kara turns to him. "It's a bull."

"It's not," Kelli replies. "Daddy just said it's not alive."

"It's dead?" Evander makes a yuck sound.

"Are there baby goats at the bar?" Kurt asks. "We petted baby goats this one time and one ate food from Kelli's hands and she cried cause she was scared." He chuckles and Evander joins him.

"They licked me too much," Kelli says and punches her brother on the arm.

"No hitting," I say sternly.

"Sorry," she mutters.

"If the bull is dead, aren't its eyes closed?" Evander asks with a serious expression.

A long breath comes from me. I look over at Z and shake my head. "We've completely lost the narrative, man."

Julia clears her throat, a smile of amusement curling her lips. She and Sugar stand together, their arms crossed. "The mamas have decided. We get a fifty-one percent vote in all things associated with safety. No axe throwing, no bull petting, no knocking apples—or grapes— off of heads, and no bars for our children."

I put up my hands, conceding defeat. "Alright, alright."

"What about a place full of pinball machines?" Z asks. "I

saw one online next to the axe throwing place. It's a huge arcade with some cool machines from the eighties."

"Is it a bar?" asks Sugar.

He lets out a resigned sigh. "Never mind."

"How about an amusement park?" I suggest quietly to the mamas so the kids don't hear and go ballistic. "I know it might rain, but I'd love to see those terrors driving some bumper cars. Me and Z will take them and you and Sugar can shop," I add, sweetening the pot.

Julia gives me a knowing glance. "You're the one who wants to drive a bumper car, aren't you?"

"Definitely. I'm gonna ram Z in one. Oh, and they have a racetrack and batting cages."

Sugar thinks. "Nash will want to ride the carousel, like, a hundred times, it's his favorite. Last year he rode it so much, he barfed all over the unicorn he was on."

Z joins our quiet convo. "I'll ride it with him. I'll clean him up if he pukes."

Sugar laughs. "Who's gonna clean you up?"

"I'm a hockey player. I'm used to spinning."

Sugar nods. "Okay, but you both need to take lots of pics. Julia, does that sound good to you?"

She thinks. "We can grab some lunch and catch up without the kids. Sounds good to me."

Later, Julia folds up her lawn chair and addresses the kids. "All right, munchkins, creek time is over. Everybody clean up. Let's go up to the cabin and chill for a while. Maybe play a game."

"Clean up, clean up, everybody do your share. Clean up…" The kids sing together as they grab toys, towels, and paraphernalia.

As we head up the hill to the cabin, my mom's voice comes from the back deck. "Who wants freezer pops?"

The kids start running toward the porch, calling "Me, Gigi, me!"

Even Z's kids call her that.

My mom laughs. "Come on up to the kitchen then!"

"Mom, it'll ruin their dinner," I grumble. Julia has taught me well.

"What are you talking about? It's literally frozen sugar water. They'll be fine," Nala responds as she joins my mom at the railing. She leans on her cane. The kids call her Nana.

My mom nods in agreement. "Right. And we get to spoil them. It's our calling as grandmothers."

Can't argue with those two.

The two grands have turned out to be friends, even though they have little in common. Julia's mom lives near us in Virginia at an assisted living home. We tried to get her to move in with us, but she said she didn't want to intrude on the newlyweds. After the triplets were born, she stayed for six months to help us out, then left because she said she didn't want to intrude on our family dynamic. I get it. She still wants to be somewhat independent.

My mother isn't the shell she was after my brother's death. She's vibrant and content, and I guess having grandkids has softened her grief. She visits a lot, but only for a few days at a time. Whenever she does visit, she picks up Nala and they shop, visit the monuments, or just hang out. I truly have no idea what they talk about, but it seems to involve a lot of laughter.

"Your father called," Mom adds. "He isn't going to make it. He says we should enjoy our vacation without him. He sends his love to everyone."

Julia crooks her arm in mine and kisses my bicep. She doesn't want the fact that my dad isn't here to bother me, but, of course, I'm not surprised. It doesn't hurt like it used to. Life goes on. He is who he is and he's the kind of person that can't change. On the surface he seems to be over the fact that I chose my own path, but he rarely visits even though business brings him to DC occasionally. His fund is still going strong, and he has a junior executive that's designated as his successor. When we do see each other, we're cordial, and he treats the kids great. It's the best it can be. And I've accepted that.

After playing *Sorry* and *Candyland* for an hour or so, Z asks if the kids are ready for hotdogs over the firepit. They say they are and we head to the kitchen to grab what we need to start dinner.

Julia wraps her arms around my neck and smiles up at me. "While the big strong men make a fire to burn meat, I'm gonna sneak in some work, okay?"

"Sounds good." I smack her ass as she walks away.

When we were first married, she did some photography work for a few websites around the DC area and maintained an Etsy shop of her butterfly drawings, but once the kids came, she focused on taking care of them. An author saw one of her drawings on social media and asked her to turn it into a book cover. The book ended up being a bestseller. Now, she gets requests for illustrations several times a year. She's able to work as much as she wants and do it all from her studio in our house.

Z and I are stacking wood for the fire when my phone rings.

I answer. "Coach? What's up?"

"Eric, glad you picked up. No one wants to talk on the phone anymore," is the gruff voice that greets me.

"You usually only call when you have bad news. I thought I'd rather hear it from you straight rather than a voice message. Give it to me, what's going on?"

"No, no. Nothing bad. It's good actually, well, for you. Jankovic is retiring. He just left my office. The injury last year still hasn't healed, and he's decided twelve years is enough. He's hanging up his skates, and he recommended you take his place as captain."

I blink, stunned for a minute with all the information he just dumped on me. "Are you sure? Jank wants to retire and he recommended me?"

He chuckles. "Yes, Eric. You."

Jankovic was my mentor when I joined the Capitals. I didn't set the NHL on fire like Z did in his first few years. In fact, my first few were spent on the penalty kill line, and I was constantly worried about getting cut. Haru Jankovic was our captain. He took me and some other young guys under his wing, showing us the amount of work we needed to be putting in to get into true NHL shape. It paid off in my fourth year when I started getting extended minutes on the ice with him. For the last two years, I've been on the first line and made the all-star team. Being captain on an NHL team is a big responsibility and knowing that my mentor recommended I take his place means the world to me.

"Wow, of course. I'd be honored. Do I need to come back to DC for this?"

"No, it can keep. We'll announce all of this next week before pre-season starts. You enjoy the rest of your vacation. You have a lot of work to do when you get back."

I hang up the phone and Z has a huge smile on his face.

"Congratulations, man! Hawthorne Lions always rise to the top." He gives me a slap on the back. "Best winger I ever had."

I text Julia immediately and let her know. I'd run up and tell her in person, but I need a minute to process—plus there's a fire to maintain.

Later, as the sun is setting, the temperature drops to a nice seventy degrees with a cool breeze. We sit out in lawn chairs, monitoring the kids as they cook the hot dogs for themselves and the adults. They begged us so we relented. Now, we sit and eat the half-burned, half-cold hotdogs like they were from a five-star restaurant.

The kids are now burning marshmallows for dessert.

Evander gets a little too close to the fire and Sugar calls out, "Don't play in the fire or ya'll will pee the bed."

All five kids snap their heads to look at her and then each other. They aren't sure who exactly she was scolding, but they all take a step back—except for Nash.

"I pee bed. Don't care."

The rest of them giggle but stop when I give them the "you better not make fun of him" look.

Sugar's phone beeps and she looks, smiles, then hands it to Julia.

"Now that deserves a celebration," she responds handing it back.

"What was that?" I ask.

She glances at the kids and says under her breath, "Our old classmate was denied P-A-R-O-L-E."

Sugar knows a few lawyers in Minnesota and asked them to keep tabs on Parker. He ended up with multiple charges of sexual assault, and some were truly horrific. Julia dreaded testifying, but he ended up taking a plea deal for leniency. He received a fifteen-year sentence and is now up for parole. Over the last few months other women started coming forward with accusations dating back to his high school days. The cases were beyond the statute of limitation, but the parole board agreed to hear their victim impact stories. Getting denied is great news and hopefully he'll stay in that cold Minnesota prison for his entire term.

After a few campfire songs and unscary ghost stories I stand up. "I'm gonna grab another drink. Anyone need a refill?"

"I'm good," Julia says.

I notice her glass is still full. "Did you not like the wine?"

"It didn't go with my hotdog, but it's fine. Just don't want a headache later."

I kiss the top of her head. "Wanna water?"

She nods.

Sugar holds up her empty glass with a smile. "I thought it paired well with tonight's pork. I would love a refill."

I bring Sugar a refill, Julia her water, and beers for me and Z.

A few minutes later, Kara and Evander lean against each other in a lounge chair, their eyes slowly closing.

Z stands up and stretches. "I think it's time for our little crew to turn in."

A chorus of "Noooooo" comes from them.

"Yep, you heard him," I say as I rise with him. He and I are on bedtime duty tonight. "Everyone below the age of seven needs to have teeth brushed, pajamas on, and under the covers in fifteen minutes."

The girls share a room with twin beds and the boys have a bigger room with two queens. Kurt and Evander sleep together while Nash gets his own. (Bed wetter).

After turning off the lights around the cabin, I head to mine and Julia's bedroom. It's spacious with a view of the waterfall. The lights are out and the room is empty, so I quietly open the bathroom door.

"Hey, you in here?" I ask.

"Don't come in," she calls from the toilet, but it's too late. It's not like I haven't seen her pee before.

"Sorry, babe. Let me—"

I pause when I see them. Three little plastic sticks sitting on the edge of the counter. She follows my eyes then holds up a fourth that was between her legs. She sets it next to the others, a tremble in her hand.

"Uh… Is that what I think it is?" I mean, I know what they are, but the world feels like it's spinning a little and I need confirmation.

She grimaces. "Yes."

"How long have you known?"

She points at her collection of pregnancy tests, then pushes at a strand of hair in her face. "Obviously, I don't yet, but I've been queasy, and I can smell *everything*. I mean, I can normally smell, but not like this."

I kneel down next to her. "Is it like when you were pregnant with the terrors and could smell dirt?"

She nods. "Exactly like that, but I just had my period, so I don't know what's going on."

"Should I run out and get more tests, or do you think these four will be enough?"

"Ha-ha, funny guy, this is serious. We haven't even talked about having a baby, plus all of the kids will be in school this fall, and I just thought it might give us time to, you know, catch our breath. I don't think my boobs can handle another triple attack of breastfeeding."

"What are you talking about? The odds of having triplets again can't be that high. And hey, they're still the best boobs I've seen in years."

She narrows her gaze. "They better damn well be."

"I kid, I kid."

Her phone starts to chime that the timer is up. She gives me a lingering look, then, takes a deep breath.

"The first one is ready. Are you, Eric? I mean, can we do this again?"

"Abso-fucking-lutely. Let's look at the same time, yeah?"

She takes a deep breath and nods.

I take her hand and lace it with mine.

"I peed on that hand," she says and I laugh.

"I've seen so much pee since we had kids, yours isn't going to bother me. Ready?" We lean over to the counter. "Whatta we got here?"

Positive.

She laughs, tears pooling in her eyes and I smile as only one word comes to mind.

Perfection.

Dear Reader,

Thank you for reading *Boyfriend Material*. I hope you enjoyed Eric and Julia's second chance love story. If you want more sexy romance featuring college athletes, check out one of my other series and the big men on campus of Waylon University. As an added bonus you can read an excerpt from book one of that series on the next pages, or you can go to Amazon and download your copy of <u>I Dare You</u> now.

. . .

REVIEWS ARE like gold to authors, and I read each and every one. If you have a few moments, please consider leaving a rating or a review for Boyfriend Material.

KEEP READING ALL THE BOOKS.

XOXO,
    Ilsa

P.S. SIGN UP for my newsletter below and you will receive a FREE Briarwood Academy novella just for joining.

HTTP://WWW.ILSAMADDENMILLS.COM/CONTACT

PLEASE JOIN my FB readers group, Unicorn Girls, to get the latest scoop as well as talk about books, wine, and Netflix:

HTTPS://WWW.FACEBOOK.COM/GROUPS/ILSASUNICORNGIRLS/

EXCERPT - I DARE YOU

I Dare You

Copyright © 2018 by Ilsa Madden-Mills

Prologue
Freshman year

Delaney

Welcome to Magnolia, Mississippi, where locusts are as big as your hand and iced tea comes with a double helping of sugar.

It's also home to the best damn annual bonfire party at prestigious Waylon University, which is currently happening right now in the middle of a cotton field.

But...

I shouldn't even be at this party.

It's mostly for Greeks and jocks and popular people, yet

here I am, a mere freshman, hanging out with my bubbly redheaded roommate, Skye.

"See?" she says as we take in the bonfire. "Isn't this better than watching cat videos on a Saturday night? What do you want to do first?"

I sigh, feeling nervous. Ever since I moved here from North Carolina, I've been pushing myself to try new things. Might as well put a crazy college party on that list. "Let's get a drink."

She claps and excitedly replies, "Done. Alcohol at two o'clock." We weave through the crowd, headed in that direction, and eventually we reach the bar, which is really just a long collapsible table someone set up. On top are various bottles of alcohol, and I grab the Fireball to pour shots. I've just tossed mine back and set down my cup when a prickling sensation washes over me, giving me goose bumps.

My gaze moves across the crowd, stopping on a tall guy with dark blond hair, broad shoulders, and a cocky smile. *Aha.* He's been staring at me, and now that he's caught, he raises his glass as a half-grin crosses his face.

I blush wildly as I adjust my black cat-eye glasses. I'm not used to such blatant male attention.

Skye—who's followed the trajectory of my gaze—spits out part of her drink. "Oh my God, do you know who that is?"

"Obviously I should," I say dryly.

Her mouth flops open. "You really need to get out more."

My eyes drift back to him but keep moving as if I'm not staring. "So who is Mr. Hottie McParty Pants?"

"If you don't know him, you don't deserve to know. But, he's H-O-T—like Chris Hemsworth hot. I dare you to flirt with him." She wiggles her eyebrows at me, knowing full well that for some reason, I can't resist a dare. Normally rather reserved, a dare gives me permission to be someone I'm not.

So does Fireball. I sling back another shot.

"I'll bring you a donut every day for a week if you flirt with him," she adds, watching me.

My ears perk up. "The ones with edible glitter?"

She nods, and I toss a quick glance back to him. Our eyes collide again, and a zing of connection fires between us. He has a strong, handsome face and a stance that has masculine written all over it. A smile tips up his full sensuous lips, and—

Two brunettes—twins, no less—approach him, one on either side, and wrap their arms around his waist. He smiles down at them. *Oh. Well then.*

I turn back to Skye and frown. "Player. Not interested."

She waves her hands in my face. "He likes you—I saw it on his face."

I snort. "Probably gas pains. Your dare is not accepted."

We hear our names being called from the other side of the party and turn to take in the helmet-haired Martha approaching us, which is taking some time due to the fact that she's wearing stilettos and a slinky halter dress. She carefully picks her way through the crowd, nudging people out of her way—sometimes rudely—as she focuses on us. *Great.*

"Incoming mean girl," I mutter under my breath.

Like us, Martha Burrows is a freshman and lives on our floor. Rather full of herself, she announced within a week of meeting us that she'd no longer answer to anything but *Muffin*, a nickname she'd given herself.

She eyes us both, a look of superiority on her pretty face.

"I didn't know you two were invited to this little shindig. Obviously, I know all the right people, so I'm always invited." Her gaze zeroes in on my outfit and she rears back. "What on earth are you wearing, Nerd Girl?"

"Clothes." I stiffen at her name for me as I tug on my fitted Star Wars shirt and the pleated red miniskirt I made from a man's shirt. My long pale blonde hair is up in curled pigtails, and I went a bit heavy-handed with the shimmery eye shadow and red lipstick. It's not your typical look for WU—which is anything monogrammed—but I'm learning to ignore the raised eyebrows.

Skye, the peacemaker among us three, clears her throat and nods her head at the guy who's been staring. "Delaney has an admirer, but she doesn't know who he is."

Martha-Muffin follows Skye's gaze, eyeballing the mystery man over my shoulder. She gives me an exasperated look. "That's Maverick Monroe, you idiot. He's the biggest football star in Mississippi and the freshman recruit of the year. Word is, though, girls like you aren't his type—not at all." Her hand flicks a stiff honey-colored curl over her shoulder.

My teeth grind together. "Martha, if you think I care what you think about me and whether or not a quasi-famous football player is interested in me, then you are confused."

Her lips tighten. "It's *Muffin* now, and why do you have to use such big words? What does *quasi* even mean?" is her cutting reply.

Skye's eyes get as big as saucers, and I assume it's because Martha-Muffin and I are about to finally have it out. I can't stand her, and she can't stand me. We just...clash.

But that isn't what has Skye in such a titter.

She points over my shoulder, and I get it.

It's the person standing behind me, the one I can't see. I feel a nervous sneeze coming on and—*thank God*—I somehow push it down.

A husky voice reaches my ears. "*Quasi* means *seemingly* or *supposedly*. What she means is I'm probably not a famous football player but rather one that's been highly touted but is without merit."

Oh, shit. The voice is rich and smooth with just enough southern drawl to make a girl swoon. He also sounds halfway intelligent.

I turn around slowly. Mr. Tall, Blond, and Football is right in front of me wearing a cocky smile.

How in the hell did he get over here so fast?

You know that moment when everything stops and the next breath you take is the first one of the rest of your life? That's what it feels like as Maverick Monroe stares at me with his piercing blue eyes.

I glance down and take in the sculpted chest and hard biceps.

I look back up and see a chiseled jawline that's defined and lined with a slight scruff. I see the thin pink scar that slices through his left eyebrow, and it does nothing to detract from his appeal.

He's perfection.

He's air.

Which I desperately need right now, because I can't breathe.

He smirks, as if reading my mind, and I scramble to pull myself together. Someone calls his name—it's a girl's voice, probably one of those twins—but he doesn't budge.

His eyes rove over my skirt, glasses, and lips. "The question is...do you even know what makes a good football player?"

"Nice hands?"

His lips twitch. "Hardly."

"A tight end?" I smirk, feeling sassy...which is weird. I don't know who I am right now, but it's like my mouth has a life of its own, saying things I normally wouldn't.

Martha-Muffin chokes on her drink at my remark and Skye watches me with glee, clearly excited that I have the attention of someone who is apparently *very* important at Waylon.

I put my hand on my hip. "The question is...why do I need to know?"

"You don't. All you need to know is I'm the best."

I suck in a little breath at his arrogance.

A guy walks past us and claps him on the shoulder. "Badass game last week, Mav. Rock on."

"Thanks, man." Maverick acknowledges the compliment and lifts his chin, his eyes never straying from mine.

"What position do you play?" I ask. "Quarterback?"

He smirks. "Middle linebacker—defense."

"Sounds fancy."

He laughs.

Skye, who's been eavesdropping unabashedly, sighs with a dreamy expression on her face. "His stats are the best in the country." She clears her throat. "I-I only know that because my brother is a huge fan, I swear."

"Hi, Maverick," Martha-Muffin says as she edges closer to him, nudging me out of the way with her sharp shoulders. "Remember me?"

He focuses on her. "No."

She glowers. "I was in your dorm room with your roommate last week. You said *hello* to me."

He shrugs. "A lot of girls come through. I can't remember them all."

Oh. My. God. He *is* arrogant, but I like how he just shut her down.

Martha-Muffin's face reddens and she mutters something under her breath, flips around, and flounces off. Good riddance.

Out of the corner of my eye, I see Skye is drifting away too, giving me a thumbs-up.

Whatever. I am not going to flirt with this guy...am I?

He's definitely got something about him, something that makes my body buzz. I tilt my chin up, taking in how tall he is. He has to be at least six-four.

His gaze drifts over my face. "You know there's a legend here at Waylon about our famous bonfire party?"

"Oh?"

He smiles, a flash of white on his handsome face. "Legend says the first person you kiss at the party is the one you'll never forget. It might be years later, and still their face is the one you dream about."

"Sounds like hocus-pocus."

He lifts that mesmerizing left eyebrow. "I like to believe in legends—after all, I am one."

I smirk. "Probably a game made up by some frat-boy-slash-jock wanting to kiss all the girls."

He pauses for a moment as if thinking, and then he steps in closer, so close that I can see the varying shades of blue around his pupils. "May I?"

My heart does somersaults.

"May you what?" I ask, my voice low, but I know what he

wants. My body is already leaning toward him, wanting it too.

"This." He kisses me, an almost imperceptible touch as he brushes his full lips against mine. The contact of our mouths is electric, sparks of fire skating along my skin.

As if from a distance, I hear someone calling his name. It's a female, and she's pissed.

It's one of the twins probably.

And I'm jealous.

But, I don't look. We pull away, and I stare at him as he stares right back. A stillness settles over the party, although I don't think anything's actually changed. The music is still playing. People are still talking. Beers are being passed around.

Yet...

We're connected.

Two stars in the black velvet sky.

Two ships passing in the night.

Oh, fuck, stop the nonsense, I tell myself.

"What was that?" I ask, my voice breathless.

"That's your first kiss of the bonfire. Now you'll never forget me."

And then, before I can think of a reply, he's gone.

I watch him go back to the twins, frustration coiling inside of me as I exhale.

It would be two years before I kissed him again.

END EXCERPT

If you would like to read the rest of Maverick and Delaney's story grab your copy of I Dare You today. It is book one of the Waylon University college romance series. All books in the series are available on Amazon and free with Kindle Unlimited.

ALSO BY ILSA MADDEN-MILLS

All books are standalone stories with brand new couples and are currently FREE in Kindle Unlimited.

Briarwood Academy Series

Very Bad Things

Very Wicked Beginnings

Very Wicked Things

Very Twisted Things

British Bad Boys Series

Dirty English

Filthy English

Spider

Waylon University Series

I Dare You

I Bet You

I Hate You

I Promise You

Hawthorne University Series

Boyfriend Bargain

Boyfriend Material

Stand-alones

Fake Fiancée

Dear Ava

The Revenge Pact

The Game Changers Series

Not My Romeo

Not My Match

Strangers in Love Series

Beauty and the Baller

Princess and the Player

Co-Written books

The Last Guy (w/Tia Louise)

The Right Stud (w/Tia Louise)

ABOUT THE AUTHOR

Wall Street Journal, *New York Times*, and *USA Today* bestselling author Ilsa Madden-Mills writes about strong heroines and sexy alpha males that sometimes you just want to slap. A former high school English teacher and elementary librarian, she adores all things *Pride and Prejudice*; Mr. Darcy is her ultimate hero. She loves unicorns, frothy coffee beverages, vampire books, and any book featuring sword-wielding females.

*Please join her FB readers group, Unicorn Girls, to get the latest scoop as well as talk about books, wine, and Netflix:

https://www.facebook.com/groups/ilsasunicorngirls/

You can also find Ilsa at these places:

Website:
http://www.ilsamaddenmills.com
News Letter:
http://www.ilsamaddenmills.com/contact

Made in United States
Troutdale, OR
08/12/2024

21949885R00202